House of Pigs

Christopher Ritchie

First published 2013
Published by GBP George Boughton Publishing 2013

Copyright © 2013 Christopher Ritchie
All rights reserved.
ISBN: 9780957297050

A catalogue record of this book is available from the British Library

Cover design © 2013 Mary Pargeter Design
Cover illustration D E Pearson

GBP
George Boughton Publishing
www.gbpublishing.org

For Madeleine and Henry

Acknowledgement
Immense thanks to Andrew Taylor for his encouragement and flattery, and to Brenda, George and Mary for all their help and enthusiasm

Contents

One – The Call

'So what is it?'

'Not sure. Dispatch said a disturbance out at Hawks Farm.'

'Ten minutes then, easily. Time for a couple smokes on the way. You sure there's nobody else?'

Tom glanced at his partner. 'Apparently not, douche. That fire over at Hart's department store's keeping everyone busy. Looks like a biggie. You'd know that if you paid some attention to the radio.'

'Whatever. I've been asleep.' Frank put his left hand in his right shirt pocket, took out a wrinkled cigarette and put it in his mouth. 'Time for a refill.'

'Just open the window, moron. *Please.*'

Frank lit the cigarette and clicked the button on the door to open the window. Cool air from outside rushed in, blowing the first plumes of smoke straight into Tom's eyes.

'Thanks a bunch, asshole,' Tom said through a cough, blinking to clear the sting.

'Whatever. Anyway, the radio is always the same old shit, so I don't bother with it. Shop fire, mugging, the occasional gang rape in an abattoir – makes no difference to me, as long as I get paid.'

'Just as well you've got me then,' Tom smiled. 'Besides, this'll be an easy one. What kind of disturbance would we get on a Sunday night at a farm?'

Frank inhaled half the cigarette, which sparked with intensity and crackled like a tiny cancerous firework. His eyes darted down. He didn't appreciate the power of fire – like the one ripping through a local department store.

'Dunno. Guess we'll find out soon enough. Maybe it's connected to the abattoir gang rape – couple of sheep gone all messed up and want revenge.'

'Man...' Tom looked over, grinning. 'You have some deep-seated issues right there. You're stone cold *mental.*'

~~~

The men stepped out of the cruiser roughly fifty feet from the house, just inside a twelve-foot gap in a stone wall where the road led into the farmstead. Under the near-full moon the immediate area was fairly visible.

To the right of the house was a narrow passage, about two metres wide, a sliver of darkness; next to that a tall barn. Left of the house was what appeared to be a paddock, to the other side of a tall wall a few feet away. All was silent.

'Never had cause to come up this way before,' Tom said. 'Let's find out what's going on.'

Frank led as they approached the house, noting two curtained windows upstairs, a large wheel bolted between them, which hung partly over the front door. He raised the knocker and thumped it against the door firmly.

Tom shone his torch at the barn. Footsteps inside the house drew his attention back to the door, now creaking open. A man stood before them was tall and bulky, the thin light upon his face giving it a creepy, weathered look.

'Police, sir,' Frank said. 'I'm Frank Willis and this is Tom Turnbull.' They held up their ID badges and flipped the wallets shut in one smooth, well-rehearsed motion. Frank noted their skill and grinned inwardly. He'd always considered himself movie star material. 'We've had a call to check out a disturbance. Mind if we come inside?'

'There any more of you?'

'No, sir. I think we can handle this,' Tom said. 'Besides, everyone else is busy tonight. There's a fire in town.'

'Ah. A fire.' The man gestured for them to enter and gently closed the door behind them. 'Thanks for coming out so late, gents. I'm Hat, Hat Smith. Can I get you fellers something to drink?'

'With respect, sir,' Tom said, 'we're not here on a social visit. Could you tell us what the disturbance is?'

As Hat turned away to lead them further into the house, Frank leant over to Tom's ear and whispered, 'It's Sunday, 1am, we're miles from anywhere and with some weird old man. I could *do with a drink*.'

Tom smiled and playfully punched his partner's arm. They followed Hat into the kitchen. 'There, out the back, you can just about see it.' Hat raised his arm to point beyond the back fence, about a metre high, into a further field, which neither of the men could make out.

'That's the pasture. I've got over one hundred sheep out there, usually. Now there's none. Well, half.'

'What do you mean, sir?' Tom's expression bore simple confusion. 'You've lost an entire flock of sheep?'

'No son, I've lost all but half of one sheep.'

Frank stood with his face an inch from the window, straining his eyes, but for all he could see there were no sheep in the field.

'That pasture is about fifty by a hundred metres and it's mostly flat. Even in the dimmest light you can see 'em in there. There's one gate in and out, and I've been here all night.' Hat looked at Tom grimly. 'I'm telling you; there's *half* a sheep in that pasture. Half.'

Hat led them into the next room, weaving between furniture to reach a back door, open it and move out into the rear paddock. Tom and Frank exchanged confused smiles – *What's with this guy?* They followed him up to the back fence, which they stepped over and into the pasture.

'I'm telling you boys.' Hat stopped, turned and fixed Frank with a glare. 'This is the most messed up shit I've *ever* seen.'

Hat raised his arm again. 'Over there.'

Tom followed the arm with his torch, casting the beam over as much of the field as he could. 'Over a hundred sheep?' he asked. 'Really?'

Hat didn't answer. Frank and Tom's torch beams danced over the grass as they walked slowly over to what looked like a lumpy mound. Closing in, Frank spoke quietly, glancing back at Hat and then at Tom: 'Is this for real? This guy is a cracker; a certified nut-job.'

'I'm inclined to agree,' Tom whispered, 'Let's see what's what before we do his kneecaps.' Frank chuckled like a child watching his favourite cartoon.

Ten strides on, their beams rested on the mound, indeed half a sheep, head and forelegs intact, but cleanly cut – too cleanly – just in front of where its hind legs would have been.

The sheep was prone, left eye facing the sky. There was no discernible gore – no evidence of anything around the scene, just grass and half a sheep lying on it.

'What...the...fuck?' Frank stood slack jawed, staring at the body.

'Um...' A good twenty seconds passed before Tom spoke again. '... I've no...idea. It's half a sheep, for sure. Hat!' he called loudly, turning with his torch picking out an empty landscape and landing on the man. 'Would you come over here?'

Hat was already two metres behind them. He held up his arm to shield his eyes from the beam. 'You mind?' he snarled.

'So let's get this straight – all your sheep just disappeared, apart from...'
He pointed around and down, in a theatrical, sweeping motion. '...this?'

'That's right feller,' Hat nodded. 'All messed up. I ain't ever seen anything like this before. It's a bad practical joke or something worse, I can't decide. You guys want to head further down and have a look?'

Frank flicked his torch up and shone it out towards the back of the paddock. The beam didn't appear to penetrate anywhere. 'Nah. I mean... let's take some details.'

Hat gestured and the three men turned to head back to the house. It was then that Frank thought he glimpsed something in the back bedroom window, perhaps a face pulling quickly away from view.

He decided he was mistaken. Things were already spooky enough out here. No need to start seeing things, too.

'You live alone, Hat?' Frank asked.

'Sure do. Sometimes the kids come to visit, but usually it's just me and the sheep.'

~ ~ ~

'We're gonna have to wait till morning to check this out,' Tom told Hat, back in the kitchen where they were waiting for the kettle to boil. 'Simply no way of seeing much with these piddly torches. We've got some equipment in the cruiser.'

'I getcha, but now you've seen it I'm gonna do some investigating of my own.'

'Hat...' Tom shot in. 'It could be a crime scene. You can't dist...'

'I'll do whatever I like on my property, feller. I'm not waiting around to see what's what here. You do your shit, I'll do mine.'

The muffled sound of a door closing came somewhere else in the house; Frank appeared, expressing his gratitude for use of the facilities with a nod to Hat. Hat nodded back.

'Sir, we can't stop you,' Tom continued, 'but if you do disturb any vital evidence, it's going to interfere with our chances.'

'Chances of what?' Hat laughed, in a way that showed he wasn't laughing because anything was funny. 'You don't have a clue any more than my dead aunt about what's happened out there; shit, you don't even believe me. I can see that. You've seen it but you can't explain it. You fellers finish your coffee and then let me back to my business.'

4

'Uh, *you* called *us*,' Frank said, quietly.

Hat looked worn out but riled. Tom, who had maintained eye contact throughout, broke away and looked out of the window. 'Sir, we will find your sheep, one way or the other ,' he said. 'How can a hundred sheep – *minus a half* – just disappear? There's always a reason, and we'll always find it.'

Tom and Frank decided not to stay for coffee and Hat let them see themselves out while he disappeared upstairs. The tired policemen headed back to their cruiser.

'Let's call in,' said Frank, lighting up a cigarette. 'Then let's go get a drink, sleep a bit and let some other mugs deal with this weird shit.'

Tom looked at Frank. The moonlight cast an unpleasantly pallid hue over his face. He started: 'Frank-' but broke off. 'Frank. We're gonna stay. I want to have a look around. This dude might be crazy but we just saw some weird shit that I've no idea how to explain. Five minutes – drink later, okay?'

Tom leaned in to the cruiser, opened the glove box and took out his weapon, a steel revolver by Roderick Firearms & Ammo that had seen more action than any other gun in the police department – not all that surprising since, out of a running stock of around ten police at any one time, Tom had been there the longest, with over thirty years behind him.

In league with his finger his gun had stopped over twenty men, a couple of very violent and rabid women, three dogs – half as rabid as those women – and Tom's marriage. He didn't expect to use it tonight, but any field investigation, so the police regulations declared, required a firearm. Frank also collected his gun, a weapon that had never seen any action and, going by the usual strategy that Tom did all the shooting, likely never would.

'Let's start with the barn,' Tom pointed with one arm, holstering his gun with the other. 'Could easily fit a hundred sheep in there, if you sawed their little legs off.'

'Right. Here we go. If we don't find anything in here, I'm off, and that's that.' Frank looked as pissed off as it was possible for him to look.

'Prick,' Tom said, quietly.

Torches up, beams dancing over the barn, the lawmen strode to the door, as tall as the building at about thirty feet, and twelve feet wide. It was made of wood, but had sheet metal covering. The rusted handle was askew. Frank grabbed it in one hand, his gun in the other, and Tom stood back, gun up level with his chin, firm and ready.

'Open it.'

Frank pulled the handle and the door swung open as expected. Torches and guns screened the area, about thirty feet deep by fifty wide. As far as they could see, the barn was mostly empty. A long ladder led up to a second level, typical of a traditional barn. The two men ventured inside, beams flashing light into dark corners but revealing nothing of interest.

They approached the ladder. 'You first,' Frank said.

Tom groaned, nodded and started up the ladder, clutching his torch and gun. At the top he set them down on the wooden floor to hoist himself up.

'What the-' Tom lurched back, nearly falling off the platform. 'Get up here, now!'

Frank holstered his gun and torch and scrambled up the ladder.

'Holy shit – what *is* that...?'

Rooted, both men began to shake. Caught in Tom's jerking beam in the silent, dark barn was a corpse of a man – naked, bloody and rotten. Two hooks curved from his shoulders, their ends attached diagonally to the barn wall. The hooks looked about eight inches long and spiked through to emerge about an inch from his nipples, which had been detached.

There was a grim dent from his windpipe down to his belly, caked in shiny blood. Below this, his genitals were missing and his legs had been sliced into three strands, connecting back at the feet, which at least still resembled feet.

Tom and Frank stood up together, breathing as heavily as the weight of the hooked body looked. Tom's throat burned red-hot from rising stomach acid. Frank's mouth was already full of vomit.

'This is insane. Is this – is that Hat?'

Tom remained speechless, his eyes widening, back straightening. At last he blurted, 'No way! We were with him two minutes ago. There's no way this can be Hat. Hat is in the house. Hat is in the fucking house!'

'It sure looks like him,' Frank took a step nearer; Tom shuffled back. 'We've gotta call this in.'

Frank got as close as he could to the body and kneeled down without taking his eyes off the face. Tom's torch beam danced around in small, inconsistent arcs as he struggled to find his comms unit with his other hand. Then he realised it was back in the cruiser.

'It's him, *definitely*,' Frank said. He had noticed a mole on Hat's throat just minutes earlier and sure enough, this mole was in the same place, albeit now caked in blood. Tom looked up, saw and nodded.

'What mad trick is this? Half a sheep and now a man in two places at once, alive in one and dead in the other? Bullshit!'

'Let's just get out of here and come with some backup in the morning,' said Frank, cautiously stepping backwards. 'Okay...we go back to the house, we knock, and if no one answers, we leave. Right?'

'Right!' Tom shifted around, got back onto the ladder and descended as quickly as he could. Frank followed. Cautiously they moved out of the barn, flashing torches and guns left and right.

'Get the visors, Frank. No chances. This whole shit is running crazier.'

At the cruiser, Frank leant in to grab two visors off the charger on the dash. Blue lights indicated they were ready to go. He shuffled back to Tom, passed one visor over and the men mounted them on their heads.

'I hate these things,' said Tom grimly.

'I know you do,' Frank snapped. 'Every time you tell me. Whatever. So you hate the shit. Saved your life a hundred times or more, dick.'

'A hundred times? I've not even worn it more'n twenty!'

The visors flickered into life. Dark was no longer dark. Sounds entered their ears that had not been audible earlier.

The tiniest crunch of ground under foot registered as a crisp snap in the lawmen's ears. The technology had been developed to give the wearer that extra edge, and, at least in cases where their opponents did not have them too, the visors proved invaluable.

They headed towards the house, faster than before, weapons ready. The door was half-open. Tom and Frank glanced at one another, before Tom stepped into the house. The lights were off.

'Hello! *Hello*! This is officers Turnbull and Willis. If anyone is in this house, identify yourselves.'

'Tom!'

'Yeah ... what?'

'Tom! Look at the walls.' Frank pointed his torch and gun and traced along the length of the hall. 'This isn't the same house. The walls here were patterned.'

He was right. The walls were white, all around them. Down the long corridor into the kitchen; half way down where the stairs started, and going up, it was all white. The carpet looked the same and the furniture was the same as Frank remembered – a small stack of occasional tables at the bottom of the stairs in particular.

'Is anybody here?' Tom shouted again. Although mildly unnerved by the walls, his visor was picking up movement upstairs; a small line tremored above his right eye – the only indicator of anything at all on the visor. Frank's showed the same. The technology had been tuned to ignore the wearer and any other members of law enforcement.

Frank gestured towards the stairs, edging closer to the kitchen; Tom mounted the first step. A loud thump came from upstairs, followed by a crash, sounding as if something had smashed through one of the front windows.

'Back out the front!' shouted Tom, bolting for the door. Frank turned to follow.

'Where is it? There's nothing here!' Tom shouted.

They craned around to see the windows either side of the large wheel above the door intact. The visors registered nothing; the small tremor was gone.

'What the – oh shit! Back inside! Now!'

Frank turned to see what Tom had spotted. Their cruiser was sinking into a widening crack, further ripping the ground open and heading for them – fast. To a sound like ripping paper, they just managed to re-enter the house as the crack hit the outside wall and stopped dead. Frank slammed the door shut and they backed away fast, stumbling and breathing erratically.

Tom slammed his fist against the wall, not noticing it had reverted to the original reddish-green paper pattern.

'This is *insane*!' he screamed. The visor showed nothing. Apart from their heavy breathing, there was no sound – inside or out; no movement, just disquieting silence.

The lights went out – and then on for about half a second. Frank saw Hat's smiling face right in front of him, his teeth black, his lips grey. The light went off again.

'Tom…' He felt a hand close over his mouth and pushed his arms out to the front, around to the back, flailing and hitting nothing. His breathing became heavier, heavier still and then weak. Frank passed out.

Two – Welcome

'Frank...Frank! Fraaaaaank!' At the top of the stairs Tom stood in total darkness, visor offline, torch lost in the darkness. He could hear nothing, see nothing. Stumbling backwards, he felt for the wall to his left and right and connected. Following the wall, fingers bumping over imperfections in the plaster, his fingertips met with a different texture – painted wood; a frame. He felt the smoothness of glass – the window. He could see nothing out of it. There was no moonlight, no light at all. He'd heard the phrase 'pitch black' but never known it till now.

Turning, he fumbled for his gun and held it out in his left hand. Consciously trying not to make any sound, deliberately calming his breathing, he cautiously edged forward, right hand on the wall. Slowly, he shuffled on for about twenty feet, passing into another room identified by the feel of a doorframe. Directly above the kitchen, he estimated. He reached up to flick the visor off his head. Awkwardly he folded it into his jacket pocket.

Standing as still as he could, Tom listened. He was rewarded with only the sound of his own quick breathing. He felt his entire body trembling. Seconds later he moved forward again, a bit faster. His left shin connected with something – a bed? He felt his way around it and reached another window. This one was different – in the distance he could see something.

Two figures moved across the landscape, lights beaming out in front of them. In about twenty seconds they stopped to look at something on the ground. One of the lights turned and highlighted another figure standing several feet behind them. The light flashed on his face. Tom struggled to see it. The face lifted to look directly up at him, followed by the faces of the others. He drew back quickly against the wall. Had they seen him? Almost certainly. Who were they?

'Oh shit...' The words dropped from his mouth, slowly and breathy. *That's...us. Shit.* He leaned slightly off the wall and peered over the rim of the window, keeping his head low but just enough so he could see back out onto the pasture. The men were in the same spot. *What is going on?* This time they raised their arms and all three pointed straight at him.

Before he could press back against the wall, he saw the men run towards the house. Tom gasped. He felt as if he'd been kicked in the balls. 'Frank!' he groaned through gritted teeth. He felt around for the bed, with some vague idea of hiding under it. The side was solid – this bed had no *under*. 'Dammit!' His teeth ground tighter together as he mounted the bed to clamber over. Something blocked him – an arm. 'Arrgh…'

A hand closed hard over his mouth and nose, pushing him down into the bed. Tom waved his arms and kicked his legs, but connected with nothing. His gun clattering to the floor jarred with his muffled attempts to scream. Tom's world turned black.

~ ~ ~

'Hold the line please, sir.' Louise clicked the *hold* button, leaned back so she could see into the adjacent room, and called, 'Gully – have Frank or Tom checked in?'

'Not yet.' He paused. 'Wassup?' Feet up, Gully was trying to enter a competition in *Serve + Protect* magazine by filling in his name, address and badge number with a pen that scratched inklessly unless held exactly upright.

'It's the man at the farm…' Louise called, '…says they came to see him but disappeared. Their cruiser's still parked out front but they arrived two hours ago and he's not seen 'em since.'

'Tried the VICOM?'

'Sir, thank you for holding. I'm going to try to raise the officers by radio. Thanks for your patience, sir.'

Louise propelled her chair to the right, gliding to the intended spot, and leaned over to grab the VICOM headset. She found the code for Officer Frank Willis, tapped his entry onscreen and pulled her visor down. 'Gully. Come here a sec?'

'On my way, little lady.'

'Look – it's weird. Frank's visor is online but it's not on his head. Look – it's on the floor. It looks like a barn.' Louise tilted her head slightly to get a better angle. 'You can see some…feet…looks like they're…hanging.'

Louise passed the headset to her superior, who calmly put it on. For a few seconds Gully said nothing as he peered intently into the visor to make sense of the scene.

'Louise, who is the man on the phone?'

'Mr Hat Smith. He's up at the farm.'

'Have him transferred to my station please.'

Louise walked back to the phone and reconnected the caller.

'Mr Smith?'

'Here,' replied the voice.

'Thank you again for your patience. I'm going to transfer you to our deputy sheriff.'

Louise punched in the phone code and Gully immediately picked it up at the other station. Removing the VICOM, he placed the receiver to his ear.

'Mr Smith – Hawks Farm?'

'Yes?'

'Do you have a barn on your farm?'

'Yes sir, right out front. Can't miss it.'

'Mr Smith...Would you mind telling us please where you last saw the two officers who came to see you? Did they...did they go into that barn?'

'I guess they checked it – they went all around, shining their lights and pointing their guns. Last I seen 'em they were getting something outta that car.'

'Mr Smith. Thanks for your patience. Is the cruiser still there? Can you confirm that?'

'Yessir, yes it is. Hasn't moved in two hours.'

'Mr Smith. Hat...if you can see the car, can you see the barn too? Can you tell if there's anyone in the barn from where you're standing?'

'I've been in the barn. There's nothing in there, nothing at all. I told you. These guys are *missing*.'

Gully picked up the VICOM and held it in front of his face.

'Hat...um...Mr Smith, I'm going to drive out there and take a look. Should be there in twenty minutes. Please hang tight, don't leave your house ... in fact, lock the doors. Don't answer the door to anyone but me – Officer Joe Gullidge. I'll have identification.'

'Okay sir,' came the voice. 'I'll be here. Looking forward to it.'

Gully ended the call. 'Louise,' he said, 'Try Tom's visor next. I'm going to get my shit together. Last thing I need tonight. Where *is* everybody anyway?'

He knew where everybody was, dealing with the fire in town. It had claimed more than fifteen lives now, two of them police officers and the fire department was not getting control of the blaze by any means. This was easily the most action the town of Shenbury had seen in years. Not good action. Bad, very bad.

Gully returned to his 'office', opened a tall locker, took out his IR suit, a revolver and rifle, two battery clips and his visor. Meanwhile, Louise had punched in Officer Tom Turnbull's visor code and was again donning the VICOM.

'Gully! Gully – come here, you gotta see this.'

Gully, halfway into the suit, stopped, stepped out of it awkwardly and strode over to Louise. He noticed her worried expression as she handed him the VICOM, and quickly settled it over his head. Gully's eyes grew wide, his jaw slackened. Tom's visor also seemed to be on the barn floor. To the right side of the view Gully could see Frank's VICOM. To the upper left he could see feet dangling. Further back and to the right, out of the view of Frank's visor but visible in Tom's, a man lay, prone, his head up. He was smiling into the visor – straight at Gully.

'Gully?' Louise demanded unhappily. 'Gully, don't go. Wait for the others to get back. This looks *majorly* bad.'

'I've got to, Lou. Don't worry. I'll be protected.' Gully was still taking in the smiling face before him – young, clean-shaven, wearing what looked like a black dinner suit. Suddenly the smile was gone. The man began to crawl slowly towards the visor. Gully edged back. The man eyed him narrowly. 'What the fuck you lookin' at?'

Tom's visor went offline. Louise inwardly refused to turn her VICOM back to Frank's frequency.

~~~

Officer Joe Gullidge's cruiser was the best in the force. It was also the only cruiser privately owned and, as such, the only one decently looked after. 'Louise, lock me in at ninety, fire straight to Hawks Farm.'

Back at her workstation, Louise tapped her screen in the appropriate places. Gully's cruiser registered a low sine beep and the wheel snapped back into the dash, the computer taking control. Gully flipped his visor down, enjoying his own presentation – like the IR catalogue guy, swathed in the best technology known to law enforcement and military alike, sitting proud in his fancy cruiser saying: 'Hi, I'm Joe Gullidge, the badass who only wears Intelligent Response.'

Leaving his cruiser to deal with the travel arrangements, Gully reclined, closed his eyes and let his mind wander. *Two officers down... potentially...a deranged man in a suit who put those officers down...potentially... and a farmer who doesn't know anything about it...* The cruiser slowed for a junction. Two cars flashed past. The cruiser got going again.

'Joe, be careful.' Louise's voice was crisp in his ear. 'Whatever is going on out there, I don't know...just be careful.'

Eyes still closed and calmly relaxed, Gully told her, in his best *hero* tone, 'Fear not, my sweet. I shall vanquish the enemy and return with flowers.'

He sat up. Louise said nothing more. Gully reached for his revolver. Taking a battery clip off his chest pad, he clicked the two together and twisted the barrel one full click, settling on *lethal.* 'I'm the man who puts the *gent* in Intelligent,' he said to himself, remembering the common retort, 'You put the *ponce* in Response.'

Two minutes later the cruiser parked adjacent to a tall stone wall, short of the farm entrance. Gully stepped out, leaned in to grab his rifle from the back seat, and shut the door. With a brief pneumatic hiss the cruiser shut down and went into protected mode. Gully could see neither the entrance, house nor barn from his position. He crouched low, taking short, firm steps along the wall. Where the wall stopped, so did he. Flipping his visor down he surveyed the scene, then flipped it up and used his eyes for the same. Nothing. If Mr Smith was in the house, as he should be, the tremor wouldn't show up this far away.

Likewise, if Mr Creepy Suit was in the barn, he would have to get a little closer to find out. However, in order to get anywhere near he would have to pass the missing officers' cruiser – which would at least provide some cover – but that would mean that anyone in the house, or barn, would be able to spot him.

Softly, softly, he thought, crawling as close to the ground as he could. Gully got to the cruiser intact and, he thought, unnoticed. He went to its left side, shielding any likelihood of being spotted from the barn or the house, and peered through the driver's window. *Nothing out of the ordinary.* The visor docker was empty; the glove box open.

Gully had to make a decision. Left or right. House or barn. *Officers down in the barn, so better check the barn. Here we go.*

Gully stood up, readied his weapon, and jogged over to the barn. He could see it was light inside – it was approaching 4am and the sun would be coming up in the next two hours – but his visor registered no movement inside. If the light was on, at least, he thought, someone was in there at some point; if not Mr Smith then Mr Creepy Suit and his missing officers.

Carefully he gripped the barn door edge to pull it slightly open. Through the crack he could see a ladder, little else. He pulled some more, revealing more of the barn, but nothing out of the ordinary. No hanging feet, no visors, no sinister dinner-jacketed crazy man. Gully stepped inside. The visor was quiet; only his own breathing disturbed the silence.

Gully moved to the ladder, his visor lighting every dark corner to which he turned. Half way up, a voice stopped his cautious ascent. 'I wouldn't come up here if I were you.' The voice came to him slow, calm and *velvety*. It cut above the silence as if dubbed on top of a recording.

Gully jumped confidently backwards off the ladder, raising his gun. 'Police!' he shouted. 'Show yourself and throw down any weapons.' His artificial light covered the sound's source.

'I do not need weapons – nor do you,' came the voice. 'If you turn back now, go to your car and leave right away, I will not come after you. If you stay in this barn for any longer than, ooh, ten seconds, I'll show you why I do not need any weapons.'

Gully noted that not one word from Mr Creepy Suit had registered on his visor. 'I am looking for two missing police officers,' he called up. 'Please identify yourself.'

'I know what you're looking for, officer. You now have only five seconds... 4. 3... 2. 1... Are you still here?'

Gully backed towards the barn door, eyes and gun trained on the upper level. Still in slow reverse his back ran into something soft. Heart jumping, Gully spun round. Up close and uncomfortable, Mr Creepy Suit was smiling at him. They stood roughly the same height, both appeared well-dressed, and Gully realised that this horrific apparition was just another man after all.

'Now then,' Creepy said softly. 'I warned you and you didn't listen. Now you have seen my face, you will not forget it. Do you think I should let you leave?'

14

Gully, frozen to the spot, tried to speak with authority. 'What's... what's going on here?'

'None of your business, dear chap. I see that you think it is, but this is actually my business, and *I do not like* people interfering in *my* business.'

Forcing himself, Gully managed to step back. He was still holding his gun, but down on his side. As his wrist twitched, Creepy's leg shot up and forward and into Gully's chest, sending him shooting back into the barn wall with a crunch. His IR suit vibrated aggressively. He landed on both feet, raised his gun and let off two shots.

Creepy instantly appeared at his left side, punched him in the back and launched him over to the left side of the barn. Gully rolled straight onto his feet, turned to shoot and squeezed off eight shots, which all hit the far wall. Creepy was nowhere.

Gully surveyed the barn – nothing at all. The battery clip on his revolver expelled a sharp shot of hot air as it recharged. His visor picked up a tremor to the right and level with him. *Must be outside*, he thought. *But first, let's see what's up that ladder, and then find out where the hell Creepy went?*

Gun up, Gully moved cautiously back to the ladder and began to climb, watching his back on every step. At the top, he turned to hoist himself up. He had felt no pain from Creepy's blows – the suit had taken care of that – but he sure did suffer from the creeps.

On the upper level he found what looked like a body – well, more like a mound of flesh, riddled with holes, covered in a thick layer of black oil, or something like oil. There was no head or face. As he neared it, the smell became unbearable. He gagged and covered his mouth.

Gully moved to the far corner of the level, away from the fleshy pile. He held his breath and tried to decide what to do next. At risk of running into Creepy, he would have to go outside to get to the house. *The visors...* he had almost forgotten them! *Where are they?* He surveyed the whole upper area again and could neither see them nor any parts of them. *Creepy took the visors*, he thought. *Creepy has them in his pockets or he's eaten them, along with Tom and Frank – and some sweet mayonnaise.*

Why had Creepy disappeared? Was it because he realised he couldn't hurt him in the IR suit? For now, it didn't matter. He had to get out of this barn and into the house. He supposed another encounter with

Creepy would not go quite as well, but he didn't have a choice.

Gully moved warily to the ladder and peeked down. Seeing the way clear, he shot down the rungs and in one sweeping movement reached the barn door. Looking into darkness, he flicked his visor down and all became light. There were no tremors, no movements. The cruiser stood forty feet in front of him, the house twenty or thirty to his right. He bolted for the house, flashing his weapon once left and right. At the door he knocked loudly and frantically.

Footsteps...the door opened and a man, mercifully not Creepy, stood in the corridor, smiling. 'Officer Gullidge?'

'Yeah...yeah, Officer Gullidge,' he confirmed through panted breaths. 'You must be Mr Smith. Mr...are you alone?' He pushed through, glanced back, and shut the door quickly behind him.

Hat eyed Gully's gun nervously. 'Yes indeedy sir – but hold on a second...what's up with you, and what's with the gun? You look like you've come straight from the arena.'

'No...sorry, Mr Smith. I've just had a minor combat encounter in your barn, and my assailant has vanished. Do you...do you know what has happened in your barn sir?'

'Nothing? I was in there this morning, I mean yesterday morning – sorry, it's been a long day here – but not really since. Not had call to. Just keep some tools in there. What's going on? Who attacked you? One of them officers who was here earlier?'

'No...no, sir.' Gully regained more even breathing and felt his heart rate slow a little. 'Mr Smith, there is a corpse, or something that looks a lot like a corpse, in your barn. When I was in the barn, I was attacked. The assailant has now disappeared, as have my two officers, and their equipment, which we knew was in that barn because we could see it through their visors, which are no longer there. According to your call earlier, your entire flock of sheep is gone. There's a whole lot of disappearing going on here – would you care to tell me why *you're* still here?'

'Shit...I mean, dammit. Darned if I know.' Hat smiled. 'Just lucky, I guess. Come on in anyway. I'll make some coffee.'

Gully followed Hat down the corridor to the kitchen, reconstructing images to form a picture of what might be happening but, more peculiarly, trying to guess who this Hat character was and why he presented an apparent calm within a very strange storm. Hat turned

16

back as he entered the kitchen, glancing and raising a smile.

'Mr Smith. Do you have any identification? Pardon me, but it's due process. We have to make sure we're dealing with the right person, you know?'

Hat filled the kettle. 'Sure. Um, I think so. I'll go get something. You need a photo or something? To show this is my house?' Gully nodded. 'No problem. I'll be right back.' Hat flicked the kettle switch, walked back to the living room and disappeared around the left corner calling, 'Help yourself to a biscuit!'

Gully grew more relaxed. Something about the house, this kitchen, and that kindly, eccentric and rough but *good* man made him feel at ease. He flipped up his visor and sat on one of two chairs tucked under a small, tidy table.

'Won't be a minute,' Hat called from the next room. 'Got something right here, just blowing the dust off.'

Gully didn't respond. *I don't have time to relax. This is messed up. How come this guy has all this shit happening around him and doesn't even notice? What the fu…*

Hat appeared from the next room, in an instant raising a long shotgun and squeezing the trigger firmly. The shot mostly hit Gully mid-chest, crumpling into his suit and sending him flying backwards through the chair and into a wall two feet behind him.

'Damnit, should have taken the head shot!' Hat shouted, gleefully. 'Here we go! Don't wriggle!'

Gully's ears rang. The IR suit crumpled outward; the shot fell to the floor. He stood up, winded but undamaged, and charged at Hat, tackling low with his shoulder to the old man's pelvis, taking him down to the ground. Hat's finger squeezed the trigger and sent a blast up to the ceiling as his head connected with the side of the kitchen bench. The corner was rounded but gouged a good inch into the left side of his head, spraying a thick jet of blood at the wall and on the floor, like a kid taking his thumb off the end of a garden hose.

Gully leapt up, drew his gun, and within a second had it stuck in Hat's cheek, kicking the shotgun away with his left foot. He screamed: 'Who the fuck are you, where are my officers, and what the fuck is going on here?'

Hat smiled and raised his head slowly and shakily. A thick stream of blood poured from his head wound and puddled beneath. His teeth were covered in the red stuff too. He looked like a vampire who'd just awoken from a short nap after a fulsome takeaway. He spluttered uneasily: 'Go fuck yourself.'

Gully stood up, gun still trained on the mad man's head, and let off two rounds. A second later the gun fizzed with the familiar short, sharp air release. Hat – if this was Hat – was dead. Gully looked down to check his IR suit, flicking his visor back down to survey the immediate area. He decided to check out the rest of the house. It was the last thing he wanted to do right then but it was necessary.

He walked out to where Hat had gone to get his shotgun and saw a living room like any other: a little untidy, old-fashioned and, well, drab. At one end, almost level with the end of the kitchen, was a bookcase full of varying sizes of books and some ornaments, a bureau and a table with some flowers in a vase, an ashtray and a notebook. Behind these was a wall – *funny, no door*, Gully thought. He didn't remember seeing a door off the entrance corridor when he came in, but from the outside of the house it was clear a room had to be there. *Maybe you get in from outside.*

He moved quickly from the thought and headed to the back window and door, which led out into a small garden area and then, as much as could be seen, a low fence before a big field stretched away into the darkness. *No TV in this room either*, Gully noted, *but it feels like it's a set for TV.*

Gun raised, Gully checked the door. Locked. *Good. He* headed for the kitchen, glanced briefly at Hat Smith's corpse, and passed on to the corridor to reach the stairs, at the same time glancing up the corridor. *No, no door.* He took the first two steps up and stopped. *No tremors.*

One step at a time, careful not to make any noise – even though it would be unlikely that anyone in the house would not have heard the four loud gun shots mere minutes earlier. Gully's ears were still ringing. He reached the landing uneventfully. To the right was nothing but a corridor with a window at the end. Left, the corridor led to a bedroom. The light in that room was off, but the corridor's light was on.

This is some shit odd house, Gully thought: *Like half of it's here and the other half isn't.* The idea elevated his unease. He moved on. Entering the bedroom, gun still raised, he flicked the switch with his left hand. Nothing happened. *Great! Artificial light then…*

Keeping on the move, he checked the room, especially to the left.

18

There was a wall but no door. This half-house was growing spookier by the minute, not from any other stimulus, just the fact that there was half a house hidden from view. At the window he could more easily see the back field. Two figures were moving towards the north-east corner of the field, torches lighting their way. *Tom and Frank! Shit!* There was no handle to open the window. Scanning the frame he saw that these windows did not open without force.

One of the figures turned, torchlight flashing back onto another figure who Gully immediately recognised. *Mr Dead Hat Smith – what?* Unable to take his eyes off the three figures gathered together, he saw them turn to head back to the house. Gully's instinct was to run downstairs fast and back into the kitchen, but better judgement won out. He stood, transfixed.

One of the figures stopped and raised an arm in the direction of the window and pointed straight at Gully. The other two glanced up. Gully gasped, shrank back from the window and headed for the corridor leading back to the stairs, moving purposely slow, gun raised. If those guys were Tom and Frank, and Hat Smith, he was even more confused than he thought.

Of course, he could try to make contact.

At the top of the stairs one tremor registered on the visor. It was approaching fast from beneath. Pointing his weapon, he leaned around, flush against the banister, and waited. When another gun appeared at the bottom of the steps, he sharpened his aim. Officer Tom Turnbull's inquisitive face emerged into the light then, and stared up at him.

'Tom?'

'Gully? What the hell are you doing here?'

Three – Time to die

Tom Turnbull, Frank Willis, Joe Gullidge and Hat Smith – alive and well – were standing in the kitchen where only minutes earlier Gully had blasted two bullets in the face of their host. Now, instead of being a warm corpse, Hat was holding court.

'So what are you doing here, Gully?' Frank asked. 'We didn't know anyone else responded to the call.'

Tom looked at Gully, expecting an answer. He felt aggrieved that his superior had come out all this way, as if to check up on them. Yes, they were good friends, but Tom had been in this game a lot longer than Gully. He knew the job – and never got into a situation he could not handle.

Gully, sweating inside his IR suit, felt very uncomfortable. 'What's bothering me here is that you two have been missing for three hours, and Mr Smith here has me the most confused.' He paused, not noticing the puzzled look exchanged between his fellow officers. He directed his next question directly at Hat: 'Sir, have you ever seen me before?'

'Nuh-uh,' Hat replied. 'And what's all that about your men being missing? They've only been here five minutes.'

Gully flipped down his visor, checking the time – 4.27am. He flipped the VICOM up again. 'Frank, what time do you have there?'

'It's 1.10am, Gully. We only just got here. Why are *you* here? We sure aren't missing, as you can see. Only thing that's missing here is ninety-nine and a half sheep!' Frank glanced at Tom, who was grinning. He chuckled quietly, too, flashing a look at their host to ensure he hadn't noticed.

'Okay then – these sheep. Any idea where they could be? In my experience, sheep, other animals, things, whatever, don't just disappear.' Gully was still sweating, his heart pounding. 'I've had a look around and seen...uh, nothing. Exactly nothing. Come on gents, time to leave. We'll send a forensics crew out tomorrow, once the fire in town is dealt with...'

'Whatever you say, Gully,' Tom said, mustering another faint smile.

'Take a statement,' Gully continued. 'I'll wait outside. I'm gonna call Lou, tell her what's what. That okay with you, Mr Smith?' He eyed his host suspiciously. Hat didn't seem to notice.

'Sure, whatever. I'm tired. Been a long day. I can't see for shit anyway. Wait for your boys to come back tomorrow, yep.'

As Gully turned to leave, a splotch of red in the corner of the floor held his eye. *Hat's blood?* Purposefully, he walked to the front door. Tom and Frank set up a recorder on the kitchen table. Gully turned to go back, hesitated, and then did so anyway.

'Mr Smith?'

Hat looked over at Gully. 'Hmm?'

'Do you own a gun, sir?'

'Nope. Never had cause to keep a gun. Well, not these days. Used to have an old rifle, somewhere.'

'Thanks...' Gully left the kitchen and opened the front door slowly, surveying the area beyond. Still deeply unnerved he headed for the cruiser, but turned to take in the left side of the house. There was a lower window there, blacked out it seemed, but a narrow alley beside the house suggested he could get down there.

First, he headed back to the front door, purposely left open. His officers and Mr Smith were still in there. They were speaking but he couldn't hear what they were saying.

Sticking close to the front of the house, he shifted along stopping just once to peek into the large window of the front room. Beyond the glass, he could make out nothing – not even a curtain; giving him an odd sensation, like he was really staring into *nothing*.

Reaching the alley he flipped his visor down, hoping for readings as he entered the passageway.

In a space some four feet wide he searched for a door, something to show that the half house was only an odd design and did not hide anything – no mystery.

He walked the length; there was neither door nor windows, up nor down. Gully returned to the front, his mind entertaining the possibility that there was a door hidden inside, or at least built into the wall.

At the front door he saw Tom and Frank walking towards him. 'All wrapped up for now,' Tom said. 'Let's hit that bar, Frank. You coming, Gully?'

'No ... I mean, wait. I need to talk with you guys. Debrief.'

'Debrief on what?' Frank asked.

'Just come over here.' He led them over to their cruiser. 'Guys, something really, really messed up is happening here right now. Would

21

you mind explaining everything that's happened to you since you arrived?'

Frank and Tom exchanged a worried look. 'We got here just after one, entered the house with Mr Smith, who showed us out to the pasture, where we found half a sheep,' Frank explained. 'Seriously, half a sheep. We saw you in the window, walked back to the house and ... and here we are.'

'Have you been inside that barn?' Gully pointed and their eyes followed.

'No, we haven't had much of a look around. We think this guy's a bit of a fruit, and he's either making this shit up or someone's been up here with a giant transporter and had his livestock away while he was napping on the shitter.'

Tom nodded. 'Probably. Anyway, what the hell are you doing here, Gully?'

'Listen to me, guys. Just listen. Something is majorly wrong here. I'm here because that man, who may or may not be Hat Smith, called the station to say that you two had turned up, but gone missing. Lou took the call and pulled up your visor feeds, which were prone in that barn over there, taking in a corpse hanging from the rafters...'

'Gully!' Tom shrugged aggressively, accompanied by a look of sheer bewilderment.

'Shut up, Tom. Hear me out. When I got here, I immediately checked the barn, whereupon I was attacked by a man in a dinner suit who somehow moved faster than the wind. He just disappeared. Looked like he'd been eating the corpse in the barn and then...'

'Gully, uh...'

'Tom, I am *deadly fucking serious.*' His expression reinforced his oath. 'That house, Hat's house...has no doors leading to the rooms on the left. There's half a house missing, just like your half sheep, except it's there and I just can't see how. More importantly – *most* importantly – that man, Hat or whoever the hell he is, just attacked me with a shotgun.' He pointed to the mark on his IR suit as evidence of the claim. 'And I put two bullets into his face. Now he's walking around as if none of this ever happened. My time shows about three hours up on yours, and Hat's blood is still on his kitchen floor. The blood I got out of him.' He held out his watch and nodded at it. Tom and Frank didn't look at the watch but exchanged worried frowns.

22

'Gully, I...um...this is crazy. We've been here like twenty minutes, no more. None of this makes sense. You been drinking?' Tom looked concerned.

'I haven't been drinking, Thomas. Not a drop, not a sniff. We have two choices here. We stay or we go. Whether or not you believe me, I'm inclined to stay and have another look in that crazy shit-up barn. You coming?'

'Uh...sure,' Frank said. 'I'm in.' He walked to the cruiser, pressed his palm against the window to unlock it, leaned in and took out his and Tom's visors. 'See, Gully, here are our visors.' Gully felt as if his brain flipped, as if someone was folding it to make a wild origami.

With a playful wink Frank passed a visor to Tom. Frank walked towards the barn, Gully and Tom following. At the same time, Gully studied the house, the front door, side window, and then the barn. Frank confidently swung the door open.

~ ~ ~

'Gully, are you there? Come in, come in. Gully. Gully! Please acknowledge.'

Louise had desperately been trying to get through. The VICOM was connected to Officer Gullidge's feed but it was all black, apart from some strange back and forth movement, like a curtain swishing in the breeze, or some digital interference. She couldn't tell which. She had tested Tom and Frank's visors several times and saw they were still offline. She felt sick – a sensation heightened by Gully's similar vanishing act. It wasn't a dead feed, just a very dark feed. There was some sound, like white noise, but low and somehow *dark*, she thought.

Attempts to reach Gully had gone on for the last hour. No one had called anything in apart from the fire updates. That was turning into a major drama and was promising a long, long night for everyone on the scene. Several officers had been taken to the hospital. Now, however, Louise had a doom-laden feeling in her gut that Hawks Farm was the site of the real drama.

Louise checked the time. 4.40am. She had been up for nearly 24 hours, working for most of them. Sometimes she loved this job, mostly when nothing was happening and she could chew the fat with the guys, but times like these sucked balls – big time.

'Gully – please respond. Can you hear me?' Again no response, as the black grainy view from his visor feed shifted again.

~~~

Frank leaned against the door, holding it open. Tom was first into the barn, followed by Gully. They found nothing out of the ordinary, yet somehow, Gully couldn't tell exactly, the barn felt *different* – it was *colder*.

'You've already checked the barn, Gully?'

'Yeah, Tom. Take the ladder.'

Tom started up the ladder. Gully covered the area. Frank came in and closed the door behind him. It clanked shut.

'Nothing up here; coming down,' Tom warned.

Gully's relief was instant until he remembered he had no good reason to relax. Whatever was wrong here was *very* wrong. They needed to know what.

'Hold on...' Tom called, standing right at the top of the ladder and pointing, 'what's that? North-east corner.'

Frank and Gully turned. Frank walked to the corner. 'Looks like a trapdoor,' he called. 'Open it?'

'No,' Gully responded quickly. He couldn't recall a trapdoor there before. 'I'm in the suit. I'll open it.'

Reaching Frank at the trapdoor, he knew he hadn't seen this before – because it hadn't been *there* before. If these were all some kind of alternative realities, was he back in the real world now? No weird shit – and that *blood* in the kitchen could have been something else altogether. The thought eased the tension in his shoulders. But still – so much was strange, unanswered, unexplained. Everything had all happened, he was *sure* of that, but could anything else happen? Regardless, the trapdoor was in the here and now, and they were going to take a look. Could be nothing, perhaps sewerage, a generator, whatever ... but something told him it couldn't be that simple.

'On three. One – two – three!' Frank pulled up the hatch, a wooden door about three inches thick. It swung open easily, revealing a dimly lit shaft around ten feet deep. The sides were not wood but earth; dug straight out of the ground. Tom joined them at the open hatch.

'You going in, Joe?'

Gully didn't answer but turned to lower himself down backwards until his knees were firm against the earth wall and his fingers clutched the ridge at the top. He relaxed his knees, let his grip loosen and dropped to the bottom. 'Here we go.'

Flipping his visor up to deal with the small surrounding space, Gully saw a tiny opening ahead. With his orientation this would have the opening leading east – out the back, behind the barn.

'There's an opening,' he called. 'I think I could get through here.'

'Okay Joe. We're right here. You be careful.'

Gully closed his hands together as if about to pray and brought his arms tight, pushing into a thin opening not much bigger and then jerked them apart, crumbling the earth around them.

'Do we...uh...do we really need to start burrowing underground?' Frank called.

'Just...let me have a look. I'm nearly through.'

Gully twisted his body around and upwards to enter a gap just big enough to get his head through, which at least would let him see what was down there. With some wriggling, he managed to push his head to the other side, keeping one foot on the earthy pile behind him; his shoulders caught snug in the bottleneck he had created.

Tom looked over at Frank: 'Why is there a hole under this barn anyway?'

'Maybe it's a food store, something like that?' Frank shrugged. 'Doesn't mean shit to me anyhow. I say we get out of here-'

'Guys!' Gully shouted up from below. 'Guys! You gotta see this. This is fu...'

From below came a crack like a thunderclap in reverse. Tom and Frank lurched backwards, shock rupturing through their feet and shins.

'Joe,' Frank called croakily as he struggled up. 'Joe, are you okay? What the fuck was that?' He leaned over, peered into the hole and saw Gully's legs, hanging out of the hole, his IR suit ripped cleanly away at the top, as if Gully had been sliced down the middle with something very, *very* sharp.

Frank recoiled, stumbled backward into Tom, knocked him over and ended up like a passed out drunk on an armchair – awkwardly shaped by Tom.

'What the hell is going on?' Tom demanded, struggling beneath Frank. Managing to straighten up, he glanced down and saw a look on

Frank's face he'd never seen there before. 'Frank! What is it?'

Tom stepped slowly towards the hole, peered in and glimpsed a head poking through. Gully's – swivelling around to look up at him.

'You coming down or not?' Gully asked again, face bright, glowing even. 'This is insane.'

Frank stiffened. Light returned to his eyes. 'Joe?' he called out. 'Joe? Whose legs ...'

Tom backed into the hole, dropped down and looked ahead. The tiny gap Gully had found had given way under his colleagues' weight, collapsing into a man-sized entryway to what looked like – *how?* – a body of shimmering water with grassy hill on the other side. The oddest part of this view was the bright daylight that bathed it. Tom ventured through to join Gully and they stood silent, mouths slack, staring across the water. Gully had no doubt who was standing on the far side – Mr Creepy was back.

The water – *it looks like water, so it must be water* – stretched out as far as the eye could see in all directions, except for where the figure stood on a small island some twenty feet wide, going back to the hill and possibly beyond, and an area of about six by six feet upon which Tom and Gully held their ground. They hadn't even looked down at their tiny island. The vista ahead was breathtaking in every way – like a Dominican picture postcard. Right about the spot where the grassy hill raised into the sky, the sun squatted as if glaring at them.

Frank dropped into the hole, hunched down and looked out, but struggled to see anything but the legs of his colleagues. 'Joe? Tom? What's happening in there?'

Eyes fixed on Mr Creepy, standing still as the air in this place, Tom whispered: 'Frank. Get outta here.'

Arriving nearby, Frank's expression matched theirs. Within seconds, Creepy moved. He took several steps towards them and put one foot onto the water, followed by the other, and headed straight for the trio, pace quickening. His feet touched but didn't splash the surface.

Gully, Frank and Tom shuffled backwards expecting to hit the wall. They hit nothing. Isolated on this tiny island, with only water in any direction, apart from where Mr Creepy was rapidly advancing, Frank's anxiety put him off balance. As he rolled backwards, his right arm splashed into the *water*, causing an enormous sound much like cymbals clashing together at the height of orchestral fervour. He quickly withdrew his arm and discovered it was not even wet. Something moved in his stomach. A thin breeze lifted his hair. He turned to face it, held out his arm towards it and felt...something that simply wasn't there. He pushed out into the nothing and let his body flow forward, calling back to Gully and Tom to join him. They did not hear him.

'Shit...Frank!' Tom called. He and Gully circled the small island, like bees in a glass jar. 'Did you hear that splash? He's gone into the water!'

Mr Creepy, now just thirty feet away and getting closer by the second, lifted one arm to the sky and clicked his fingers.

The sun went out.

Tom and Gully each felt a hand close around their neck, lifting them into darkness. Gully recognised Creepy's voice: 'How did you get in *here*?' it smoothly snarled. 'You're not supposed to be *here*.' Creepy might have been speaking in two voices, with two languages melding into English.

He expected no answer. He had compressed their vocal chords.

Then, mood altering, 'Come on then – I'll show you something,' he said.

~~~

Frank stood with his back against the earthy wall, staring into the blackness ahead. From above, the light of the barn provided his only comfort. Breathing heavily and fast and trembling with real cold fear, Frank could not move. In seconds he had understood that whatever lay the other side of that hole was not real – *it couldn't be* – but it was *there*. He realised the half-body he'd seen of Gully was only because the other half of Gully had stretched off into this *otherness*, and for that brief time he'd left his other half behind, as if it was some other body in another time zone. Frank acknowledged he was scared half to death, had no idea what might be happening to his friends, and that he wasn't about to stick his arm back through to find out.

He pulled himself out of the hole into the light of the barn and headed for the door. Opening it without any sense of caution, he went out and turned to look at the barn and then set off to the right of it. Up the side he came upon an alley about a metre wide, flanked on the right by a tall wall.

He made his way to the back end of the barn, pressed his body up against the wall and leant out to the left, just enough to see around the back with one eye. With light breaking through cracks in the wood, and helped by the moonlight, Frank could make out a low wall, running from the tall wall to his right along to the rear of Hat's house and beyond, into the darkness. No water, no sunlight, no Gully and no Tom.

What now? Back into the barn, through that hole and into who-knows-what? No, back to the house, to see if Hat was okay.

As Frank turned back to his right a fist smashed into his nose. The sound told him it broke. Blood sprayed from his nostrils, down onto his suit and outward, splattering on Hat Smith's shirt. Hat punched Frank again, squarely in the gut. Frank reeled back, fell over the low wall, head hitting the ground first.

'You're not supposed to be here,' Hat called into the silence. Slowly, he hopped over the low wall to bring his boot down onto Frank's neck. The force snapped it. With face half buried in earth, blood still spurting into the ground and seeping across his face and chin, Frank's last breath came short and quick.

Hat walked along the low wall, reached the rear of his house, took a shotgun that was leaning against the kitchen wall and headed for the paddock to which he had lured his visitors not many minutes earlier. He strode purposefully over forty feet or so and, with the half-sheep corpse a little over to his right, stepped into the *otherness*, marked by an enormous thunderclap – with no one around to hear it.

~~~

Mr Creepy flicked the sun on.

Gully and Tom swung gently from ropes that stretched up yet appeared unattached to anything. Their eyes were barely parted slits, their necks sporting barely open slits, with pulsating rivulets of blood slowly draining away their lives. Pooling beneath their feet, it glistened under blazing sunlight.

In front of their bodies, stretching as high as the ropes they hung from or perhaps further, was a kind of tower – a cylinder of black stone, with one single window about half way up. Only a steep bank of lush green grass led up to the tower. There were no steps but, in any case, there was no door either.

Gully mustered enough energy to twist his head a few degrees to see where Tom had died. He felt like a drunk first thing in the next morning, eyes adjusting to a world edging back in. There was no life left in his body. It was the most horrible sight, but he didn't have the energy to care. He closed his eyes.

Mr Creepy flicked the sun off.

Four – Echoes and shadows

Frank opened his eyes and was faced with blanket darkness, but he could hear breathing. 'Tom?'

No response. Louder this time, 'Tom?' Tom jolted awake, also faced with darkness. 'Tom? Is that you?'

'Uh...yeah. What happened?'

'Dunno. Last thing I knew was that old man sticking his hand on my face, and here I am.'

'Shit. Same here. Can you see anything?'

'Not a thing,' Frank said. 'Are you tied up? I don't think this is a chair. I don't know what it is.'

'This isn't a chair. It's cold, stone I think. My hands won't budge.'

There was a raking sound, like fingernails on a blackboard but not as shrill. At first it was slow and then faster, more urgent. The sound turned to scraping.

'Shhhh,' Tom warned. 'Keep still.'

The scraping turned to something like sawing and a dim light appeared through a tiny crack. The light disappeared then came back, followed by an almighty thud as a large object crashed through the wooden wall, splinters splaying outwards. A pair of arms pushed through.

'Guys? Are you okay?'

'Gully? What the hell are you doing here?' Frank was relieved.

Tom looked around the small room and in the weak light he could see very little: four walls, one of which was half-destroyed, and not a lot else. His partner was sat on a large stone slab, his hands bound by something to the top of the slab and his feet likewise to the lower side. 'Gully, thank God. Can you cut us free?'

'Hold on a second,' Gully said, calmly. 'How'd you two get in here? The only way in is the way I came in.' He moved over to Tom, looked down at the leather figure-of-eight grip and bolt that was cuffing him to the stone slab and looked back up again to survey the room. The visor gave nothing away. No tremors, no *nothing*.

'Was it Hat? Did Hat put you in here?'

'Yeah, I think so,' Frank said. 'Where is he?'

'Hat is dead. Who wants to get out first?'

'Quit messing about Gully and get us out of here!'

Gully's knife made quick work of the leather bounds. 'Let's get out of here. Grab your visors.'

Tom and Frank stooped to pick up their visors. Tom stretched a little to iron out some muscle creases. His junior by some years, Frank had no need and moved towards the lit room in front of him. As he emerged into the living area, he saw ahead and to the right the body of the house owner slumped in the corner, a pool of blood by his lifeless head. Tom followed, letting out a laboured sigh as he neared the kitchen.

'What the fuck, Gully? What did he do?' Tom answered his own question, spying the shotgun on the floor and the sprawled, splintered table and chairs over to his right. 'He attacked you? Got us too, I think. The whole place went dark and we wound up in that room. This place is really fucked.'

Gully was only half-listening. 'Guys, come over here and sit down.'

'Can't we just get outta here, Joe?' Frank asked.

'Nope, not yet. Just come in here and sit down. Please.' The expression on Gully's face was half blank, half exasperation.

Tom and Frank did as they were told, sitting down on opposite sides of the room in identical armchairs, each with a small table to their flank. Comically, the pair simultaneously put their visors and guns down on these tables and looked up at Joe with his serious, head-teacher expression, like he was about to tell them off. He wasn't.

'I don't even believe this myself,' Gully started. 'It's...uh... unbelievable.' He stood with his back to the hole he had created a minute earlier, feeling a little exposed, like something could crawl out of that room, something with giant jaws and sharp teeth, and pull him back in. He shuddered.

'Tonight, I believe I have seen and met around three versions of you two, and this dead Hat feller, who is dead here, but...um...not actually dead because I've seen him alive since shooting two bullets in his damn face.' Gully looked over to the body, and back again at Tom, his gaze shifting between his and Frank's faces, hesitating on what to say next.

'Gully...okay,' Tom said. 'Some pretty unexplainable stuff happened to us too. We saw the world disappearing around us, a corpse in the barn...'

'I saw a corpse in there too, guys, which is what brought me out here,' Gully interrupted. 'But the corpse you saw is probably not the same one I saw, although it could've been the same guy.'

Frank couldn't hide his confusion. Tom was concentrating on his own interpretation of these events.

'Y'see,' Gully continued, 'I watched you die, Tom; I saw your throat bleed out. And Frankie, I found your lifeless damn body out the back of that barn not two minutes ago. Your neck was broken, and your nose was taking up most of your face.'

'Joe,' Frank started. 'What the *fuck* are you on? I don't understand any of this – you talking about time warps and shit? That's all sci-fi. The way I read this, Hat Smith is a lonely lunatic who pulled us out here on false pretences and boarded us up in that room.'

'The walls, Frank,' Tom said. 'The walls *changed*. The cruiser disappeared into the ground! D'ya remember that stuff, Frank?' His tone was harsh. 'The body, the half-a-fuckin'-sheep? You not detecting anything a bit weird about all this?'

'Shit Tom, I don't-' he began, before Gully finished his sentence: 'No, you don't, Frank. Tom doesn't, and I don't.'

He looked down at his feet, then back up. 'The three of us, just a few minutes ago, were standing on an island in a giant...*ocean* in glorious sunshine while Mr Creepy, who I have put bullets in, ran over the water, *actually on it*, and turned the sun out like a lamp. Then he hung me and Tom up and while we hung there dying, he showed us a tower. There's a window in that tower, and this house, I believe, is that tower. Somehow.'

'Uh, we ain't dead,' Frank volunteered, quietly. 'Alive and kicking and ready to get the hell outta this place. Sir.'

Tom's expression didn't change. He was staring at Gully's mouth, waiting for the next volley of bullshit.

'When Mr Creepy last turned the lights off, he cut my rope and pushed me the hardest I've ever been pushed and I ended up underneath the barn, which you guys won't remember we all found a hole in just now...' Frank looked over at Tom and shrugged. Tom didn't notice. '...and so I left the barn and saw Hat Smith walking back into this house – a man who, incidentally, was dead a few minutes before I went into the barn in the first place – and so I decided to go round the back of the barn – where I found Frankie's body – and kept going, until I saw Hat literally disappear in the field out back. Yep, disappeared into thin air, into the black. Gone! And so I came back in here; sure enough there's Hat's cold, dead body, and I hear a voice from behind this wall, and here we all are – happy families.'

Gully's face had lit up and, Tom saw, his eyes reflected a quiet panic, or something that certainly he'd not seen in Joe Gullidge's eyes before.

'Joe, if you're serious, which I can see you are, and I'm not saying I have any other explanation, but what exactly are we dealing with here? How can Hat be there, all dead and deader, and also somewhere outside, having just killed me? None of this makes any sense.'

'I know Frank, but we're not even looking at this the right way, whatever the right way is. Tom...Tom! Wake up man. What's your take on this?'

'Geez, guys, I have even less of an idea.' He slapped his palms down on his knees and stood up slowly. 'Gully, you've seen a lot more than we have. We certainly haven't seen any island or ocean, or this Mr Creeps feller, but if what you're saying is one hundred per cent, we open that front door and our cruiser is back where it should be, and Frank here's body is not. I mean, it is, and that's here, *on him*.'

'So this tower...we're in it?' Frank asked? 'This is not, I can tell you, a tower.'

'No,' Gully retorted, 'but it is an approximation of a tower. Here's my crazy theory: there are rooms, without walls, without boundaries that *we can see*, and when we cross over those boundaries, shit changes. There's some kind of grid down here, and crossing over into the next square, or whatever, takes you up or down a level in this tower. And it's outside too. It's above and below us, and we're in it right now. I guarantee, if one of us goes up those stairs, or outside, and then back here again, Hat's body will be gone; we'll all be gone. We'll be here to us, but gone to whoever comes back.'

'I can live with that,' Tom said, brightly. He picked up his visor, put it on his head and picked up his gun. 'So we got to stick together. When we split up, the shit hits the fan. I guess as we're all here, we're on the same *level* of this tower or whatever it is. The shit I'm struggling with is how and why, but none of that really matters beyond survival, and if I already died a couple times tonight, I'm happy to keep hold of this life and get the hell out of here.'

'I don't think it's that easy, Tom,' Gully said, thoughtfully gazing just over Tom's shoulder into the wall at the back of the room, then down to Hat's body. 'I can't be sure this is the right instance of us. What happens if we leave now? I can see we are all here and now, but how many instances of us are out there? Which is the right one? Does it even matter?'

'What matters,' Frank started, 'is that we get out of here alive. If there's a tower around here somewhere, I don't really want to go up it, y'know. Let's just get back in that cruiser and get outta dodge. Let's find a bar and sit in it till the sun comes up.'

Tom had started to try figuring it out. 'Okay, so there are echoes of ourselves in different parts of this house, right now or not, for *some* reason.'

'He told me we're not supposed to be here,' Gully said.

'Yeah. Hang on a minute, Joe. These echoes come about when we move from one place to another, so I don't think we can avoid creating more echoes. Keeping together, we can get out of here, I'm sure of it. Well, sure according to a logic that I don't comprehend, but sure as I'm unsure. Fifty-fifty. Maybe if we die again we'll sprout up somewhere else. Shit, maybe the three of us are already in that bar anyway!'

'Let's take it as we are, then,' Frank said. He too stood up, put his visor back on and picked up his gun. 'We don't know what's out there in any direction. I say we follow our host, into the vanishing point and see what he's up to.'

'Agreed,' Gully said, solemnly. 'It seems like they aren't keen on letting us leave anyway. Let's go.'

Tom forced open the back door. 'Do we cross into another level by going out here?' The three men shrugged at each other. 'Stick it then. After me.'

Gully led, with Tom and Frank just behind, hopping over the low back wall, and out towards the original spot where Hat had showed two of them the half-sheep. They walked past it and carried on about twenty paces before Gully stopped.

'There's nothing here. Nothing. You guys see anything?'

Tom and Frank indicated a negative response.

Gully took two more steps forward and a light came up on the horizon. Looking back, he saw nothing. The house and the kitchen light were gone. Nothingness surrounded them on all sides, but the light ahead beckoned progress.

Taking a few more steps, Gully realised they were facing the same kitchen light they'd just walked away from. Sure enough, to his left, on the ground, was half a sheep. He took two steps back – 'Gully, what are you doing?' – and saw the other half. Forward again, the hind legs; back again, the head and forelegs. 'This is the crossing point,' he said, matter-of-factly. 'Up there is where we just came from. Up there is living, breathing Hat. We may not even have met him at this point.'

Tom nodded. Frank shook his head. All three proceeded towards the house, the two who had watched their superior dancing back and forth looking to his left then realising why, and being absolutely dumbfounded.

Echoes. Crossing points. A tower made of many levels, all on the same level.

Gully stopped again. 'Wait!' Tom and Frank did as they were told. 'You guys have your torches?'

Frank did and raised it up to confirm the fact. Gully passed his to Tom. 'Right, stand here and shoot your beams at that sheep for a few seconds, then back at me.'

Again, they did as they were told. 'Now, point up at the left bedroom window. Now, quick!' He pointed to make sure they knew which one.

The beams danced around the window, lighting a face which drew quickly back out of sight.

'We're going back to the barn,' Gully said. 'Follow me.'

Skirting low and fast, to stay out of sight of the house, they reached the low wall, staying on the right side of it as they scampered along to the rear of the barn. *No corpse*, Gully thought. *Good.* They rounded to the front of the barn and inside. A quick check up the ladder – no corpse and no Mr Creepy.

'Okay, we're back here,' Gully said. You guys won't remember it but we've already done this. There's a trapdoor over there. Open it.' He pointed; Tom and Frank jogged over.

'When you open that up, it will be a hole, an empty hole. Tom, jump in. You'll see a tiny light through the east side.'

Tom shrugged at Frank, who lifted the trap. Tom lowered himself down. 'What next, Joe?'

'You see the light?'

'Yeah, I see the light, your grace.'

'Smash a hole there but do not, *absolutely do not under any circumstances*, go through that hole!'

With the butt of his torch, Tom thumped against the earthy wall,

35

which politely gave way enough so that he could see, as if looking through a ship's porthole, the scene Joe had described.

'Okay Tom, what do you see?' Gully asked.

'Water, grass, sunshine. How's this even possible? I've seen some shit bu-'

'Never mind about that, just come on up outta there. We should have his attention.'

'Mr Creeps?' Frank asked. 'Why'd we want his attention, exactly?'

'Because we need to kill him.'

Five – The waiting room

Joe Gullidge, Gully to his friends, had once shot dead a man in cold blood. It was his only regret, but still an act he felt justified in doing. As an officer of the law, he had a duty to serve and protect, and break the occasional neck, in the line of carrying out that duty.

The first kill was the sucker punch, an act of such horrifying intensity that it took the wind out of him for six weeks or so. After that, though, it became a strangely numb experience. Pointing and shooting was a part of the job and before he had transferred to his current position, his previous patch in Chicago had seen plenty of action.

In those days Gully had felt like a superhero, untouchable and immortal, and this was before IR suits had reached 'the pinnacle of protection'. Nowadays he simply was untouchable, or just about anyway, so long as he kept his wits about him and expelled his weapon after every few shots.

But back then, as he often let his mind wander to *that* day, he had a lot of anger, and although he had never been what one might call trigger-happy, on *that* day he had been, and increasingly so since. A combination of sleep deprivation, some special 'nose powder' and watching a man beat his six-year-old kid to the ground was enough. He had nearly killed that poor kid, breaking his back and sentencing him to the rest of his life in a wheelchair.

Gully was too late to stop him. He was dealing with a disturbance next door when he heard the child's screams. The mother was at the door shouting for someone to help. Replaying this memory in slow motion, Gully's version of it had him striding into the hallway and past the mother, pulling up his gun and watching the father rain down heavy blows on the kid's neck and back; he didn't say a word – just squeezed the trigger and put four holes in the perpetrator. The memory always ended there.

So much more happened outside of that memory, but it wasn't information he could access anymore. A few weeks later he became a small town man; adjusting to a different way of life – one where his firearm would get dusty from lack of use, and one where his friends didn't see the need to carry one, although from his colleagues' stories he knew that it hadn't always been that way; Tom in particular had been forced to use his weapon many times, but he was also quite a bit older than Gully.

In this barn, however, nothing was more important than being weapon-ready. He would happily shoot an unarmed Mr Creepy, cold blood or not. As soon as he saw that smug face, he was going to send him the same way as Hat Smith – one, two, even three shots to the head, and make them all count.

Gully was furious – and that fury welled up inside him, creating a panic, an urgency he hadn't felt in a long time. He had plenty of back-up today too, with Frank up on the second floor, ladder kicked down and blocking the barn door, and Tom, in the top corner, hunched down with his gun trained on the hole in the floor. Gully was the bait, or so he hoped. Did Creepy know who was where, and how? Which levels of the tower he and his friends were on? Did Creepy think any of them were dead? Come to think of it, why *weren't* any of them dead. Gully didn't want to think about that at all.

'Anything?' Frank called. His visor immediately registered a tremor, from the direction of the hole. No one answered. Gully stood as still as he could, weapon ready. He saw the tremor too. Tom did not, the source of the sound bring directly underneath his visor – a blind spot. 'He's coming,' Frank said quietly.

'Gentlemen!'

Gully swivelled round to see Mr Creepy standing three feet from him, back to the barn door.

'Please don't shoot me. I am unarmed.' He held up his hands and pirouetted theatrically on the spot to prove the point. 'My name is Edward, and you are in my house. It would not be very polite to shoot an unarmed man in his own house, would you say?'

Gully's finger squeezed the trigger in; Frank was crouched up forty-five degrees on the balcony, laser sight painting a target on Edward's nose. Tom's gun was down.

'Mr Gullidge, I did not appreciate the intrusion or the violence the first time we met. Please stop pointing that *thing* at me.' Edward smiled. 'You have seen how fast I can move anyway. Save your energy, perhaps?'

He continued: 'So I have foiled your little ambush, but what puzzles me is why you want to do this anyway. Curiosity, is it? You have seen a different world tonight and you want to see more. Did you notice that I spared your life earlier? Did you also notice that you are together with your friends, all unharmed, and that I am not venturing forth any violence on this occasion?'

'I-' Gully started. 'Frank, stand down.' He lowered his own weapon. Frank kept his up.

'You want some answers then? I understand that. Let me say that I cannot give you many answers, but I can tell you some things. You are alive because I want you alive. You are here because I want you here. I am pleased to say that there is a party here tonight and you are *all* invited – nay, my guests of honour. Especially you, Mr Gullidge.'

'Who are you? How do you know me?' Gully demanded.

Edward the Creep was still smiling, broadening to a grin. 'I have known you for a very long time, Joe. Longer than these two have. But they are your friends, so they can come along too. It just would not be the same without them!'

He let out a long belly laugh, snapping down to a stern, serious look and staring straight into Gully's face. 'You want to see what's in that tower? You want to know *where* that tower is? All in good time. You see, down here we have some geography that...that is a little different to what you might be used to. Walls aren't walls. Thoughts are enough to move the props. You are on a stage, and I am the director of this play. How it ends is entirely up to you – not *them*. You.'

'Just what does anything here have to do with me?'

'As I said, friend, all in good time. Right now I have some important matters to attend to. You can go down that hole, play around in my little lake, but there's nowhere to go. That lake goes on forever. I made it to show off my sunny side. If you like, I could take away the water and just leave a void. Have you ever stared into the void, Joe?'

Edward was smiling, apparently entirely relaxed and not bothered by the laser target dancing around like a moth on a lightbulb, hovering around his chest, occasionally heading back to his head. He didn't even register it.

'Or you could go back to your cars, get in and drive back home, maybe stop off for a drink somewhere. Why, if I could get the time off, I'd come on with you!'

Tom stood up in the corner. 'Just what are you?'

Edward laughed, his perfect white teeth bared: 'I am a gatekeeper of sorts. That is all I can tell you. The man you know as Hat, he is one too. He made you kill him, Gully. Did you *enjoy* that? Did that make you feel like a real man?' He roared with laughter.

'So we can...uh, go?' Frank called down. 'Just get in our cars and go?'

'Well, yes and no. You are welcome to try, but your cars are no longer accessible. I am truly, terribly sorry about the inconvenience. Oh, and the road isn't there anymore either! This really is embarrassing.'

'Enough tricks,' Gully said. 'What happens next?'

'This!' With a snap of his fingers, the barn was plunged into darkness for two seconds, then back into light again, but Edward was gone.

Tom started forward, but looked down to avoid the trapdoor and saw that it wasn't there. Just the barn floor; no hole. 'Huh? Gully, look at this.'

As Gully turned his gaze away from the spot where Creepy had disappeared, Frank jumped down, landing with a thump and what sounded like a nasty click in his knee. He got up uneasily.

'So what now? Do we just wait here?'

'Fucked if I know,' Frank said.

Tom shrugged.

~~~

Tom pushed the barn door open and in an instant saw that the door had swung into another barn. The *same* barn. He walked in, turned back and saw a mirror image apart from the two figures of Frank and Joe staring back at him.

'I don't believe this shit. Are we stuck in a loop?'

Gully turned his back and looked to the trapdoor spot again, as Frank ventured forth into the second barn. 'Holy shit!' He had nothing else to say. This was testing his sensibilities a little too roughly.

Then: 'That guy talks like a lizard. He's something *else*.'

'Agreed,' Tom said, leaning against the far wall, looking back at Gully in the mirror-barn. 'This whole thing's like some stupid sci-fi. I don't *believe* in sci-fi. I don't *believe* in God. I don't believe in *any* of this.'

'That's not really an option right now,' Gully said to Tom. 'I'd also say it's not an option to wait around to find out what this party is. Let's get out of here.'

Apathy turned to a renewed sense of urgency, Tom and Frank hit opposite sides of the barn, scouring the walls for some crack, *anything*, that might indicate a way out. There was nothing, no sign of moonlight outside, and no sound. *Four walls, no way in or out*, Frank thought. It reminded him of their previous predicament, but at least then Gully had smashed on through.

Frank walked back into the first barn and picked up the ladder, swinging it around uneasily and then walking it through to where Gully and Tom were. 'We haven't looked up *there*,' Frank pointed. 'What if these barns aren't identical?'

He set the ladder in place and Gully stepped up. Reaching the top, so that his eyes were just above the floor level, there was nothing out of the ordinary. He carried on up and stood on the balcony, looking over at Tom, who was tracing the outline of the roof with his laser sight.

'So?' Frank called up.

'Uh-' Gully turned and started to the back of the balcony area. 'Yeah... yeah, there's something here.'

A tiny metal ring, big enough for a little finger to hook into, protruded from the floor about a foot in from either side of the sloped roof. The floor was dusty but this ring gleamed, almost inviting closer inspection. 'Hold on...'

Gully put his finger in and found that it raised quite easily; it felt surprisingly light. He raised it further, bringing up a wooden panel, dust falling off it. The barn was plunged into darkness. Gully dropped the panel but the barn stayed dark. At this point Gully realised his visor wasn't doing its job: no artificial light.

'Gully? What the fuck just happened?' Frank called.

'There's someone else in here!' Tom shouted.

Gully heard footsteps shuffling urgently towards him. Frank had been holding the ladder but was now half-way up it. Tom ran right into the side of the ladder, knocking it sideways and sending Frank flying. He managed to get a hand on the balcony edge but the sharp wood cut his hand open. As he landed awkwardly, an inch or so from the barn wall, he screamed. Tom and the ladder had become close friends on the floor too and his head landed on something soft. He also screamed.

As suddenly as the light had gone out, it came back on. No flicker, just light. As his eyes adjusted back, Frank saw something hairy and with teeth advancing at him. 'Shi-' Tom tried to scramble to his feet, but there was something around his neck.

Just as a very angry dog managed to close its jaws around Frank's neck, Gully let off two shots, both hitting the dog in its left side, the force pushing it against the wall with a loud yelp. Frank quickly rolled right, stopping as he bumped into Tom's leg and seeing the corpse of Hat Smith, his dead arm wrapped around Tom's neck, holding him close; looking up at his face, Hat was smiling, his teeth caked with blood.

'Tom!' Gully jumped down, landed cleanly and prised off the arm, with Frank dragging Tom backwards off the body. Tom clambered to his feet, pulled his gun and swivelled desperately, looking for threats. Frank did the same. Gully was looking over at the *other* barn. Mr Creepy, Edward, stood in the doorway.

'You know,' said Edward, glaring at Gully, 'that a magpie can't resist touching something shiny. Are you a magpie, Mr Gullidge?' He chuckled. 'The other guests are arriving. It won't be long now.' He raised both arms and in a sweeping gesture flung them back across his body. The barn door flew shut.

'Fuck this!' Frank screamed. He turned around to kick the corpse of his attacker, but the dog's body was gone, as was Hat's. There was no sign anything had been there.

'We're just supposed to sit and wait for this sick bastard to play around with us? What'd you *do*, Gully? What'd you do up there?'

'You know what, Frank?' Gully looked furious. 'I didn't *do* anything you wouldn't. You brought me here, not the other way round. Hat-fucking-Smith called the station saying you two were missing, that's why I'm here. It was your idea to-'

'Guys, stop. Just stop. This is what he wants. This is some kind of test and we're failing it.' Tom's voice was calm but firm. 'We can't leave here and we can't create a strategy and we can't shoot a guy who can disappear into thin air.' He shrugged, rolled his neck around twice, and sighed. 'You got a ciggie, Frank?'

'You don't smoke, *Tom*.' Frank felt for his cigarettes. They were there, as expected. Reaching in for the packet took the edge off already. 'Want one Joe?'

'No, thanks. That shit'll kill you.'

Frank tossed a cigarette to Tom, who caught it easily and put it between his lips. Frank did the same, clicking the flamer button on the top of the packet and holding it up to the cigarette, which sparked into life. The flame went out after two seconds. He threw the packet to Tom, who fumbled the packet to the floor.

'Nice one, dick,' Frank sniggered, letting out a thick plume of dark smoke with a sound like wind rushing through a pipe.

'Whatever.' Tom bent down to pick up the cigarette packet. Considering he had never smoked, he wasn't familiar with the button on the top, which linked a circuit to a small reservoir of gas and then back to a tiny outlet from which came a flame about an inch high. Standing up, he clicked the button and missed the end of the cigarette, flailing around at the end of it.

'Retard!' Frank called. He was calm again and happy to see his friend struggling with the simplest of devices.

Tom clicked again, this time catching a little fire on the end of the cigarette, which was enough to begin his adventure into the cancerous unknown. As the first drag hit the back of his throat, he lurched forward, spluttered and dropped the cigarette to the floor. With his hands on his knees, bending forward, he let out a loud, raspy and smoky cough, looking up to see Frank giggling like an idiot.

Gully was not amused, but he wasn't really watching. *Why put a shiny ring up there? Why even suggest there's a way out? Why give us something only to take it away?*

Tom picked up the cigarette and packet. 'Round two,' he announced, uneasily. The three men, shellshocked to varying degrees according to their capacity to be shellshocked, stood in near-silence, staring into space; two with the benefit of a chemical boost, the other deep in thought.

Walking over to the door Edward had just closed, it dawned on Gully that they were in the wrong barn – a facsimile of the real barn, if in fact either of them could be called real. But this barn was the less real of the two.

Gully's expression lightened: 'Tom, can I have that packet?' Tom looked at the packet in his hand, then back at Gully, and nodded.

He threw it to Gully, who examined the flame outlet. 'Any way to make this flame bigger, Frank?'

'Uh... sure. I guess so. Just gouge the hole. Why? What're you thinking?'

43

'I'm thinking we burn this fucking barn down, with us in it, and see what that asshole has to say about it.'

'We'll burn alive, you crazy bastard,' Frank offered.

'I don't believe we will.' Gully looked over at Tom, who did the usual shrug, followed by three gentle nods of his head.

'Sure, Joe, why not? I've already started smoking; might as well take it to the next level.'

~~~

Edward and Hat sat within a void. Without speaking, they had a conversation. The true voices of these 'men' were alien to humans, but they were not aliens. They had lived here for a very long time; far longer than humans. Speaking in what the human mind would have processed as a sound similar to cars rushing past an open window, Ed and Hat discussed how Hat had messed up. He was supposed to kill Joe Gullidge, for it was the wrong echo of Joe Gullidge; that echo had displaced the geography – for the wrong Joe Gullidge had freed the right Frank Willis and Tom Turnbull, and the three of them should not have been together.

Hat argued that he was not aware of the capabilities of the special suit that Joe Gullidge was wearing. Ed replied that it was their heads that were the weakest as that is where their brains are. Hat apologised for this and asked if Ed had any plan in mind to bring the correct Joe Gullidge, not an echo of him, back with his friends. It was entirely necessary, Ed agreed. Hat said he would go to find the Joe Gullidge they need, but didn't know where to start looking. Ed said there was still time and that they would find a way out of the barn soon, so then would be the perfect time to bring in the new and cast out the old. He would particularly enjoy killing Joe Gullidge, but it would have to be the right one. Killing the wrong Joe Gullidge would undo all their hard work.

Six – Crossing the line

Frank had managed to gouge a larger outlet from the cigarette packet and, after spraying some liquefied gas over the barn wall, passed it back to Gully. Tom hunched down, still smoking his cigarette, uneasily puffing out plumes of dark grey smoke. His mouth was stinging, his eyes were sore and his throat burned.

Gully had gathered a small mound of hay and barn detritus in the corner furthest away from the door. He leaned down, clicked the button in and watched the flame for a second, completely still to confirm the lack of any air currents from outside. Was there even an outside? He was about to find out.

The flame connected with the mound, which gleefully took hold of it and spread the flame over, sending a thick plume of white smoke up, with the gentle, soothing crackle of a bonfire doing its thing. The flame hit the barn wall, gradually rising up it as the wood caught fire and yet more smoke plumed out and upwards.

Frank stood back a few feet away, mesmerised by the show and shaky in anticipation. Tom was still hunched down, but he too was watching. He stood up, walked over to the fire and threw his cigarette in to join the fun. 'And there, ladies and gentlemen, ends my short sojourn into the world of burning my face off,' he said. Within seconds the flame had engulfed the entire wall and was riding underneath the ceiling like a giant, fluid and sparky tiger clawing at the wall as if trying to get through.

Gully stepped back and then raising his right leg, slammed it into the burning wall, hoping to smash a hole through. As soon as his foot connected with the wall, the barn once again went dark and although he didn't see it, or have much time to experience the feeling of it, something very sharp, and very cold, smashed through his skull from behind and ended his life in an instant.

As the light returned, again so suddenly that a blink would have masked it happening at all, Tom and Frank stared at each other, eyes as wide as they had ever been. The fire was gone and so was Gully. A loud thump behind them startled the men and they both turned to face the barn door, in time to see Joe Gullidge pushing the door open with his shoulder. Next to him stood Hat Smith, smiling, pushing Gully in front of him.

45

'Here they are. I told you they would be!' Hat chuckled. 'How you fellers doing? Found anything yet?'

Frank lurched backwards; Tom stood fast, but his mouth dropped open. He could see that Gully's hands were tied behind his back; his mouth was gagged with what looked like a dirty cloth. Frank stumbled to his feet and reached down for his weapon. It wasn't there.

'Now we're all back together again,' Hat said, pausing to let out a roar of laughter and jerking Gully's body backwards with a snap, 'It's time to go. Everyone's waiting!' He roared again, this time jerking Gully forwards and backwards; he turned and gestured for the men to exit the barn.

'I'm not going anywhere until-' Frank started, and in the space of a second the world disappeared and returned again; when it did, the three lawmen found themselves lying face down over what appeared to be a giant pit, with a tiny, dim light reflecting off a fluid surface maybe eighty feet below.

'I'm sorry guys, no time for chit-chat,' Hat said. 'We don't wanna be late.' He turned and whispered something that sounded like wind rushing through a pipe and a few seconds later, Tom, Frank and Gully were pulled to their feet, swivelled around and pushed down a narrow, dark corridor, one by one, towards an opening from which more dim light came.

First in line was Tom, who couldn't see what was pushing him or his friends. Behind him was a figure dressed in a suit, wearing the mask of a caricatured pig's head, covering its own head entirely, with the pig faces on the front and back of the mask.

This was the sight greeting Frank, second in the line of prisoners, who after catching this deranged, horribly unsettling sight, cast his eyes down and away.

Gully had the same view of Frank's captor and assumed the figure pushing him had the same image. However, his view did not shift at all from the pig face in front of him and as he glared at the empty eye holes in the mask, he saw a blink and two bright eyes stared back at him. He gasped, stumbled and was kicked upright immediately, before he too decided to look elsewhere.

Hat emerged through the opening, followed by his six companions. He began to speak in wind-voice again, and other voices came out of the darkness, beyond the dimly lit area which seemed featureless. Hat

46

wind-spoke again and then turned back to his captives, smiling. 'Have a seat.'

In another instant the world disappeared and came right back, this time bringing a bright, red room, furnished and full of chatty figures, all in pig masks with faces on both sides, and the three lawmen, now unbound and dressed in dinner suits, wearing pig masks but initially unaware of this, were sat next to each other on a long, comfortable and cushioned seat, looking out into something resembling a masquerade ball.

Music played softly, violins and piano gently rolling over each other, brushed jazzy snares and cymbals washing in and out. The room was warm, full of people – *people?* – some holding glasses of red or white liquid, raising these to their masked mouths and sipping through the exterior without any incident.

Despite the horror of the last few seconds, Tom, Frank and Gully immediately settled into a calm atmosphere and each was smiling underneath his mask, feeling a warmth akin to comfort in the womb. Frank was first to stand up and he looked back and down at his friends, who joined him. They ventured forward into the throng. There were around thirty other figures in this room, some in dinner suits and the rest in long, silky dresses. The room was high, wide and bright. Ornamental coving decorated the ceiling and several crystal chandeliers cast light all around. The walls were a light, soft red and the floor a glimmering marble surface, reflecting the light and figures which stood upon it.

Over to their left, a bar was tended by another figure in a dinner suit and pig mask, but there were no bottles or taps, just crystal flute glasses each with red or white wine inside. Further left, behind where they had been sitting on arrival, the band sat, heads eerily still but their limbs appropriately moving around their instruments.

Tom looked at Frank and spoke, but there was no sound. He had tried to say 'I don't remember.' His lips had moved but for nothing. He didn't care. Gully had moved through a group of human pigs to the bar and taken a glass of red wine. He raised it to his lips and sipped the most beautiful wine he had ever tasted. His smile broadened. Inside he felt a further rush of warmth, almost overwhelming. Tom and Frank joined him. Tom chose red also; Frank took white. They turned back to face the throng.

47

Inside their masks, sickly smiles and dozy eyes resembled those of junkies directly after their hits, but they did not know or care about this and they did not notice that of everyone in the room, they were the only figures not wearing gloves.

The chatter died down and the band carried on as a large set of doors over the other side of the room opened slowly, but there were too many figures in the way to see what was through those doors. A high, gentle and short bell sounded and the figures began moving towards the open doors, with Tom, Gully and Frank compelled to follow.

Seven – Feeling the burn

Joe Gullidge opened his eyes, rolled over a little to his right, and swung his arm around Louise, who was still sleeping. He reached over to bang the top of the alarm clock – a traditional, last-century model that could threaten to produce enough annoyance to wake the dead.

Louise stirred, rolled over a little and locked lips with Joe, the two sharing a gentle and warm kiss before both rising onto their elbows.

'Sleep well?' Joe asked.

'Yep, like a log, thanks. You?'

'Same. We got any bacon? I'm gagging for bacon.'

Louise yawned and stretched her body out flat on the bed. 'Think so. I just want some coffee.'

Joe rolled out of bed, onto his feet and caught sight of himself in the tall mirror on the wall. He *hadn't* slept well, and it showed. His face was worn, slightly stubbly, and his eyes sagged within dark bags. This was about the tenth consecutive night he had experienced a nightmare. Not the same one, but at least two of them had featured similar imagery.

'I'll bring a mug up, honey,' Joe said, making his way around the bed to the door, walking out into the open plan apartment he had shared with his lover for close to six months. They hadn't wanted to move, but their old apartments being burned down with the rest of Shenbury had made that decision for them and had provided a good excuse to move in together – something Louise believed was long overdue.

In Joe's nightmares, sometimes he saw the fire spreading across the town from a position high above it – the flames sprouting out of the old department store and then quickly engulfing everything else, ripping through houses, apartment blocks, across parks, skirting over the lake and devouring the trees at its edges, through the two schools, three churches, and always ending at the police station. As the station burned, he always heard laughter in his left ear, then filling his head, to his whole body, and always at this point he would snap awake, usually sweating and breathing heavily.

This nightmare was a vivid exaggeration of the truth; yes, a lot of the town had burned, but certainly not all of it. Joe had got back to the station just in time to save his lover, Louise, his most precious possession. She had shut herself in the back office, using an oxygen tank and staying low under a table to avoid the fumes. By the time she had realised the building was on fire and her exit was blocked, that had been her only option. The table had also shielded her from the ceiling caving in, and Joe had smashed through the door, his IR suit hot but protective, a face mask taken from his cruiser keeping his head safe, grabbed Louise and dashed through the building to safety outside. A closer call there couldn't have been. Seconds later the station was completely destroyed.

As the town tried to rebuild itself, painful memories and too many deaths of friends and colleagues told them it was time to move on, so twenty miles away they had settled in Coldharbour, a beautiful tourist trap stuck on the side of a lake, opening out via an estuary into the ocean. The lake was busy on all three sides, with water sports of every kind available; shops, bars and restaurants came alive at night; a couple of piers were home to several craft traders and religious nuts and from there the town backed up and out into forest country, with residential areas in the hills before soaking the earth up with rock and Redwood for several miles to the next town, with the highway linking the two and, further down, the rest of the country in its spaghetti network of roads, forests, towns, cities and lakes.

Joe and Louise had been fortunate in that their collective insurance had paid for an incredible location in the hills, looking over the town and out to the lake. Their open plan apartment was set in an exclusive block of six, with clever design keeping the walls thick enough to kill any noise between them and huge, apartment-length windows providing the best views available in the town.

Joe poured his lover's coffee, flicked the grill on and leaned over with his elbows on the white, shiny counter, his robe sparing the birds outside his manhood, and let out a long breathy sigh. The clock to his right confirmed he had one hour before he needed to show up at the station, long enough to shower, dress and make the journey on foot.

Louise emerged from the bedroom, tying her robe tight around her body and made her way to the counter, grasping the mug in both hands and feeling the warmth spread up her arms.

'More nightmares, hun?' she asked, putting the coffee down and stroking her hand over Joe's back. 'I can tell, y'know. The bed's wet in sweat, and you don't normally stick the grill on without any bacon.'

Joe smiled at Louise. 'Yeah, it's pretend bacon. The real stuff's too

50

salty and fattening. This way it's much more palatable.'

He reached down into the refrigerator, found the bacon packet and stuck two rashers on the grill surface. 'Happy?'

'As Larry, Harry and Barry, Gullywully,' Louise said, softly. She picked up her coffee, moved across the floor to the C-shape white leather sofa, and curled her legs beneath her body as she slunk into its comfort, looking out at the view to see a clear day, with the only noise and movement coming from the various birds flying past.

She took a big gulp of coffee, and leaned her head back over the sofa: 'Have you called him yet?'

There was a long pause, punctuated by the sound of bacon fizzing on the grill. 'Yes, last night. We're meeting for lunch today.'

~ ~ ~

Joe turned up at work four minutes early. He had taken the fastest, but also prettiest route down through the woods and then hitting the stream at the bottom of the hill, ascending gradually to the main road between two large old New England-style buildings – to the left an old outfitter and to the right a grocery store set over two floors (he loved shopping there) – and snaked his way through two parades until he arrived at the station. Frank was already there, leaning on a cruiser and smoking.

'Morning, boss,' he called.

Joe smiled. 'Morning to you, Frankie. Any drama yet?'

'Not a sniff, chief.'

Just like back in Shenbury, there was not a lot for the police to do on most days in Coldharbour. The occasional shop theft, some rowdy tourists or one of the town drunks getting in a fight was about the routine of it. Every now and then, there would be something that made the front page of the *Herald*, but it was a good couple of years since anyone had been murdered, gone missing, or run their car into someone. It was, genuinely, a lovely place to live and free of the social problems felt painfully elsewhere.

The *only* homeless man, Ged, had elected to live 'rough'; that is, he had fashioned himself quite the street-level marvel of grand design and everyone knew he was harmless, good-humoured and good-natured. He always waved and said 'hi' to Joe and Frank, asked them how their ladies were doing and never asked for anything. Joe didn't know the full story but assumed Ged had money stashed somewhere and for some reason had turned his back on traditional housing and living.

His dwelling was impressive. Fashioned entirely from reclaimed materials, driftwood, discarded textiles and decorated with an eclectic, fascinating assortment of bric-a-brac and ornaments, from Russian dolls to twentieth century war memorabilia, African tribal masks and more unrecognisable items, there were three rooms in this 'house' – a bedroom complete with floor-mattress, a just about working washroom and a lounge with a concessionary kitchen section.

Ged had arranged for electricity to be wired in and water to be plumbed in, and always paid his bills on time. That his home was built into a small hillock to one side and the lapping lake shore to the other rounded off what was a most quaint and fascinating landmark of the town.

The old man usually spent his mornings and evenings sitting out the front, under his sturdy brown canopy, with his collie dog Whistle. Together, Joe thought, they lived the happiest existence, as he never saw either of them looking unhappy or bothered.

Joe had passed Ged's place the night before and thought he heard Ged call out to him, but when he turned to look there was no one there. He had been carrying a bag of take-out seafood home anyway, so didn't go back to check. He had forgotten all about that now.

Joe put his arm around Frank, gave him a playful squeeze and said, 'You joining us for lunch then?'

'Yep, wouldn't miss it for anything, chieftain,' Frank said, stamping out his third cigarette of the hour.

~~~

Another uneventful morning out of the way, spent mainly walking up and down the main Coldharbour parade and at one point taking the cruiser out to Herman Point just for something to do, looking out to sea and smiling at tourists, Frank and Joe stepped off the promenade and into the Royal Wharf restaurant, which was already busy. A beautifully refurbished boathouse facing out onto the centre of the lake, with its second floor decked out in mirrors along every surface

52

and with the cosiest of atmospheres anyone could want while dining, this was everyone's favourite local restaurant and was famous as the town's best-loved landmark.

Joe had a table reserved on the second floor and after enquiring about the reservation, he and Frank were led by a girl of eighteen or nineteen, smartly dressed and very pretty, up the winding staircase and to their table. Tom was not there, but they were five or ten minutes early, so Joe supposed they wouldn't mind waiting for him.

'Can I get you guys some drinks?' Melanie asked.

'We're waiting for someone,' Frank said. 'I'll have a ginger ale, Joe here will have a-' He looked at Joe, raised his eyebrows and waited for the nod... 'Also a ginger ale, and Tom, when he gets here, well, he'll tell you himself.'

'Gotcha,' Melanie smiled and turned to head back down the stairs.

The mirrored surfaces dispersed the natural light all over – it was like sitting in a giant mirrorball, with sun rays dancing off the walls, ceiling, tables, eyeballs – and Frank and Joe loved the warm feeling it gave them.

'How'd it go yesterday?' Joe asked. 'With Jackie?'

'Um... you know,' Frank looked out to the lake and then back at Joe, smiled and said, 'We made some headway. I think. There was some weird stuff. Difficult to express.'

'Go on.'

'Well, ah, for the first time we tried some regression, or whatever it's called. Jack talked me down into a trance, I think, it was weird... and asked me about the night of the fire, how it made me feel. It was freaky. Then she woke me up and we talked a little more, and then my hour was up, so I hit the bar.'

'What was freaky?'

'I dunno. The strangest shit. I just don't remember anything. There was the fire, but I don't remember the fire, I wasn't in it, but I don't know where I was. Me and Tom headed out to that farm after midnight, and then you came out, but I think we were back by two, and I don't get anything after that. The fire happened, but I didn't *see* the fire, you know? I can't even remember why you came to the farm either. I can't remember what was going on at that farm, why we were there. It freaks me out.'

'It's classic post-traumatic stress, dude. That fire cost everyone a lot

– life, money, their homes – and we didn't know how to deal with it.'

'But you can't remember that night very well either, Joe, and neither could Tom. Why have we all suppressed the same memories? Doesn't that make you wonder?'

'Sure it does, sure. But you know, I see it all in my dreams, and I feel that same pain every time and it's something I am happy to let go of. Frankly, Frank, I am happy to forget whatever it is I forgot. Frankly.'

Joe smiled broadly at Frank and as Frank jokily snarled back at him, Tom appeared at the table, himself broadly grinning, and sat down. 'Afternoon, my darlings,' he drawled, in a southern accent designed to mock the residents of Coldharbour, despite it being in the north-east.

'Afternoon,' his friends replied in chorus.

'You guys look pretty as a picture. God, I miss this place.' He smiled again, the light bouncing off his face and lighting up the room even more. 'You ordered?'

'Nope, we're bred with manners down here, mister. Some drinks on the way though.'

Melanie arrived with two tall glasses of ginger ale on ice and smiled at Tom. 'What can I getcha?'

'Vodka and lime, hun,' he said. 'Lots of ice.'

'Ooh, the hard stuff, eh?' Frank leaned over and gave Tom a mock stern glare.

'The only thing that takes the edge off, so I ain't shy about it,' Tom said, shrugging.

Joe ordered swordfish steak; Tom ordered a ham and pickle sub; and Frank asked for chicken and ribs. Melanie smiled again, pirouetted and disappeared as the men got down to business.

'I've been having the *strangest* dreams,' Tom said, 'except they're not like dreams. I'm seeing them while I'm awake. And I'm sorry Joe, this is gonna come up eventually anyway, but it's still you – you're still there, doing something I can't see but I know it's horrible. There's a kid.'

'Stop it, Tom. Seriously, stop it. I don't want to hear this again, not today. Please.'

Tom looked put out; Joe did too. Frank interrupted the pause: 'So, um, we're all a bit in the woods here, right? I was just telling Joe before you got here about my regression to the night of the fire. My memories just aren't there, but they're supposed to be. My therapist,

Jack, can't make sense of it. She says memories can't just disappear. They're in there somewhere.'

'Well my memories can go wherever they want to,' Joe said, sternly. He looked back at Tom. 'And I'm sorry, but just because you see some shit in your head doesn't make it real, Tom. Can we just get past this, please? I've been looking forward to catching up for ages.'

'Okay, okay...' Tom replied. 'As you wish, boss. Frank...' he looked over at him; 'What's this regression about? Is it helping?'

'I guess so. I dunno. Some stuff is coming back to me but there's a lot that's just blank. I don't ever remember what happened out at that farm. It bothers me, man.'

'Same here!' Tom's face lit up again. 'We got out there, Joe came along, I remember that, sort of...ah...and then we came back, and found the station on fire, and then Joe ran in for Louise.'

'I'll never forget *that*,' Joe smiled, and with a wink, 'And neither will *she*.' He chuckled. Tom and Frank did too.

'You know, I have some weird dreams too,' Frank said. 'Like we are at some party and everyone's wearing weird masks, and there's this music playing really loud so that you can't hear anything, and there's this girl who takes off her mask, and her face is so pale, but smiling like she's blind drunk. It's kinda sexy, I guess, but you guys are there too, and we can talk but can't hear each other. I always wake up sweating.'

'Weird,' Tom agreed. 'But dreams are dreams, right? I definitely dream more since the fire. Most of 'em are nightmares too. I guess it's that post-trauma shit.'

'Bang on,' Joe said. 'Trauma makes its own rules in the fragile minds of the best lawmen in the state.' He winked, rolled his shoulders back and presented a cheesy grin.

Conversation graduated onto Louise, the lake, the funny old guy sitting outside his lakeside shack, and as the food arrived, the three old friends reminisced about the five or so years they had all worked together, and wondered if they ever would again, as a fearsome threesome.

'Not a chance,' Tom said. 'You guys are loose cannons. I'm happy in my own backwater – even less happens over there!'

Tom was referring to his post at the station in Upstanton, a small mining town twenty or so miles the other way past Shenbury. There had been so much to deal with; questions were asked of these men, difficult questions from difficult people. It had made sense to the authorities to separate these men, even if they personally didn't understand why. Frank was originally posted up to Kopperton even further back upstate, but after a retirement came up in Coldharbour within a few days, he had applied and been given the spot almost instantly.

Now here they were back together, for the first time in six months, for the first time since losing so much. Their friendship dynamics had changed, for better or worse, but at least they were still a unit in spirit. So many lives had been lost on that night, with nearly all of their colleagues fried in the chaos, an unexpected explosion killing five of them in one shot. There had been a mass funeral and the national press had been all over it. These three men and a lady escaped death so fortuitously that the country wanted answers, and there weren't any to give.

Fortunately, Coldharbour's residents had warmed to their new arrivals pretty quickly. Not a lot of respect for the media among those folks. Most of them could smell bullshit.

The sun gleamed off the lake, bounced onto the many mirrors of the Royal Wharf restaurant and basked the whole place in glorious warmth. Lunch over, the friends elected to take a stroll down to the east pier and dangle their feet in the cool water. There was nothing else going on, so why not?

Turning right out of the restaurant, waving back at Melanie, who looked a little hot and bothered, maybe grimacing, they walked towards the shore and then along, reaching the pier and starting off along it. The pier stretched out maybe eighty feet into the shallow area of the lake and the water was clear as the sky, the sun bouncing off it somewhere on the horizon.

Tom caught the eye of crazy old Ged, waved a friendly wave and carried on. Ged stood up and called: 'Hey you there. Old man, come over here. I've somethin' for ya.'

Tom turned as he walked, clocked Ged again and turned back. 'Hey! Hey! Old man, come over here. Come on over. I gotta tell you something.'

Tom stopped, turned and saw that Ged was indeed hollering at him. *Old man?* he thought. *Old man?* He walked back towards Ged's shack, waving back at Frank and Joe to imply he'd catch them up.

As he approached the shack, Ged's eyes were fixed on his and a wave of discomfort washed over him. Those mad eyes staring, piercing right into his brain. Tom was shaky enough these days, without crazy old hobos evil-eyeing him.

'What's up, sir?' Tom offered his hand. Ged wrapped it in both of his.

'You're new round here, right? But I *know* you. I've *seen* you before. Do you remember?' Ged smiled a little maniacally.

'Uh, no, sorry,' Tom said. Ged's grip tightened. 'Sure I would remember you, sir. I've been here a few times before, but I'd say we've never met.'

'Oh, we've met all right,' Ged smiled. 'You came to my party. Life and soul of it, I'd say. Hah!'

Tom's discomfort grew. 'No, no sir. You must have me mistaken for someone else. I don't *do* parties, as a rule. Now if you'll excuse me.'

'Those friends of yours too, they were there. Great party it was.' Ged's smile widened, his gaze intensified and Tom tried to pull his hand away, shuddering as he noticed the colour of Ged's teeth.

'I...I'm Tom,' he said. 'Pleasure to meet you.'

'I'm Ged. You really don't remember? That's a bitter shame, bitter. Well, pardon me.' He let Tom's hand go. 'Sorry for wasting your time today, Tom. I'll see you again.'

Tom smiled, uneasily. *I hope not. I really fucking hope not.* 'Pleasure to meet you, Ged. See you around.'

He turned and walked briskly, but not *too* briskly, back to the pier. Frank looked over and saw what he thought was Tom making a face. Joe was looking out over the lake, splashing his toes gently in and out of the water.

'What was all that about? You know each other?' Frank asked, looking puzzled.

'No idea man, no idea. He's freakier than you said he was, for sure. *Real freaky.* Said we'd all been to his party, but I couldn't remember it at all. Told him that was bull. We parted ways.'

Frank laughed, looking past Tom's thigh as he too sat down to take his boots off, to see Ged staring right back at him, nodding. 'Well, he's definitely interested in you, Tommy boy. Reckon he's on a promise. What kind of party does he throw for *you?*'

'Funny!' Tom's sarcasm was a little too loud. Joe looked back from the lake at his friends.

'Forget about it,' he said. 'Harmless but mad as a sack of cats. Two, no three sacks of cats.'

'Does he sit there all day?' Tom asked.

Frank chuckled. 'Pretty much. Walks his doggie at some points.'

~ ~ ~

Joe and Louise curled up on their white leather sofa with the blinds drawn and half-watching an old film; something about dinosaurs. Louise was drifting in and out of sleep and Joe was staring into space, deep in thought. *Our lives have changed so much, but we're missing pieces of the puzzle. Why can't we remember what we were doing? Why is there no proof? How could they want to pin that fire on us? How did the fire spread so quickly?*

The state department had banned the three of them from returning to Hawks Farm while an internal investigation took place. They had been up there and found no evidence that the police had visited. The man who owned the farm, whose name he couldn't recall, had said there was no call-out, no police, *no nothing*. Reckoned they were up to mischief, skiving off while their friends and relatives died, and made the whole thing up. Not that they had invented any particular story that explained at all what they had been doing. The media had jumped on this fact: was it post-traumatic stress in nature or stupidity not to have formulated a decent excuse?

In any case, the media circus had died down within a few weeks and Joe had been able to live a normal life again, in fact considerably better than before. He had loved Louise for some time before the fire and moving in together had proved the right decision for both of them. Despite the missing memories and the night terrors, Joe had a good life – no complaints.

Louise's breathing matching his own, their heartbeats seemingly in the same rhythm. Joe's eyelids dropped, flickered a little and closed as he entered a light sleep. Within one minute he had entered a dream state and within two more he was in that dream. Dinosaurs chased humans on the TV.

Joe had dreamed this dream a thousand times, remembering maybe a tenth of them, but enough to know where he was and most importantly how to get out. He stood at the foot of a steep grassy bank. Atop the bank was a tower, reaching high into the sky, but with the top easily visible. Up there was a single window; the only window in this tower. As he stared up there, he could make out a face looking back at him. The face was featureless from this distance, but it chilled him to the core.

Joe looked back down at the steep incline. He desperately wanted to get inside the tower. He tried to move forward, but his legs sank into the ground. His pulse quickened and back on the sofa, his legs stiffened and his arms tightened around Louise, who sleepily responded to this unwitting affection with a low moan and a smile.

A figure appeared from behind the tower, rounded it to face Joe and stood just a few feet from him at the top of the grassy incline, eyes wide open, before advancing down the slope towards him, in wild, jerky movements like a marionette controlled by a drunk.

It stopped right in front of Joe, put its face right up against his, and spoke: 'It's your time again, *Gully*.' The voice was like three at once, in different pitches. 'Time to serve your purpose.'

Joe stared into the evil eyes and saw raging fire. 'What purpose?' His words came out slow, dry and barely audible. His eyes looked up briefly to see the face in the window, still looking at him. It looked like the face was smiling.

'The next time you see me, you will know it is time.'

The figure leant in as if to whisper something in Joe's ear. There was no sound, but Joe felt breath followed by a warm stream of something on his neck. The figure pulled back, and as he bared his teeth, Joe saw that they were sharp and covered in a dark liquid. It pointed at Joe's neck. Joe reached his hand up and felt a wetness, then raised his fingers so he could see them. They were covered in a gloopy, dark red substance.

'See you soon!' The figure laughed and, still maintaining eye contact, backed away the same jerky way it had approached, up the incline and around the tower, out of sight. A huge shadow enveloped the sky within seconds, casting the top of the tower into darkness, then the bottom, then the grass and then everything.

Joe's eyes opened in a flash. He leapt up, sending Louise falling to the floor with a thump. His eyes widened, searching the room for the threat, before he realised there wasn't one. He picked Louise up and carried her to the bedroom. She had barely woken – Joe laid her on the bed, covered her with the duvet, and headed back out to the lounge where he sat for three or four minutes, with his head rested in his hands.

I've been there. That tower. The face. I know these things. Who was that man? Was it even a man? I have to stop these nightmares...

Eight – Home comforts

Joe had barely slept and arrived at the station over an hour before he was due to clock in. Frank hadn't arrived yet, which was good. Joe could access his desk and find what he needed and no one had to find out. He went in the front entrance, waved and smiled to Colleen (Louise had been offered a transfer to Kopperton too, but chose to follow her heart instead, and there wasn't a job here for her) and walked on back to the office, a well-lit room of about twenty by thirty feet – big enough to keep Coldharbour's law enforcers in reasonable comfort.

He made his way to Frank's desk and surveyed its surface. Frank usually scrawled contact numbers on tiny scraps of paper and left them dotted about on his desk, a life organised by chaos. Joe had always used his PDA – much easier, and satisfying his mild lust for gadgets big and small. Sure enough, after a little shifting of the various desk-detritus, Joe found what he needed: Jackie Brayburn's number.

Jackie had been assigned to Frank on an original programme of four sessions, immediately following his transfer, as the central authority had deemed him a 'mild but considerable risk' in the police force. After all, Frank had lost most of his friends, his whole family and his apartment, car – and a whole lot of happy memories – to the great unexplained fire of Shenbury. He had, as men often do, kept these emotions in check until boiling point, at which began a meltdown. Jackie had suggested extending their programme beyond the initial investigation – coaxing out his feelings, working through the trauma – to move into regression therapy and other techniques which she felt could bring him some peace of mind.

Joe had been offered the same four sessions, but in his first psychiatric examination was deemed to have dealt with the grief differently, and was not 'at risk'. Sure, he had lost a lot too, but nothing close to Frank's losses. Joe's most important possession, at least as he saw it, was his girlfriend, and as long as he had Louise, to have and to hold, he didn't need anything else. The grief was there, but it was different to Frank's. Tom had been affected too, of course, but his seniority over his colleagues and the assumed wisdom he had accumulated over the years were held by his examiners to have taken him down a less dangerous lane on the grief highway.

Grief was still very much in evidence back in Shenbury. There was a positive consensus to rebuild most of what had gone up in smoke, and that was pretty much everything. About five thousand people had survived the fire, but their homes had not. The one area spared of any flame was situated about a half mile from the main town, across a raised ridge that took the old railway line, which in days long past was Shenbury's lifeline to the rest of the world. Now it had acted as a giant fire door, and the industrial area it had preserved housed a group of warehouses, which were now mostly turned out to become makeshift shanty towns for the homeless and refugees.

The first warehouse to become a maze of grim dormitories belonged to an animal feed wholesaler. Most of its new inhabitants didn't mind the smell, the damp or the harsh cold as the nights drew in. There were over five hundred people living in there, some families and some alone. Although grief filled the air for much of the time, there were some who were glad just to be around people. Those who had never really had friends found each other, grief becoming less personal for them as a result.

Outside the bank of warehouses, outhouses and sheds was an enormous construction provided by the military to house fifty or so bathrooms, a giant mess hall which could accommodate close to two thousand people at any one time, and a selection of merchants with a range of 'essential supplies' at not-so-bargain prices.

An imported police force occupied another, smaller military construction, close to the railway ridge. Considering the downscaled population, crime had gone up in Shenbury since the tragedy. Two murders, a good number of thefts, criminal damage and affray were all reported in the town's new paper, *The Aftermath*, run by Peter Johannsen, a hobbyist publisher who had at last found an audience. The paper had two star columnists – Mayor Ernest Tifton and Peter Johannsen himself – along with children's art and poetry, news and views from Shenbury and further afield and an ongoing editorial line that petitioned for an end to the six-month investigation which was stopping any regeneration projects from getting under way.

Chief Silas Bangay and his team of around twenty investigators had set up as close to ground zero as they could – but the real problem and the reason why they were still here six months after the event was that ground zero was apparently impossible to pin down. No one had been able to ascertain the cause of the fire, although the initial two hundred-strong investigative team did successfully catalogue more or less everything that had been destroyed.

Most of the investigators were living in a separate settlement not too far from the warehouse district in fairly well-appointed caravans. Those slumming it down wind unaffectionately referred to it as Posh Park, and naturally the Mayor had one of the nicer caravans there. He had been out of town when the fire rampaged, but the flame did not discriminate and his house was burnt to a crisp just like any other. Those who had money in the bank had either left town or settled in this caravan park.

Although over the long recent months a real 'us and them' resentment had developed, the better off had at least made attempts to share the wealth. Around every two weeks, enough money was raised by the residents to bring in a new caravan and give it to a needy family. The Mayor was behind this campaign in name as much as financial donation, and made sure everyone knew about his good deeds in *The Aftermath*. It was a charitable operation that was very important to the morale of what and who was left of Shenbury.

Over at ground zero, Silas Bangay was standing with Peter Johannsen, surveying the charred landscape ahead of them which used to be Shenbury Medical Centre. Fifteen men and women were lifting, sifting and marking anything that looked like it should be catalogued. Peter had been lightly ribbing the chief over the news that with corporations and government breathing down their necks, the investigation was going to be shut down very soon, results or not, and in the case of the latter he would be a laughing stock. Silas thanked Peter for these kind comments and said he would be pleased to read all about it in the next paper. They then arranged to meet up for golf and a few beers at the weekend.

A car pulled up a few feet behind them. Out stepped a tall, well-dressed man who walked over to Chief Bangay and introduced himself. 'Chief Silas Bangay? I'm Paul Motta – pleased to meet you.' He put out his hand, shook the chief's firmly and turned to Peter. 'And you must be Peter, right? You run the paper here. Pleased to meet you too.'

Peter's surprise was clear, but he shook Paul's hand all the same. The chief said: 'Looks like you know your stuff, Motta.' He turned to Peter and smiled: 'Motta's our new star player. He's been out of the game for a while – make a nice feature for your asswipe paper.'

Paul Motta was six-foot-three, wearing a pressed black suit, white shirt and red tie and pointed black shoes, shined that morning. Peter was dressed in jeans, an old white T-shirt and trainers. Chief Bangay was uniformed, but scruffy. It was the kind of first impression that could breed resentment from the off.

'Motta, we got work to do,' Silas said. 'I'll ride with you.'

'Pleasure.' Peter nodded insincerely to both men and went back to surveying the blackened, ground-levelled medical centre.

~ ~ ~

Joe had picked up the phone eight times and put it down again before dialling Jackie's number. Part of him wanted to get to the bottom of his mysterious dreams. The other, much larger part did not.

Memory to Joe was not a big deal. The here and now mattered far more. He had never really been one to care much about the future either. But there was something really niggling at him – these dreams and the memory loss, whether a symptom of trauma or not – were annoying because he couldn't explain them.

Answerphone: 'Hi. This is Jackie Brayburn. Please leave a message.'

Joe was relieved but irritated. He did as he was asked: 'Joe Gullidge, Coldharbour 558-4212.' That was his badge number, and Jackie would be able to contact his PDA directly.

'Shit,' Joe muttered.

'What is?' Frank appeared in the doorway, looking mildly concerned.

'Ah, nuthin', just the usual. Or, actually, maybe it was just what I could smell a couple of seconds before you walked in!' Joe grinned at Frank, who grinned back.

'Another sleepy day in Coldharbour, which is fairly welcome I'd say.' Frank sighed. 'Another non-sleepy night in Coldharbour. How was yours?'

'No drama,' Joe lied. 'Coffee?'

Frank nodded. Joe closed the door behind them, waved and smiled at Colleen on the way out, as did Frank, and they walked out and around the corner towards the lake promenade.

If he had been looking, Joe would have noticed that Ged was not, as he always seemed to be, out on his makeshift porch.

Frank stopped suddenly. 'You know, Joe, I don't really want a coffee. How about a beer?' He was smiling and Joe stopped too, turning to see this.

'Beer? It's just gone nine, Frankie. For one we're police officers, and for two we are police officers!'

'No one gives a shit round here, Joe. We could be snorting up hundred-foot lines of heroin off this pier and no one would even blink!'

'You're over-qualified for this – just wasted in law enforcement!' Joe winked. 'And no, no beer. Maybe later. Let's just settle for coffee, huh?'

Frank mock-sighed to show he was not entirely in agreement but that he would go along with it.

Behind them, in Ged's shack, a single eye glinted in the sunlight, peering out at them through a crack in the wooden wall. Even if they had been looking, they would have been too far away to notice this. Ged's eye disappeared briefly and a different eye replaced it. Only someone standing right outside the shack at that time would have heard the giggling inside.

~~~

Another hard day of doing nothing much came to a close and Joe looked down at the desk he had just tidied for the fifth time in as many days. His PDA buzzed in his pocket. Taking it out, he saw Jackie's number on the screen. He accepted the call.

'Joe Gullidge.'

'Hi, Mr Gullidge. Jackie Brayburn. You called?'

Joe hesitated. 'Yeah – yeah, it's about...I was wondering. Maybe you could help me out with something? Are you free this week any time?'

'Great, great,' Jackie said. She was writing something down. 'Sure... how about tomorrow? You're Frank's friend, right?'

'That's right, yep, but...but I'd rather he didn't know I'm coming to see you.'

'Absolutely, Joe. Absolutely. We don't deal in tittle tattle here. Your secrets are my secrets.'

Joe felt relieved again. 'Marvellous!' He didn't think he had ever used that word before. 'Um, I mean great. What time and where?'

'I'll buzz you the details in a flash,' Jackie said. 'See you then.'

The call disconnected and immediately the PDA buzzed, a small black 'JB' icon appearing on his screen. Joe looked but didn't touch. He put the PDA back in his pocket, stood up, left the police station and headed for home. His PDA buzzed again. This time it was from Louise – a message saying simply 'pizza pleez'. *Great*, Joe thought, *takeout again. I should've got with someone who could cook*. She could do a whole lot besides, but cooking was his domain. Whatever – he had mild cause to celebrate. Tomorrow he was going to start wiping his dream slate clean.

The walk to The Coldharbour Pizza Experience was very short – one minute, roughly. Decorated in similar New England fashion to many of the shops and restaurants in the town, the unique selling point of this establishment was that you just selected the base, the toppings and anything else and waved your credit marker over the terminal. Two minutes later, your food appeared from underneath the terminal. If you wanted the personal touch and atmosphere, you could dine in the restaurant proper, but this walk-through approach was considered the pinnacle of convenience at front of house.

Pizza boxes in hand, Joe left and walked back up the road to his usual shortcut. In the winter he would be able to see the top of his apartment block poking out above the trees, but now, just coming into autumn, he could see the stream, the banks and the narrow path through the trees leading up. He was yet to see what kind of winter Coldharbour would have, but this wasn't on his mind anyway. The sun had just disappeared from view, leaving a rosy pink colour in the sky, competing with the oncoming darkness.

He set off up the path and no more than twenty yards into the forest, his pocket buzzed again. *Louise*, he thought, *telling me to hurry up*. He didn't look but carried on another fifteen steps before it buzzed again – and then again. Joe stopped. He leaned over, placed the pizza boxes on the uneven, dirty ground, and reached into his pocket. On the screen was written, in capital letters, 'TURN AROUND'. Joe looked up, bewildered.

'Turn around, Joe.' The voice came from behind him.

Joe gulped and as he turned, reaching for his gun, his PDA fell to the floor and he kicked the pizza boxes over, one opening and spilling its contents onto the earth.

'Ged, geez – what, what do you want? How did you...' His grip relaxed on his weapon. He let it drop back into the holster.

'Funny, eh?' Ged's voice was elated but his face was serious. His eyes widened at Joe. 'That gizmo there.' He pointed at Joe's PDA, now casting a dim light and the previous instruction into the earth. 'I don't got one, don't want one neither. This here's all I need.' He pointed down at Whistle, who was also staring, eyes wide and with a serious expression, at Joe.

'Ged, what do you want?' Joe looked rattled, and irritated.

'I just got a message for you, that's all. Just a quick message. You wanna know what it is?'

Joe's irritation grew. 'Uh, yeah. Yeah, Ged.' His breathing was heavy. 'What? What is it? Can it wait?'

'Sure, if you wanna take your lady some dirty pizza first and come back, I can wait.' Ged opened his mouth wide, revealing a black hole with nary a tooth in sight. His expression was of surprised delight.

'Just spit it out, Ged. What's this *message*?'

'Don't go digging, Joe. That's the message. If you dig, you will find *shit*, that's all.' He repeated, slowly: 'Don't. Go. Digging.' He pushed his head forward on the last word. Joe's body instinctively moved back a few degrees. 'Now you have a nice night, sir! Enjoy the food!'

Ged turned and walked down the path, as if disappearing into the sunset. Joe stood, motionless but for his shaking hands, for a good thirty seconds, his gaze fixed on the stream rolling gently a few feet away. Eventually he turned to see the pizza flopped unceremoniously on the ground. He picked it up, put it back in the box, and took the intact box under it, followed by his PDA, and then carried on up the path, looking back once with the feeling that he wasn't alone.

'Hi honey. Pizza delivery boy!' Joe called. The rest of his journey home had been without incident. He walked to the kitchen, placed the dirty box in the waste and the clean one on the bench. His hands were still shaking. 'Honey?'

There was no answer. 'Honey!' Joe walked across the lounge to the fork. Left to the bedroom; right to the bathroom. He stood in the centre, peered into both, and saw no one. 'Lou?'

He picked his PDA out of his pocket, dusted it off and turned back to face the kitchen. 'Louise,' he spoke. The call connected. Two seconds later he heard it – Louise's PDA and its distinctive ring tone. It sounded like trumpets and horns blowing all at once. The sound was coming from the bedroom.

Joe rested one hand on his holster, gently put the PDA down on a table next to the sofa and turned back towards the bedroom. He walked slowly, softly, stopped at the doorway and leaned in to flick the light switch down.

'Surprise,' Louise purred. She was reclined across the bed, draped in a cream silk nightdress that hung loosely from her shoulders, going down and hugging her figure to just above her knees.

An hour later they were wrapped in a blanket, with low music playing in the background, enjoying each other's warmth. The empty pizza box on the floor rested on top of Joe's PDA. It had buzzed three times, but Joe didn't want to look at it. He said as much to Louise. She didn't care.

~~~

The alarm woke Joe at 5.45 am. He rolled out of bed, put his robe and slippers on and softly stepped out into the lounge. It was still dark outside. He found his PDA and blinked down at it. Three messages: the first, Jackie Brayburn – *Let's make it 9*. The second, from Frank – *Call me!* The third, sender unknown – *DON'T GO DIGGING*.

He stared at this last message for almost a minute, blurry and hurried visions of the previous evening's disturbing encounter running through his mind. He dropped the PDA onto the sofa and moved into the kitchen, hitting a large round red button below the word 'Coffee'.

'Lou?' he called back into the bedroom. 'You fancy a holiday?'

Louise appeared in the doorway, silky nightdress intact but creased. 'This town *is* a holiday, hun.'

'I mean – can we just head off somewhere...I mean, somewhere a little more exciting?'

'Last night was *exciting*,' Louise smiled. She paused, noticing her lover's concerned expression. 'Hey, what's up?'

'I just think...I just think that there's more to life than enjoying the peace and quiet of Coldharbour...' The vision of Ged's dog staring at him rushed back in. 'Maybe the boredom is getting to me a bit, that's all.'

'Maybe you should come back to bed then.' Louise's eyebrows

lurched upward, her smile going for cute and sexy. She dropped one strap off her shoulder and shrugged, raising a leg and letting her toes dance in the air while her nightdress slipped around on her thigh.

'You know...' He looked straight at Louise's face, trying to smile. 'Hold that thought. I gotta do something.'

~~~

Joe was out of the apartment just as the sun was coming up. Louise had gone back to bed while Joe got dressed and drank his coffee. As he drank it, the words and images tumbled around his mind. *Don't. Go. Digging. Turn. Around. Don't. Turn. Around. Go. Digging. Don't.* As the words echoed, the sound of a dog growling got louder and louder. He snapped out of this trance in an instant, getting his bearings back. For those few minutes, he didn't even know where he was.

He was almost at the bottom of the forest hill, with the backs of the buildings on Coldharbour's main street in sight. It was 6.32 am. He had stopped at roughly the same point where Ged had surprised him twenty-three hours ago, but for no reason he could work out. There was no evidence of their meeting. The trees and stream were the only witnesses, but he wasn't about to ask them.

Joe rounded the corner of the main street and headed up towards the lake, keeping the line of sight between him and Ged's shack obscured by a fishing store on the far right corner. There were only a few sounds around – a car some several roads away, the usual chattering of nature and the distant almost imperceptible sound of water lapping over a shore.

Joe arrived at the corner. He peered around at the shack, which was all quiet. Leaning further round, he looked out to the lake. In the distance he could see some fishing boats, with the sun rising up and glinting off the water's surface. He looked back to the shack, and let his body follow, walking briskly up to its right edge, nestling back into a hillock. There was a window at the front, but it was covered over inside. He looked around for another way to see in.

'Morning, Joe!' A cheery call from back on the street startled Joe and he turned quickly just to see the waving arm of young Johnnie Hollister, local paper boy, disappearing on his bicycle into the main street. Joe turned back to the shack. He felt a warmth spread across his chest and then a tight, stabbing sensation on the left side. This caused him to draw a deep breath in, letting it out slowly through his nose. He felt the breath on his left arm, pulling him sharply back to the task at hand.

Moving cautiously around to the front left side, Joe found what he needed: a thin crack in the wood. He leaned in close and bobbed his head around gently until he caught the right angle. He could just see a sliver of the room and thought he could make out Ged's legs and feet lying on a floor-level mattress. He raised his head a little, trying to look down. As he did, a sound behind him of The Mariner lakeside bar opening its doors didn't register. His eye caught something bright. It took only two seconds to realise that this was the eye of Whistle, who immediately jumped at the wall and began to bark.

Joe jumped backwards, turned and sprinted around the corner into Main Street. He ran up as far as a break in the buildings about sixty feet up and took a right, coming out just between his favourite restaurant and a beach shop selling all manner of tourist tat. He leaned up close against its wall and peered back towards the shack. The door swung open. A dishevelled Ged appeared, buckling a belt on his dark brown trousers and stood, surveying the area. His dog knelt at his right side, as always.

Out the front of The Mariner, a man of about twenty-five was laying out tables and chairs. He hadn't noticed Joe a few buildings over, but he waved over at Ged. 'Morning sir!' Ged raised his arm half-heartedly, keeping it there for longer than he had meant to. He closed the shack door behind him and started off towards The Mariner.

Joe pulled back against the wall, thought for a moment and hurried back up the alley, turning left onto Main Street and sprinting back to the shack. Reaching the corner, he edged round to see Ged and Whistle in conversation with The Mariner man. Keeping low and facing them, he edged back against the shack, opened the door behind him and slipped inside.

Choosing not to attempt to lock the door – *was there even a lock?* – he ventured forward, passing a stack of books to his left and a dusty old armchair to his right, into the back area of the shack. Shelves on the walls were filled with all manner of interesting items and ornaments and a good selection of same hanging from the ceiling. There was Ged's mattress, another stack of odds and sods and off to the right a sink with a mirror on the wall above it; next to all that, straddling the back and lounge areas was a small stove with some food packages and associated implements around it on a table and the floor underneath. It was fussy without being messy but most of all, a cosy and *atmospheric* place.

Joe knew what he was looking for: any sign of a PDA, a computer... anything electronic. He had been lying awake after his passionate encounter with Louise thinking about this over and over. If he could find whatever Ged had used to send him those freaky messages, he could perhaps find out a little bit more – anything at all – about what was happening and why.

Of course, he could just approach Ged in the light of day and ask him straight out. But the thought of that repulsed him. Ged had turned in an instant from a figure of fun and an unlikely tourist attraction into a scary, disturbing figure. Trying to rationalise the experience had not been successful: Joe had been rattled then and he was rattled now. The thought of him coming back in with that dog had his pulse racing. Scouring the area, he could see no electronic equipment at all, except for a small and old-fashioned television perched on a round wooden stool back towards the door.

Joe raced back to the front wall, looking for the crack so he could see out without disturbing either the door or the curtain. He found it and looked out, bobbing until he could see straight down the promenade. Mariner Man was still arranging furniture, but Ged and Whistle were not with him anymore. Joe felt that same warmth across his chest and dropped to a squat. His choices were slim pickings: stay and hide or risk bolting out the front door and being seen by – or worse, running into – his new enemy.

Choosing the latter, he pulled the door open just enough and slipped through, dashing back and around to the right, then over towards the forest path leading back to his apartment. It was not until he stopped half way up there that his heart stopped pounding.

Outside, around the corner from The Mariner in the alley where Joe had hidden a few moments ago, Ged and Whistle were waiting patiently. 'We'll catch him later, boy. No hurry right now. Later, boy.' He smiled, knelt down and patted a grateful dog on the back, moving his hand up to stroke the tufts on his head. 'I've got a feeling he'll be 'specting us.'

Nine – Jack in a box

Joe didn't make it home. He stopped just a few hundred feet shy and rested, sitting against a tree out of view of the main path down. A couple who lived in the same block had walked past him, ignorant to his presence, chatting happily about the day ahead and making plans for the evening.

He checked his watch – 8.43. He wasn't sure how long he had been there until then; he had again fallen into a kind of trance with his head full of thoughts, images and sounds swirling together like a storm. *Turn Around. Turn Around. Turn Around.* Every time he heard this, the loop seemed to go faster, the words going over each other.

Getting to his feet, Joe brushed his trousers down. He saw his PDA had fallen from his pocket and picked it up. He found the icon from the day before, pressed the screen and noted the information: 10am, Hollister's Holistics. Touching that name yielded the address, and a guide arrow on his PDA with a rough on-foot travel time. He knew where it was anyway.

Joe made it back to the apartments, opened his and Louise's garage and got in the car. He drove out with the windows open and down the winding road that joined Main Street after a mile, and then out away from the lake – *and Ged's shack* – taking the eastern route out, which would eventually pass through Shenbury. His stop, though, was just about two miles up the road, in a sparsely residential area with a large house converted into Hollister's Holistics.

Geoffrey Hollister, the father of the boy who had startled him a couple of hours earlier, had set up the practice, a fairly old-fashioned one that dealt with the 'alternative' systems that had been suitably debunked many years earlier. Those surviving practitioners tended to be in out of the way places, avoiding the big-city cynicism and ridicule that had all but closed down the lot of them.

Jackie Brayburn rented a small, cosy room from the practice. She had come to the area from the south quite recently, pretty much hounded out of the town she had lived in forever because she had branded, professionally, a local official as dangerous to himself and the world around him.

Coldharbour had been much nicer to her. The initial joint police/central authority assignment to evaluate and psycho-analyse The

Shenbury Three had been funded by the central authority and had brought her some good publicity. Despite this, generally the people of Coldharbour did not like to be analysed, although her regular client list meant she made a decent living.

At 9.13, Joe walked through the front door, approached the desk and apologised for his late arrival. The receptionist, a short and plump, but not unattractive woman in her fifties pressed a button on the monitor on her desk and seconds later, Jackie appeared at the top of a wide, curved staircase, smiled and beckoned him upstairs.

Joe followed Jackie and once upstairs they entered into her room. Light brown walls, darker brown carpet and some uplighters that subtly set the atmosphere joined one fancy leather armchair, a small desk in front of it and then, on the other side, a two-seater with soft cushions where Joe sat down.

He watched Jackie open a draw under the desk, pull out a folder and spread it open in front of her. 'So,' she said, 'what can I do for you, Mr Gullidge?'

'Nightmares... um, just nightmares, I guess. Missing memories maybe. A bit of a mid-life crisis...maybe?'

Jackie smiled reassuringly. 'Well then, you're in the right place.'

She got up from her chair and moved over to sit next to Joe, clutching the folder and opening it on her lap. 'This is your file, Mr Gullidge. I've had a quick look – can we just clarify some things before we start?'

Joe nodded. 'Call me Joe, please.'

Jackie nodded. 'You were raised in Chicago, trained at the police academy there and were transferred to...Shenbury. You served there for...eight years and following the fire you came here. All right?'

Joe was looking at the open folder on her lap. He nodded again. 'Yep. That's my life, right there.'

Jackie smiled. 'Great. You have a brother, George, and your parents...there isn't anything here about them. Why's that, Joe?'

'Orphan,' he responded quietly with a croak. 'Orphan,' he repeated with more clarity. 'My brother and I were put into foster care and then adopted a little later. My adoptive parents and I don't speak...we, uh, well...I suppose I made a few bad decisions somewhere.'

'Okay, okay,' Jackie said, smiling softly to reassure her patient. 'That's fine. It helps to have some background before any initial consultation.

Today I don't know...hmm.' She paused. 'We could go off in several directions. I guess the best thing is to...nightmares. Tell me about your nightmares.'

Jackie stood up, walked to her desk and poured a bottle of water into two glasses. She took one to Joe, who clutched it in both hands between his legs, and went back to sip her own. She settled back into her chair and looked over sympathetically at her patient.

Staring into the floor, his eyes dilating, Joe started: 'Kinda creepy stuff. You know, I've done some bad things...I suppose these dreams are my conscience reminding me.'

'I don't know about that, Joe.' Jackie typed something on the keyboard set into her desk. 'Dreams can mean lots of things. I don't want to know what you've done right now – what happens in these dreams?'

'There's one that recurs – a dark, empty place. A tower rises out of the ground, and the earth rises with it. There's a face in a window, a thing that appears from behind the tower and it...it comes to talk to me. I never remember what it says.'

'And how often do you have this dream?' Jackie was still typing.

'I dunno. Maybe a few times a year. There are others. I have another where I'm chased by a pack of pigs, but they aren't like real pigs. Their legs are much longer, like pigs running on two legs, and they have razor sharp claws.'

'Do they ever catch you?'

'No.'

'How does that dream end?'

'I don't remember. I wake up.'

'How do you feel about the fire? Do you feel guilty that you missed it?'

'Uh...I don't...I mean, the fire...I don't know how I feel about that. It was tragic, but I guess...I don't know. It sounds terrible. I don't feel anything about that fire. I wasn't there and I don't feel any big sense of...of loss. I knew a lot of the people who died. It was tragic. There's not a...well, I don't know. I have never been good at attaching to people. I guess it's...it's something that for some reason I haven't managed to process.'

Jackie stopped typing and looked up at Joe. 'You saved your girlfriend from the fire, so I hear. I mean, patient confidentiality doesn't mean I can't tell you I know that. Your colleague, Frank, has talked about you a lot. So I kinda know quite a bit about you already, from his perspective at least. Were you...*are you* attached to Frank?'

'Sure, I mean...well, yeah. And Tom.'

Jackie nodded.

'They are my closest friends, not that I get very close with them. I only really see Frank at work and Tom is miles away. I mean he works miles away. You know, I'm...I'm not a very social person. They were there when I transferred. We kinda connected. It was always about work though. I'm into my work.'

Jackie resumed typing. 'So your girlfriend. You have an attachment to her, right?'

'Yeah, absolutely. I love her more than anything. I guess she's my only real friend. She has this way of knowing everything about me. She gets me, figures me out. Effortlessly!' Joe's face turned from vacant to a broad smile. 'And she's *hot*.'

'Okay, Joe.' Jackie stopped typing again. 'Frank couldn't – *can't* – remember the night of the fire. How about you? What do you remember?'

'Not a lot. We got a call at Hawks Farm and headed out there. It was a false alarm, so we came back to hit a bar but found the whole town on fire. Pretty much everything. Couldn't get Lou on the radio so we got back to the station and I went in to get her. Close call.'

'The three of you were investigated. How did that make you feel?'

'I'm not the kind of guy who sets entire towns on fire. I got nothing – you know I don't remember exactly and I guess that's one of the reasons I'm here – but nothing to hide. The investigation isn't over though – we've been told we're on standby.'

'Okay!' Jackie raised her voice positively, back to smiling. 'We've taken Frank down on some regression. We've got some to play with now, so do you want to take the leap?'

Joe shrugged. 'Whatever you think I need, Jackie. What's...uh, how do you regress me?'

'It's painless, Joe. You sit right there, and I'll just pop out for a minute to get my bits and pieces.' Jackie smiled, got up and left the room. She closed the door behind her.

Joe eyeballed the room. Nothing out of the ordinary, he thought. He stood and walked over to the only window in the room, which was covered by a blind but without the shutters closed. He put his index and middle finger between two notches and leant in so he could see outside. The view was to the back of the building and he could see most of a green and flowery garden. A man was kneeling down tending to a flowerbed at the far end.

The door opened and closed. 'Ready to go?'

Joe pulled back from the window and turned around. 'Sure – where do you want me?'

Jackie pointed back at the sofa and opened a small pouch on her desk. She took out one small ampoule and snapped the top off. 'Just lie back now, head on that cushion.' She walked over to the window and fully shut the blind, then back to Joe. 'Comfy? Right, close your eyes and open your mouth just a bit please.'

Joe closed his eyes and quickly opened them again. 'Don't worry, Joe. I've done this a thousand times. Just relax.'

Jackie emptied the ampoule onto Joe's tongue, gently pushed his mouth closed and walked softly back to her desk. She pressed a button on the side of the desk and carefully picked up her chair, placing it over next to Joe. She sat down and took his left hand in hers. She began to softly stroke the ridge between his thumb and forefinger. 'It's okay, Joe. It's okay. We're sliding now. Sliding. *Sliding.*' Her stroking became softer still and she watched Joe's eyelids go from slight twitches down to motionless, putting his hand gently down to rest on his tummy.

Jackie turned to face her desk. 'Regression session started with Joe Gullidge.' A soft blue light pulsed at the words. 'Joe – can you hear me?'

Joe could not hear Jackie. He found himself standing in a thick fog, which dissipated over a few seconds to reveal that he was in a garden – the one he had just seen out of the window. This time the garden had high walls all around, maybe twenty feet high and blue sky everywhere he could see above the walls.

He looked back down and saw a man ahead of him, kneeling down and pressing his hands into the earth. He had his back to Joe, as before. From somewhere came the soft tinkling of piano. He cocked his head towards the sound but couldn't pinpoint the source – it was all around. A hand pressed down on his left shoulder. He turned his head slowly to see a white-gloved hand there, with a blurry face coming into view. It was the face of a pig. The hand squeezed his shoulder.

'What are you doing, Joe?' The voice was muffled, as if spoken through a wall.

'I...' Joe tried to speak.

'Joe, what are you doing?'

This voice came from his right. He turned that way. A figure, also with a pig's head, came into view as if appearing from the fog. That figure's hand settled on his right shoulder.

'Joe. Did you call Frank yet?'

Back in front of him, the figure stood up from the flowerbed. 'Hey Joe,' it said in a soft, but loud and clear voice. 'Why didn't you call? Why didn't you call, Joe?' The figure began to turn. Joe felt his chest tighten. His hands clenched into sweaty fists. The piano sound was louder now, much louder; the tune playing faster.

'When're ya gonna call, Joe?' The figure was facing him now. Joe tried to make out the face but it was...*too far? Just blurry*. He strained his eyes, as his body began to give way beneath him. Joe fell to the floor, his knees taking the initial impact and then his body falling backwards and his head flailing as if semi-detached from his neck, dangling in an abyss. The figure stood over him. Joe could now make out the face, a human face with two piggies to the left and right.

'You really fucked up, Joe. We had to take something.' The figure clicked his fingers and the lights went out.

~~~

'I don't know what happened to him – he was here, I swear it. There's no way he could have got past me without me noticing. Is she...?'

'Okay, ma'am. Just calm down. Calm down, can we...' Paul Motta caught the attention of one of his new deputies. 'Can we get a glass of water for Miss...uh...Miss?'

The receptionist was ashen-faced and astonished. She let out a harsh sigh. 'Carter. Mrs Carter.'

'Sorry, ma'am.' The agent looked back at his deputy. 'Get Miss Carter a glass of water please.' His gaze went back to the distressed woman at the desk. Her hands were manicured, moisturised and pretty.

She didn't wear a wedding ring but there was a dent of one that had sat there perhaps two or three years before; her clothes smelled faintly of dogs.

'Now, Miss Carter. Just tell me, slowly and clearly, what you saw and heard.' He looked up at the second floor to see one of three police officers who had been searching upstairs shaking his head, mouthing 'nothing'. The other two were evidently still looking.

'I. I saw him, Mr Gullie...Mr Gullidge. He came in and went up the stairs with Jackie.' The receptionist stopped to gulp down an emotion. 'I guess they were up there five minutes, and Jackie came out – I can see her door from here. She came out, and, uh...she went across the hall.' Paul followed her gaze and Mrs Carter embellished with a point of her finger. 'She came out with her medicals and...'

'Medicals, you say, Miss? Medical whats?'

'You know, the drugs and...the drugs.'

'Drugs for...?'

'It's the...stuff she uses for the repression. The regression, I mean. I think it's like a sedative. I don't know. I'm sorry.'

'Okay ma'am. That's fine. So what happened after that? She went back in *and...*'

'Yeah.' Mrs Carter was trembling. 'She closed the door behind her and then it was all quiet. I took a phone call from...' Mrs Carter looked down at her monitor, embedded in the desk. 'Mrs Ronson. I was talking to Mrs Ronson for maybe a couple of minutes. Then I hear this loud bang, like a firework or something, or a gunshot. Next thing I know, the door has flew open and slammed against the wall up there. Then you guys showed up.'

The receptionist looked up at the agent with hopeful eyes. 'Is she? I mean...is Jackie *okay*?'

'You need to go home, Miss Carter. We'll have to do some work here. You live alone?' Mrs Carter nodded and looked over to her right, out the door to the front where several people were gathered – police and her *and Jackie's* colleagues, as if embarrassed by the question and her answer to it.

Paul rounded the desk, helped Mrs Carter up and walked her to the door, her colleagues greeting her with similar distress.

'Officer...Brady?' A stocky man in police uniform stopped what he was doing. 'Would you make sure Miss Carter makes it home okay, please?' Paul smiled a comforting smile. Brady and his long-time partner, Lopins, exchanged a look that Paul interpreted as 'sure thing, prick'; he went back inside, started up the stairs and stopped at the top and stared across the hall to meet the gaze of Officer John Sharpe, standing in the doorway of the psychiatrist's rented office.

'Found anything?'

'Just prints.'

Paul winced. 'People *can't* just disappear.'

Sharpe responded with a shrug. 'Whatever you say, boss. Not a body up here. He *was* here though. Bio says his prints are down. No sign of the lady either.' He gesticulated for Paul to follow him into the room.

As he walked to follow Officer Sharpe, Paul stopped at the door, which had been flung open with such force as to make a handle-shaped dent in the wall behind it.

Looking closer, the hinges on the door were bent out of alignment. He went in, over to Jackie's desk. There was an empty phial on the desk, an open pouch containing a few more, each labelled with a scrappy piece of coloured paper. Over to the couch, he found Joe Gullidge's file – a quick glance at which didn't tell him much.

He continued over to the back window, pushing aside the blind. There, down below, was a well-tended garden and a man wearing overalls was talking to one of the officers, but Paul didn't recognise which one.

He turned back to the room. 'His car's still here – can't have gone far. I want roadblocks in and out of Coldharbour and an APB on this Gullidge all over the district.'

Officer Sharpe nodded, turned to walk back out to the hallway and reached down for his communication unit. Paul put his hands on his hips, leaned back so that he was looking at the ceiling and let out a heavy sigh. He began to speak quietly to himself.

'How does a guy just disappear? How do a guy and a gal just disappear?'

He straightened up and walked to the door, pausing to look back at the desk. He reached over and took one of the ampoules with a matching pink paper label, put it in his inside jacket pocket and made his way back down the stairs, out to the front of the building.

'Sir.' Officer Lopins approached. 'We've searched both vehicles.' He paused, waiting for his superior to acknowledge. He didn't, but for the tiniest raising of eyebrows. Motta was miles away. Lopins continued anyway and shrugged as he said: 'Nothing.'

~~~

Jackie Brayburn's eyes opened to see complete darkness. She felt that she was lying down, face to the ground and inside something. It was hot and the air was thick. Slowly she moved her arms out to the side and each pushed against a hard surface. She wrapped her knuckles against the left side. A dull thump. Raising her head, it went just shy of six inches up before connecting with another surface.

I'm in a box.

I'm in a coffin.

Where am I?

About seven metres up, a gardener stood talking to a police officer.

Jackie remained alone with her thoughts for the rest of the day, slipping in and out of consciousness, her face red and her hands bloody and sore from hitting and scratching the box where that night she would draw her last breath.

Ten – Old friends

Joe woke up. He was not sure of his whereabouts. His eyes opened slowly, his head failing to catch purchase with his neck and dropping back down onto a soft pillow. As the blur lifted from his eyes, he saw a wooden ceiling with something shiny hanging down a few inches. The blur lifted some more and he sat up straighter.

'Welcome back, Joe!'

Sitting on a short stool in front of the bed was Ged, with his dog at his feet, both staring at Joe. The dog looked like it was smiling.

'How'd ya sleep?' Ged let out an enormous roar of laughter. The dog kept smiling.

Joe followed a strong urge to lie back down, his head thumping down into the pillow. He gazed up at the ceiling again and saw that the shiny thing was an old knife, pointing down at his face menacingly. *Ged sleeps under a knife?*

'Sit the fuck up, buttercup,' Ged said with authority. 'Ain't no time to be lazing about. We got us some shit to take care of.'

Joe sat up, swinging his legs either side of the bed to rest on the floor. 'Would you mind telling me why I am in your bed?' A thought ran into his head like lightning – and his stomach turned; he remembered being on Jackie Brayburn's couch.

'Yep, and ya woke up here. Funny, huh?' Ged was grinning. 'Had to give ya some shelter, see. Them police is after you, see. What did ya do *this time*, Joe?' He let out another roar of laughter, this one cut short as it turned into a croaky cough.

Joe put his hands to his face, rubbed up and down and then set them on the bed, vaulting upwards to confront his host.

'I haven't done anything, Ged, nothing at all. What am I doing here? Can you answer me that, old man?'

'Last time I saw you, Officer Gullidge...' Ged's eyes were wide and staring right into Joe's. 'I gave you a little warning. Just a little'un. Remember?'

'Yeah, I remember...Look, Ged. What is this? You told me not to go digging – what for? I haven't been digging for *anything*.'

'Your problem, dipshit, is that you don't know who you are. You got no idea, that's for sure. And you sure did go digging – you came in here. You came in my home.' Ged leaned forward, his stare intensifying. 'You snucked in and thought I didn't know, right? Right, Joe?'

'Yeah, okay. So what? You approached an officer of the law in a threatening manner, rearing your dog at me. It's fair to say you got me a bit shaken up there old man.'

'You call me old man one more time and I'll snap both your fuckin' legs off, dipshit.' The dog stopped smiling and growled instead. 'You listen to me. People askin' questions about you and you don't have the answers. So it's best not to be in those places where those people be.'

'What people? Who wants to ask me questions?'

'That's just it, Joe!' Ged laughed. 'You don't know. This is...' Ged coughed again. 'This is just so much *fun*!'

'I'm not having fun here, Ged. No fun *at all*. How did I get here?'

'We took you straight outta there, Joe. Just swooped on in and moved you out. Just in time too!'

'Just in time for what, and how...how did you get me out of there?' He didn't give Ged time to respond. 'She drugged me, right? That's right, she drugged me. And you came in and carried me out like a baby. Why?'

'Sure, if that's the way it happened, that's the way it happened!' Ged roared. 'Just the way you want it, Joe! She was taking you down somewhere we don't want you, that's all. You can't answer questions if you don't know them answers, Joe.'

'Answers about *what*?' Joe shouted. He was getting visibly angrier now. 'What questions and what answers?'

Ged's dog growled again. 'Settle down, boy. And you, Joe, you settle on down too. Y'see, if I go tell you what you wanna know, you're gonna know too much about shit, and that shit ain't for you to know!' Ged cackled this time, his gaze finally leaving Joe's face and out to the shack's door.

'What you do gotta know is that some shit's happened and you're on a hiding to it.'

'What?'

'Okay, okay. What you been up to today, Joe? You seen your friend, what's his name? Frankie? You seen him today, Joe? And how about your lady, the *lovely* Lou, how's she doin', Joe?'

Joe mentally re-traced his steps. The image of his PDA, a message from Frank stating 'call me', shot into his brain.

'That kid's lost without you, huh?' Ged was still smiling. 'This is how it is. You did for us, but we can't always do for you. Things ain't always as you remember them. With *you*, hardly anything's as you remember it. Lot of stuff you do without even realising it, Joe.'

'I'm leaving, Ged. You're just talking…shit and I don't know what you've been drinking, but I'm leaving. I'm gonna call Frank.'

'You can't do that, Joe. Everyone's looking for you and you walk out that door, you're a dead man.' Ged at last looked serious. He stood up, walked to the door and leaned his back up against it. 'You can call Frankie, though. I think you should give Frankie a call.'

~ ~ ~

Twelve hours earlier, Frank had been in the Lakeside Bar, drinking on his own in a small booth towards the back. He got there at 9.15pm and left just before midnight. Leaving, he waved to the barman and half-stumbled out onto the pavement, catching his balance with a hand on the door frame. Righting himself, he set off west up the main street, which led to the road his apartment was on, up a steepish hill and around a corner, the road eventually leading back up and around the lake.

He passed and waved at a group of people he was acquainted with and then as he neared the bend in the road, stopped to talk to one of his neighbours, out walking her dog. Two minutes later he was back walking, closing in on his block, which was shielded to the front and back by tall trees, leading out into a forested area like much of Coldharbour. He rounded the bend into the forecourt, spotted a figure standing right outside the main lobby door, and thought nothing of it.

He drew nearer, and the figure stepped forward. 'Frank. Where you been? I've been trying your PDA.'

It was Tom. Frank threw his arms around his friend and pretended to kiss him, then backed away. 'Tom, darling! What brings you out here? Should'a come to the Lakeside. I been drinking all on my *own!*'

'It's bad news, Frank. Can we go inside?'

The two went up to Frank's third-floor apartment. Frank poured them each a glass of water, dropping a fizzing tablet in his. Tom explained that a friend of his from back in Shenbury had picked up through the good old-fashioned practice of eavesdropping the not-too-pleasant news that there had been a breakthrough in the fire investigation. Frank said that was good. Tom said it wasn't because, he had heard, the chief investigator thought he could link the fire back to Gully.

Frank burst out laughing. Tom said it was no laughing matter. How well did they know this guy? Hadn't Gully sent them on the call to Hawks Farm? Hadn't Gully joined them later?

Frank assured Tom there was no way Gully was involved – he was a solid guy, a lawman through and through and ultimately a friend. He may have a strange lack of social conscience, but otherwise he was as trustworthy as a friend and policeman could be.

Tom explained that he sure hoped so – the way he heard it, the chief investigator, a Paul Motta, was heading to Coldharbour the next day to arrest Gully. Five minutes later Tom was back on the road, and as he took the road out of town he passed Ged, sitting on a bench drinking from a red bottle with his dog hunched around his feet. Ged's gaze seemed to follow Tom, and when their eyes met for a brief moment, Tom thought he saw a flash come from Ged's eyes. His chest shivered for a moment and he drove on.

~~~

Paul Motta sat up straight, facing the window of his makeshift hotel room – a modular block behind the main HQ, the computer's bright glare reflecting into his Augmento glasses. He was uploading information into the glasses, starting with the photo of Officer Joe Gullidge, his address and his police profile; a list of the task force he would be taking from Shenbury to Coldharbour; and finally the evidence that had led him to the conclusion that it wasn't a coincidence that Officer Joe Gullidge had missed the hot action that night. He synced these data with his PDA before settling back onto his bed and closing his eyes.

Six hours later, Paul was standing in the ground-zero headquarters, addressing seven fellow officers and Chief Bangay. Spread on the wall to his left was a portable screen – like his glasses, made by Augmento – and on this screen was a picture of Joe Gullidge, his particulars and in larger letters across the top, *APPREHEND SUSPECT*.

'Gentlemen, let's begin.' Paul surveyed the room and saw that everyone looked interested enough, barring two who were in deep conversation towards the back of the room. He raised his voice: 'Gentlemen!'

'Quieten down, Lopins,' Chief Bangay said, craning his head backwards to deliver the instruction.

'Thank you,' Paul continued. 'Today we are going to apprehend this man, Officer Joe Gullidge, one of the famous Shenbury Three, and the man who I believe is responsible for starting the fire here.'

Lopins and his sidekick, Brady, exchanged a look of mock surprise.

Paul clicked a button on a small black unit in his hand. The screen refreshed to show a list of bullet points, with two large pictures to their side. 'What we see here is one – a document showing that almost two years ago, Rockefeller Demolition reported a theft of two dozen crates of plastic explosives which have so far not been recovered; and two – testimony from one Simon Shyler, former resident of Shenbury, which states that he saw our suspect at the time driving a lorry away from the scene. Shyler is...was a homeless man, and his testimony was discredited because A – it was dark, could have been anyone, and he had a history of alcohol abuse; and B – Officer Gullidge had an alibi: he was called to the Rockefeller warehouse to follow up the alarm and arrived in his cruiser – the log of which showed he had done so.'

'Right, so what's the deal? Why are we after a guy with an alibi?' Bangay asked.

'I'm coming to that. Frankly it beggars belief how this was allowed to slip. What was stopping Gullidge from parking a lorry up next to his cruiser, getting in that and heading back to the scene? No one asked that – no one asked about that at all. And why would you? Testimony of a drunk bum and his word against a respectable officer of the law. Fair enough? Maybe in these parts but not where I'm from. So this alibi wasn't tested and that was the end of that. Explosives never recovered until we found scraps of metal bearing the Accublast name. These are the same explosives which were stolen.'

'Sir?' Brady called from the back. 'Why would this guy wanna burn down his town? That's insane.' He looked over at Lopins. 'Insane!'

'Insane it may be, but these two shreds of evidence taken together – and the startling lack of evidence elsewhere – lead me to say it's at least worth bringing him in. Right, chief?'

Bangay nodded.

'I'm sure you've all read these fifteen times already,' Paul said, gesturing towards the bullet points, 'but let's go over them quickly. Number one – the day of the fire, Shenbury police station returned only a partial upload to division, which means the logs were not complete. We know who was at the scene of the original fire and we know what happened next, but we don't have any logs for the three missing officers. Number two – Gullidge does not have an exemplary record. He was suspended and shipped out of Chicago following an incident, details of which are sketchy. Chicago does not hold a complete comprehensive record of that incident. Number three – Gullidge did not lose a whole lot. In fact he picked up on his insurance.'

'But sir.' Lopins spoke up. 'Are you really suggesting that this guy, one of us, took out most of a town centre just to collect on his insurance?'

'I'm glad you asked that, officer. No, that would be...' He looked Brady in the eye. 'Insane. There's a bigger something here and we're going to find out what it is. Any crime by definition is insane, but I don't think our man is. I think he's a calculating son of a bitch and I want to pin him down.'

'What about the other two?' This came from Officer Steve Proctor. 'Frank and Tom, isn't it? Where do they fit in?'

'I don't know that either, but we're...I'm working on an assumption here that these guys lost a hell of a lot more than our suspect. If they are involved, we'll find out. First things first – we find our guy. So let's tool up and get out. I want to be in Coldharbour by 9, sharp. Dismissed.'

As the officers filtered out of the room, Bangay held back. 'Paul?'

'Yes chief?'

'You sure about this? Seems quite a leap. Doesn't all necessarily add up, you know.'

'Yeah, I know. But I follow my instincts, and my instincts...'

'Doesn't look so good arresting one of your own. Could be embarrassing,' Bangay interrupted.

'As embarrassing as turning up jack-shit in six months, chief?'

~~~

Joe picked his PDA out of his pocket.

'Go on then, call him up. What ya waitin' for?'

Joe tapped the screen, scrolled down to Frank's contact card and hesitated.

'Could tell ya what he's going to say, anyhow.'

'And what's that, Ged? Is he going to tell me to watch out for you or something?'

Ged laughed. 'Believe it or not, buck, I'm your friend here. I just saved your ass.'

Joe put the PDA to his ear. 'Frank – it's Joe. What's up?'

Frank's voice came back, quiet. 'Joe – where are you? They're...'

The PDA was snatched from Frank's grasp: 'Officer Gullidge. This is Paul Motta. We would very much like to have a word with you.'

Joe didn't say anything. He looked at Ged, who nodded. Then: 'About what? What's going on?'

'We'd like to know that too, Officer Gullidge. Just tell us where you are, and we can all have a chat. We knew where Frank was because his PDA is tracked at the station, but your tracking is turned off. Why's that, Officer Gullidge?'

'I...' Joe hesitated. 'I turn off the tracking sometimes when I'm doing something personal.'

'Like seeing a psychotherapist?'

'How d'you...'

'Like I said, Officer Gullidge, we just want to talk to you.'

Joe clicked the call off. Ged grinned. 'So you been a naughty boy, Joe?'

'What the fuck is going on here?' Joe snapped angrily. 'What do you...what do *they* want with me?'

'I told you, Joe. I'm your friend. You can believe otherwise but it's not going to help you.'

'Help me do what?'

'You remember back at your old place, over in Shenbury? You remember what happened that day when you started that fire, Joe? Hmm?'

'I didn't start that fire.'

'Oh, I beg to differ son. Those police think you did. Even my little Whistle down here knows you started that fuckin' fire, Joe!' Ged let out a long, low laugh. 'I know you don't remember it Joe because we don't let you remember it. You do for us but we can't do for you.'

'This is bullshit. I don't remember it because I didn't do it.'

Ged moved quickly from the door and with one hard shove pushed Joe back onto the bed. Whistle barked once. Ged's hand remained on Joe's chest and his other went up to Joe's forehead. With his index and middle fingers crossed together, he began massaging a circle into the centre.

'You want to remember, Joe? If I show you this, there's no going back.'

Joe's eyes closed – he tried to fight it but couldn't. Barely audibly, he croaked: 'Show me.'

~~~

A train shot past and half a minute later the barrier raised, letting traffic cross the railway line. Joe was sat in a cab, his head woozy; he shook his head a little and his ears popped slightly. 'What?' The sensation of the engine rumbling beneath him came back into his hands, resting on the steering wheel. A horn sounded behind him. He looked up, instinctively pressing his foot down on the accelerator and the truck lurched forward, rising over the short incline up to the tracks and then over and down again, following the road around to the right.

You see, Joe. You don't remember this, do you?

'No, I...'

Just watch, Joe. Just watch the show.

Joe drove the truck, occasionally slowing and stopping and followed his pre-determined path. 'How am I...? What is this?'

This is you, Joe. Just let it go. You can't change it. Just watch.

Joe tried to grip onto something and realised immediately that he was on auto-pilot. He had no feeling, no presence there. The rumbling was imagined; phantom. He *was* there, but he wasn't. He could look within the field of vision but was powerless to turn his head or even move his eyes even a degree. Like watching a movie; not a dream. *Just watch*, the voice in his head had said. It wasn't Ged's voice, though. Whose voice was it?

The truck came to the main junction just outside the town centre. Right in front of Joe's view was the main Shenbury drag – cars parked up either side, offices and shops to the left and right, but closer to him and just over to the right, which he could only see a sliver of, was a small access road which led down and underneath the imposing Hart's department store. Four floors of shopping bliss, or something like that.

Joe's hand flicked down and out of sight to push the indicator. Twenty seconds later the truck turned right and immediately left and down the access ramp. *Where am I going?* Joe thought. Reaching the bottom of the ramp, the truck stopped and Joe stepped down and onto the road. If Watching Joe was able to feel queasy seeing through Doing Joe's eyes, the motion would have made him puke.

'I didn't do this – what...I don't remember. What am I doing here?'
Keep watching, Joe. You'll see everything clearly. Just watch.

Joe approached a keypad on the wall, just to the right of a large solid but corrugated gate and his index finger punched in the numbers 9156. The gate shuddered and started up. Joe went back to the truck, closing the cab door and resting his hands and feet back on the wheel and pedals. Once the gate was fully open, the truck again lurched forward and entered a dark store. Doing Joe looked straight ahead but Watching Joe saw to his left two figures standing just inside the gate, heads obscured.

The truck came to a stop about another thirty feet in, a dim light shining down and Doing Joe sat, still looking straight ahead. The truck wobbled a little and several figures appeared just to the side and then in front of the truck, carrying small packages under the light and then back into darkness. The view didn't change for about a minute.

'What is all this? What are they carrying?'
We're nearly there, Joe. Just a little longer.

Two figures came back into view and as they came under the dim light, Joe could see their faces were warped, inhuman. One broke away and rounded the truck, while the other approached the front and as it did, Joe could see it had the head of a pig. A mask perhaps, but definitely a pig. The figure gesticulated for Joe to exit the truck.

Watching Joe struggled to see beyond the light but Doing Joe's field of view changed as he came to stand right in front of the pig-man.

'Good job. Leave the truck. Go home.'

Doing Joe nodded and turned away from pig-man, heading back out onto the access ramp, which was cast in shadow but glimpsed the sun breaking through at the top. As he walked up the road and out up to the main junction, he heard the gate shut behind him.

Joe's world went black.

'Joe, wake up. Wake up! Ah shit, Whistle, we're going to have to carry him again.'

~~~

Paul Motta and two officers readied at the door to Ged's shack. Motta took the lead with Phil Gibbons and Dirk Bundy flanking the door. All three were weapon-ready. Motta's leg drew back, thumping his foot into the door, which swung open and slammed back into a table, bouncing back a little. Motta flung himself inside, his gaze following his aim. 'Clear!'

Gibbons and Bundy were right behind him, weapons still up but not searching for a threat.

'We've had eyes on here for twenty minutes – where are they? Where are they?' Motta's face had darkened red, his brow crunched.

'Sir!' Gibbons picked up Joe's PDA and held it up. 'Sir – I'm guessing this is his. The suspect, sir.' He waved it in the air. 'His PDA.'

Motta reached out and took the PDA, then threw it down. It bounced awkwardly and disappeared under an armchair. 'That's no use *now*.' He sent a look of thunder over at Gibbons. 'Search the place. Every inch.'

'Sir,' Gibbons said, quietly. He looked over at his colleague, who shrugged. Gibbons shrugged back. Motta walked back out front. He looked left, then right, then straight ahead. Two police cruisers were sat just off to the left, lights off. A smattering of interested onlookers dotted the area. Motta turned back to the shack. Gibbons and Bundy were doing as they were told. He turned back to the cruisers and started walking towards them.

Two hundred metres away, surrounded by trees on a ridge which wasn't all that far from Joe's apartment sat Ged, Whistle and Joe. They had a line of sight through the branches down to Ged's shack and the activity that was taking place.

'Wake up, Joe. That one was close.'

Joe's vision was blurry, near. Over a few seconds his sight returned and he could see what Ged was seeing.

'How did we...'

'Told you, son. We can swoop on down and whisk you away like a hawk swoops down and grabs his dinner.'

'But...'

'But nothing. I was wrong about you, it seems. No matter.'

'Wrong about what? I didn't start the fire, you are wrong about that. But I don't remember.'

'Quiet. Just be quiet for a minute. We need to stay away from these guys. We can't let you and them...whatever. I'm not strong enough now. We wait here and see what happens.'

Joe's mind was awash with confusion. He felt discombobulated – another out of body experience. 'Wait here,' he spoke softly. 'Great. It's a nice day. Let's get ice cream.'

'Good idea son. Whistle, go fetch us all some fuckin' ice cream.'

The dog made a sound that was close, Joe thought, to a laugh. He looked over at Whistle, who was sat, head cocked to one side, staring intently right back at him.

Ged was staring down at the police activity outside his shack but without focus. He was deep in thought.

'I guess I were half-right about you, son. Just about. Maybe you ain't what I thought ya were, but you sure are in deep shit. Maybe...'

'Maybe what?'

'Maybe we can help each other.'

'Oh yeah, you're my friend, right?'

'Yeah, just happens I am.'

'You have a funny way of showing it, old man.'

Whistle barked. Something heavy and blunt cracked into the side of Joe's head.

Ged came to stand over Joe, who had fallen back and was slumped awkwardly against two trees. 'I warned you about that, son. You can keep ya legs for the time being though.'

Ged tossed his dirty stump back to the ground, reached down to Joe and pulled his arms up, righting his posture back against the trees. 'You sit tight there, prick.'

Eleven – Summer in the country

A beautiful starry night gave way to a rich sunrise, witnessed then as on most mornings by a man and his dog. He led a simple life and he enjoyed life's simplicities – the cycle of the Sun and the dim-to-bright shine of the Moon as it began a sliver and worked its way up to a full and resplendent orb; and on this morning, the dew atop crisp blades of grass, reflecting the beauty of nature all around. His dog, a warm, trusting and loyal female approaching nine years old, rarely left his side; they shared a sympathy and understanding that even long-married couples might not.

The view over Boldredown from the fenced border of their property was always magnificent, even if shrouded in fog or baked in sunlight like today. Jim and his wife, Polly, later joined by their faithful canine servant, Penny, had lived there for close to thirty years. Their nearest neighbour lived a good half-mile away, a not too dense forest separating them along the ridge of a valley in which the village sat, rolling hills leading from the residence down to a point at the village church, with the town then meandering in a rough triangle and with just one main road through it, heading out to the more built up realms of Hampshire in one direction and pointing back towards London – a good eighty miles away – in the other.

Jim looked down at his dog. 'Beauty, ain't she? A real cracker!' He smiled broadly, gestured his thumb over his shoulder, turned and started walking through the soft, dewy grass towards his house. Penny offered a happy bark and galloped over to her owner, sticking by his side and following his feet.

'Come on, sweetie. Let's get some brekkie.'

Penny barked in agreement.

They reached the back of the house, feet wet but not unpleasantly so and stepped onto the patio. Jim stamped his feet to shake the wet grass off and Penny seemed to do the same, all the while looking up at her owner quizzically.

'Let's go see if your mum's up, Pen.'

Shaking his boots a final time, Jim headed up to the back door, opened and went through it into a warm kitchen.

'Hey, Pol.'

His wife looked up from her book and raised a mug in her left hand.

'Want one? It's hot.'

Jim smiled. He walked past the kitchen table, brushing gently against his wife's arm. 'What's that you're reading, honey?'

'The usual, um...hokum.' Polly winked at him. She turned her attention back to the book, flipping the page. Jim saw over her shoulder that the two pages facing upwards showed two large diagrams, or something that looked like diagrams.

'Hokum, huh. Looks wild.'

'Lovely day, is it? Just what we need, another lovely day.' Polly reached her hand back and rested it on Jim's leg. He reciprocated, leaning over to rest his head on Polly's shoulder, nestling into the nook. He playfully ground his chin into her collar bone. She giggled.

'What you doing today, Jimmy?'

'Boring stuff. Probably walk down into town. You wanna come?'

'Can't.' Polly craned her neck to make eye contact. 'I have an appointment at 10. Remember?'

'Oh yeah, that I do, Pol. Well, I'm going to take a shower.'

They exchanged a smile and Jim disappeared from the room, a slightly hesitant dog following him once she realised her human mother wasn't about to give her any attention.

'Don't use up all the water,' Polly called. There was no response but she heard footsteps on the upper floor.

Polly rose from the table, swigged down the last of her coffee and went over to the back door. She stood, looking out to the horizon where the dewy grass met the blue sky, and smiled. Polly had found what she was looking for, and she was going to show her new friend.

~~~

At 9.45, Polly arrived at a small copse about half a mile from her house, having walked out and over the lip of the valley and down towards the village, then following a narrow path through a wooded area to the east. It was a nondescript clearing, surrounded by tall trees, leading further into denser woodland and then further down to the outskirts of the village, but there was at least a quarter-square-mile of woods and, Polly thought, it didn't look too inviting. The trees were just a little bit too close together. In any case, she was where she needed to be.

Polly had a worn brown satchel slung over her shoulder. She stopped in the middle of the copse, unhooked the bag and dropped it gently to the ground. She knelt down and opened the bag, pulled out an old green exercise book and closed the bag's flap neatly.

As she stood up, she heard the crunch of footsteps coming from the narrow path. A few seconds later, a man entered the copse carrying a walking stick, dressed in a long brown coat and with a baggy holdall slung over his left shoulder. He stopped, let his shoulder drop so the bag landed awkwardly on the ground, and rested his weight on the walking stick.

With a wheeze and exhaling quickly as he spoke, he said: 'Am I late?' Before Polly could reply, he said: 'Ralph Jensen. You must be the one, the only...Polly!'

Polly smiled. 'That's me. Pleased to finally meet you, Ralph.'

Standing back up straight, Ralph pointed his stick at the ground in front of Polly. 'So, where is it? Is this the spot?'

'Straight to business,' Polly said and smiled again. 'I like that. In answer to your question, I don't rightly know but this is where it *should* be. I was hoping you brought your equipment.' She nodded towards Ralph's bag.

'Yep, all there.' He leant down and settled on his knees in front of the bag. Although he looked fifteen years younger than Polly, he didn't seem to move quite as easily.

Rustling something back and forth in the bag, eventually he pulled out a mess of metal rods and two leather pouches, setting them down on the ground to his right. 'I know it doesn't look like that much, but well...it is!'

Ralph was exactly as Polly had imagined, if a little younger. They had been exchanging emails for nearly six months, since she first saw his profile in *Believer* magazine – which she had subscribed to for years – and took the bold step of getting in touch. Ralph had appeared to be something of an expert on supernatural phenomena, and since such frivolities had been all but wiped out by a succession of books and scientific papers 'disproving' many of the established phenomena, he was one of the few remaining practitioners who carried any weight of respect.

Indeed, Ralph Jensen had left his native Sweden to settle on the Isle of Wight, off the south coast of England, where he had 'divined', so he claimed, a great source of mystical power. Enough people believed him to create something of a following – what some might call a cult – but Ralph had found himself underwhelmed by such adulation, and now was much more likely to be found away from his base, traipsing around the countryside of wherever he happened to be.

'You know what these are?' Ralph picked up a bundle of four brass-coloured rods, the sun catching one and beaming a blinding ray into Polly's eyes. She winced and shielded her eyes with her arm. 'We need to set these up like we're constructing a bridge.' He pointed with a nod. 'First one down there, over by your bag.'

Polly bent over to pick the bag up and slung it carelessly to the right. Ralph set down the bundle of rods, picked two up again and then replaced one with another. 'That's the set. Did you bring a map?'

'Yep!' Polly opened her book and turned it around and down so Ralph could see. There was a rough pencil drawing of a straight line with a wavy line over it, within a circle, which had a kind of tail leading out and following the straight line.

'Okay, so we go here. Got a bigger map, you know...a *proper* map?'

Polly went back to her bag and took out a roll of paper. She unrolled it, found four stones and set the map down on the ground, a stone at each corner. 'Yep.'

Ralph finished placing the first two rods, which involved plunging them hard into the ground, then twisting to dig them in and finally knocking down hard until they were standing up solidly by themselves. They were placed about a metre apart. He stood up and went over to join Polly, squatting by the map.

'So this is the circle.' Polly pointed. 'We are here.' She brought her index finger down hard on the spot. 'And we are tracing this line.' She ran the finger along a straight line from their position on the map, taking it over fields, some dips of a valley and a couple of farm holdings, to the left edge of the map, where another straight line began and carried to the very edge.

'Okay, so it's a broken line but are you sure these meet up?'

'Yes indeedy,' Polly smiled.

Ralph stood up and shrugged his coat off, throwing it over to land on his bag. He stood behind his first set of rods, brought a compass out from his pocket and found it was facing just off east. He walked back towards the path that brought him into the copse, put the compass down on the ground and picked the other rods up, setting them up as close as possible to the line of sight that he reckoned was pretty spot-on.

'Drink?' Polly called.

'Sure, in a minute. Thanks.' Ralph was getting out of breath again.

The two sets of rods placed to his satisfaction, he picked up one pouch and emptied it into his left hand. Out fell a length of leather rope and another case, made of brown velour. He tied the leather strip to each of the rods in one set and then opened the other case, taking out a small pinkish crystal, almost the shape of a heart. Polly thought it looked cute. He attached a small clasp at the top of the crystal to roughly the middle of the leather strip and it hung in a gentle dip, twisting slowly in the gentle breeze. He did the same for the second set of rods.

'Wow,' Polly said. 'Exciting!'

'Not yet, it isn't.' Ralph picked up the compass again. 'Might not even be. These things are...rare to say the least. Finding one of these is...well, we'll see. It was enough to get me out here anyway.'

He settled behind the first set of rods, put the compass right up to the hanging crystal and leaned in as close as possible. 'This has to be...' he said quietly, '...*precise*.'

He stood up briskly, kneecaps cracking as he did. He winced and stumbled over to the second set of rods. He very carefully moved the crystal about a millimetre, then checked the compass and moved it again. 'There!'

'So now we wait?'

'Yes, we do.'

~~~

Around about 11.30am, Polly suggested she go home, make some sandwiches and bring them back. Ralph agreed – only one of them could leave the copse unattended in case something happened.

Polly had just made it home when back at the copse, a brisk fifteen-minute walk away, something did happen.

Ralph was half-sitting, half-lying on his bag for comfort, propped up on one elbow, watching a large cloud come over, drawing shade upon the copse. Coincidentally, the needle of the compass he had left between the crystals, aligned precisely on the hypothetical line that joined two straight, thermometer bulb-ended lines, began to twist. Ralph sat up quickly, cracking something in his back that made him wince again, and moved forward in an awkward spring to rest on his knees in front of the compass.

The needle was spinning faster than he could see; a blur. It appeared to be spinning counter-clockwise. 'Holy shit,' Ralph uttered quietly. He looked left and right at the crystals. They were perfectly still; rigid. He reached back into his left pocket and took out a small, old-fashioned video recorder. He flicked the lens open and turned it to his face.

'It is...' Ralph glanced at his watch. '...11.52am, Tuesday. We have found one. It's a real...' He shuffled backwards to get a better view of the whole area. 'It's a double. Two bulbs. Polly found them. Right by her house. Remember to...' A noise came from behind him, in the densely wooded area. 'Remember to credit Polly. She'll be back in a while. I can't wait.'

Another noise, like trampling, getting closer. Ralph aimed the camera over at the apparatus and then over to the map. He got up to one knee and felt another twinge in his back. His breath was getting faster and heavier – noisier.

'This is the map, where you can see on the right the bulb where we are. Then, over here, it's broken but picks up again, it's maybe...I'd say two miles. I've never seen...'

The trampling noise again. This time much closer. Ralph turned the camera quickly towards the sound. Holding the camera still, he bobbed his head around, trying to see into the wooded area. The cloud overhead made the woods seem denser. He couldn't see anything but trees. He turned back to the apparatus.

'Polly?' he called. 'Is that you?'

Nothing. The trampling sound drew nearer. It sounded much clearer now, twigs breaking underfoot. He thought he could hear heavy breathing.

'The crystals are dead still – it's happening.' Ralph's voice was hurried and broken. He could feel his heart pumping. He turned again back to the woods, camera shakily pointing in roughly the same direction. The sound of...*silence* filled the air. Ralph panted slowly, waiting...waiting...

He stood for just under a minute, as still as he could, as his heart rate and breathing returned to something like normal. His shoulders and back relaxed and he flicked the camera off with his right thumb. Backing slowly further away from the woods – *it must have been an animal, a* big *animal* – Ralph turned back and let out a horrifying scream as a giant figure with a pig's face slammed a large stone into his face, breaking his nose and knocking him out at the same time.

No one heard him scream.

~~~

Polly returned just over forty minutes later with a small wicker hamper covered over with a beige cloth, patterned with ducks and geese flying towards a sunset. 'Ralph?'

She surveyed the area to see the apparatus, Ralph's bag, the map open to the left side and, just further off towards the end of the copse, where it met the dense woodland, a video camera. She took a few steps forward to the camera, noticed the compass – which was still turning – and continued on the fifteen feet to where the camera was. She knelt down to pick it up. There was a small smattering of what looked like blood sitting on the dusty ground, droplets glistening in the sun on top of pebbles and dry grass. Polly gasped.

'Oh my God. Ralph? Ralph?'

Polly stood back up and saw a few more droplets of blood leading into the woods. She gasped again and whispered, *Ralph. Oh my God.*

She looked down at the camera in her hands, flicked open the screen and tapped at something that looked like a 'play' button. She held it up about thirty centimetres from her face – she hadn't stopped to put her reading glasses on – and squinted to watch the video. There was no sound and she didn't notice the 'mute' symbol in the lower left corner of the screen.

'Polly?'

Polly and her heart jumped together and she turned around in a clumsy flash, dropping the camera to land in roughly the same spot she had picked it up from. 'Wha...'

Ralph stood at the entrance to the copse. His eyes looked brighter than before.

'Polly? What are you doing? You brought some food?'

'Ral.. Ralph.' Polly frowned, her heart beating faster than it had in a

98

long time. 'Yeah. Food...I mean, where have you been? There's blood.'

'Oh that!' Ralph beamed. 'I had a nose-bleed. That's all. Takes more than that to stop me!'

Polly stood rooted to the spot, mouth open. 'Oh...so I made some sandwiches. Nose-bleed? Are you okay now? Want me to take a look?'

'It's nothing. I'm hungry. All this waiting around for nothing in the sun. Anything to drink?'

Polly nodded. 'There.' She pointed at the hamper, set down next to the map and Ralph's bag. 'I thought...I thought something had happened to you.'

'I'm *fine*,' Ralph said, firmly.

'Well, there's a lot of blood down there, and you look...*different*. So how about we finish up here and I take you home for a lie down?'

Ralph cocked his head to the right and looked up towards the sun, which was peeking over the tree line. 'Sure,' he said, softly. 'Okay, you win. I suppose I don't feel quite right. Give me a minute to pack this up then. Can you get the map?'

Polly did as she was asked. Something wasn't right about this, she thought, but she spent the next minute or so rationalising it. *A nose-bleed. Why would he lie? I'm just being silly.* Once the map was folded and free of grassy, dusty debris, she handed it to Ralph, who slipped it in his bag.

'We ready then?'

Polly nodded. 'Let's get home and eat these sandwiches before they evaporate.'

Ralph smiled. He seemed more energetic than before. Brighter.

~~~

Polly and Jim were out on their verandah, reclining on loungers and looking out over the valley. Each had in their hand a tall glass of sweet white wine, lemonade and ice. Jim's was nearly empty; Polly's half way down. They talked about what had happened that day. Jim had returned to find this strange man draped across their guest bed – in the room where Jim kept his hunting gear – passed out in a scene that looked like a tramp had crawled in from a storm and found shelter.

Polly had explained and Jim had accepted the explanation. He had no reason not to trust this man – Ralph. He had seen pictures of him, read – or glanced at to appease his eager wife – magazine cuttings about his work and opinions and once or twice overheard conversations from his wife's side as they planned to meet up one day. And this day had come.

Ralph had eaten sandwiches with Polly, drank two pints of cold water and then gone for a lie down in the guest room. He had been in there, sleeping, Polly presumed, for close to three hours.

When he re-appeared and found Polly reading in the adjacent kitchen, he said he wanted to take a walk into the village to check in at his hotel. They could take another look at the copse in the morning. Polly pointed him in the right direction and off he went.

The Boldredown Inn was in the centre of the village, looking out over the main and quite narrow road, with limestone walls and tall trees lending the scene a postcard quality.

The road dipped just up past the inn and then twisted away and up, eventually leading out of the village. Ralph stepped inside from the sun and his eyes took a few seconds to adjust to the sedate shade.

The inn was all dark wooden beams, a light stone floor and a dark brown colour scheme throughout the ground floor. A small reception desk gave way to a large tabled area, with a long curved bar at the far end, at which sat around a dozen men and women, some with dogs curled around the legs of their stools.

A large fan stood at one end of the bar, just to the right of an open set of double doors, which led out to what appeared to be a large garden.

Ralph caught the eye of a young lady behind the bar, who finished serving a man who looked like he did nothing else with his life and then briskly scuttled over to the reception desk. She was very pretty, petite at five feet and two inches, and bright-eyed.

'Hello,' she said, 'Welcome to Boldredown. You must be...' She looked down at an open book on the desk in front of her. 'Mr Jensen?'

'That's me!' Ralph smiled. He squinted down at the girl's badge. 'And you must be Becky. Pleasure to meet you.'

'Likewise, Mr Jensen. You're in room 7, which is through the doors to your left, up the stairs, then up the next stairs and at the end of the corridor. Your room overlooks the garden. It's beautiful.'

'I bet it is,' Ralph said with a grin.

'Would you like me to get you a drink ready for when you come down, Mr Jensen? Or will you be staying in your room? I can have something sent up.'

Ralph looked over at the bar and then out to the garden. 'I think that sounds just right, Becky. Rum and coke, please. Are those guys friendly?' He gestured over at the bar.

'Yep!' Becky smiled again. 'Mostly locals. Our other guests are all up at the field for the air show. No one round here's unfriendly, you know.' She winked.

'An air show?' Ralph asked.

'Oh, you're not here for that then? I just assumed...'

'No, no idea! I have some friends nearby. Just visiting.'

'Well, Mr Jensen, it happens every year and people come from all over to take part and watch. But mostly to take part.' Becky bent over and pulled out a sheet of paper from a shelf under the desk. She handed it to Ralph. 'People build their own gliders, and they start at the top of Hawks Hill, just out the back there, and see who can fly the furthest. The winner gets a big cash prize. We sponsor it a bit.'

Ralph looked up from the leaflet and smiled. 'Sounds fun. I might go take a look.'

'Well, it starts tomorrow and they're all up there preparing. I'll go get that drink for you. Do you want someone to help with your bags?'

'This is all I have.' He nodded towards his bag, hooked over his shoulder.

'In that case, I'll see you in five.' Becky turned swiftly on her heels and headed back to the bar.

Ralph pushed open the door and went up to his room. There was a wooden carving of a hawk on the door, just above the number, also a wooden carving. The room was large, brighter than the bar downstairs, and the window at the end of the room was open, a net curtain billowing gently at the right side. He dropped his shoulder, easing his bag onto the bed and then his jacket, which slumped down onto the floor at the foot of the bed.

He walked over to the window and leaned over, resting his elbows on the sill. Below was a large garden, with a smattering of apple and other trees shading several tables, two or three of which were occupied by families. Some of the tables had parasols bearing the names of beverages that were presumably available inside. Out to the left was someone else's garden and he couldn't see over to the right, beyond a line of trees at his eye level. Out to the back of the garden, another line of trees obscured most of his view but he could see beyond to the top of the hill, and in the distance maybe a quarter-mile away were some moving figures, a few tents and gazebos and some long tables covered in bunting.

Ralph took a quick look in at the bathroom, just back and to the right of the window, nodded with mild satisfaction and headed back out of the room. He stopped to lock the door and headed back down to the bar.

'Here you are, Mr Jensen. Rum and coke. You want some ice in there?' Becky looked like she had been an actress waiting for her cue; for Ralph to appear. Now that he had, the cameras were rolling and 'action' had been called. Ralph tended to view the world in filmic terms. Although he knew that life carried on around him, he had a niggling sense that certain things were triggered by his presence – as if the room was silent and still until he looked at it or walked into it.

'Yes, please. Ice is good, thanks. It's a hot day out there, for an evening.'

'Balmy, we like to say.' Becky took a white plastic scoop and shovelled four ice cubes into Ralph's drink, then handed it to him with another smile. 'We get a lot of good weather down here. Climate change has blessed us country folk at least!'

Ralph surveyed the bar area to find a free stool. All were taken but one at the far end away from the garden door. Another door with 'Toilets' – again, another wooden carving – was behind the stool. He nodded and smiled at Becky, walked past the backs of the locals, none of whom turned to acknowledge his presence, and sat down.

'Becky,' he called. Two of the locals turned to look at him briefly then snapped back to their conversation. 'Are you serving food yet?'

'We serve from 6.30 to 10, Mr Jensen. I'll bring you a menu.'

Ralph looked at the clock at the back of the bar, just visible behind a neat row of a selection of spirits and local wines. The time was 5.58. Becky appeared in front of him and handed him a menu. 'Everything is on but the game pie,' she said. 'And there's a specials board over there.'

Ralph followed her finger and saw a chalkboard but it was too far away to read it. Around the walls were various odds and sods of country life: some axes, ploughing machinery, old faded pictures of men and women and tractors, pots and pans hanging from the rafters and just over along most of the wall to his left, a bookcase with some tatty looking board game boxes on top and an untidy selection of a hundred or so books.

Becky caught his observation. 'It's homely,' she said. 'We get a lot of families in here, and people passing through. Mostly regulars though. No great need to keep it all tidy, y'know. They like it how it is.'

Ralph nodded. 'Lived in. Nothing wrong with that.' He took a sip of his drink, filling his mouth with a cool yet warming sensation. 'So what time does this air show start tomorrow?'

'I think it's around 10. People start turning up throughout the morning and they all fix their gliders up and do practice runs. The main competition's always after lunch. They're doing a barbecue and you can get drinks and snacks up there. Or down here, of course.'

Someone in the middle of the bar grunted and held out a glass. 'Excuse me,' Becky said, sliding over to the other customer.

Ralph sipped his drink and then, when his mouth had become accustomed to the cold, tipped it up and downed the rest. The ice rested against his lips as the dark liquid emptied into his throat. He breathed deeply through his nose, setting the glass back on the bar, and waited for Becky to come back.

~~~

Ralph moved to a table in the garden for his dinner – a delicate pork loin with honey-glazed potato mash, peas and redcurrant sauce – and another rum and coke to help it all down. It was his fourth such drink. The garden had filled up with families and inside the bar was buzzing with thirty or so more people – a more upbeat, vibrant bunch than the quiet, inclusive clientele of just an hour before.

'Mind if I sit here?' Ralph looked up to see a tall, handsome man, in a tidy blue polo shirt and khaki shorts.

'Sure, it's just me taking up a table for eight.' Ralph smiled. 'I'm Ralph. You can have any seat at the table except the one I'm sitting on.'

'Peter,' the man said, reaching out his hand. Ralph shook it firmly.

'Ah, American. I like Americans. You here for the air show?'

'Actually no,' Peter said. He took a large glug of his beer, the froth from the top resting on his lip until he licked it away. 'Just taking a break and entirely coincidentally I might as well check this air thing out while I'm here. And you?'

'Precisely the same,' he said. 'Out here doing a little research and I might as well stick around to see what all the fuss is about.'

Ralph and Peter chatted on for the rest of the evening. They each had four more drinks. Peter explained how he was on a sabbatical from work as a policeman in the US. Ralph gave a potted history of his work and beliefs, noting that most people seemed to think he was a mad peddler of 'bullshit' but he was convinced otherwise – and *clearly not mad*.

'So you found something here?' Peter asked. 'I gotta say, this is intriguing. Have you got any proof? In my line of work, you got no evidence, you got nothing.'

'Well, proof to me is probably not proof to you, officer.' Ralph made a face of mock pain. 'Give me your card and I'll send you a copy of my book, best seller in no countries, top of the loony charts, chopping down forests so I can peddle bullshit to the five or so fucking lunatics who bought it.'

'Hey – that is a fine idea. I've got another five months of enforced relaxation so I might as well spend some of that sucking up your *bullshit.*'

Both men laughed. An hour later Ralph was asleep in room 7 and Peter was sitting on the bed in room 3, at the front of the inn overlooking the road, reading the world news on his PDA, his head propped up on a soft pillow. He hadn't felt this happy and relaxed in a long time and, as he struggled to focus on a story about a fire that was raging in a small town in his home country, his eyes flickered a little until resting shut.

Twelve – Fight and flight

Ralph got downstairs at just after 9, joining his new friend at a table for breakfast. It had been laid out the night before in front of the bar area and was stocked with cereals, toast, bread rolls and fruit, with milk and juices and a large keg of hot water for tea and coffee. He noticed the room was brighter in the morning light, but not by much. Maybe it just seemed that way – he didn't usually drink very much, but he had enjoyed his new friend's company and conversation and the inevitable headache had not appeared. He knew that Polly would be expecting him to call, but hunger took priority.

Peter said how much he had enjoyed the previous evening. Ralph agreed. 'So why did you come here? Long way from Chicago, isn't it?'

Peter nodded as he chewed a buttery slice of toast. 'You know… I'm not so sure of the reason. I just kinda…I think I picked it at random. By which I mean, I don't exactly remember making a decision at any point to come right here, but here I am.'

'I know that feeling. Life on auto-pilot.' Ralph waved at Becky, who caught his eye as she walked from the garden and behind the bar. Peter turned to see and waved too.

He leaned over the table and said, quietly: 'Wouldn't mind a piece of that, y'know.'

'We're both old enough to be…well, too old.' Ralph winked at Peter. Becky caught his eye again and smiled, as if she knew what they were talking about. Ralph supposed she did. Pretty girls usually knew they were pretty.

'I just had to get away,' Peter said, returning to the subject. 'There was a big case – murder. Children, women. Real nasty shit. Not very *breakfasty.*'

Ralph smiled sympathetically. 'I've never seen anything like that and hope I never do.'

'It's a memory I'll keep forever, sure, but it's not the worst shit I've seen. There are too many murders to keep track of. Bad things happen to good people. It's part of the job. Or…it *is* the job.'

'Well now you're here, and I bet no one is getting murdered here today,' Ralph said. 'I'm supposed to be working but, hey, the air show sounds like fun. You want to go with me?'

'Yeah, sounds good. What time?'

Ralph looked at his watch and mumbled: 'It's 9.20. Meet Polly for an...hour? Yes, back here by 11.30.' Then to Peter: 'Okay, let's say 12. We can have a bite and a beer, a gentle stroll up the hill and enjoy the show.'

'It's a date,' Paul grinned. 'But, uh, not *that* kind of date. Oh, and here's my card, so you can send me your bullshit book.'

He grinned and handed Ralph a neatly folded piece of yellow paper. Ralph put it in his top pocket without looking. 'One man's bullshit is another man's truth. You cheeky bastard.'

~~~

Ralph arrived at Polly and Jim's house just after 10. The walk up the winding path, which was not really steep but not gentle either, hadn't seemed to trouble him at all. Ralph felt good. As he approached the rear of the house, he could hear barking coming from inside.

The curtains on the rear windows were pulled shut. Ralph drew nearer and the barking became louder. He stepped up to the back door, which had a blind pulled down to where the glass window met the wooden bottom half. He hesitated for a moment and rapped his knuckles twice gently on the glass.

'Shit...'

Ralph went stumbling backwards as a monstrous canine head slammed up against the glass. He landed awkwardly on his elbows, unable to look away from the dog's face, pressed up against the glass, its teeth bared and bloodied and now barking louder and faster, red saliva dripping in wild streams and its paws chaotically scraping against the glass.

Ralph scrambled backwards and up to his feet in one smooth motion, bending over but keeping his gaze fixed on the mad dog at the window.

'Penny – Penny! Penny, calm down. Penny!' He took tiny, deliberate steps towards the door and Penny stopped barking. Her face was still pressed against the glass, her paws shaking but not scratching. Ralph smoothly raised and lowered his hands in a calming movement that said *Hey, take it easy. Ralph's here. Take it easy.*

Penny's breathing slowed. Now her face backed a little away from the glass, leaving behind a red, sticky mess on the pane. Ralph made it to the door. 'Hey Penny, hey. What's the matter? What's going on in there? Where's mummy?' He tried the door, pushing down a small metal catch. It opened easily. He hesitated before opening it fully. 'Okay, girl. Just keep it calm. Calm. It's okay.'

He eased the door open and put out his right hand towards Penny's head, whispering now: 'It's okay. Penny, it's okay. Shh. It's okay.'

Penny's expression told him it wasn't okay.

~ ~ ~

At 12.15, Peter looked at his watch for about the hundredth time since noon had passed and his new acquaintance had not arrived. Becky had asked what he was waiting for and revealed that she had been in the bar area all morning and not seen Mr Jensen come in. She called up to his room but the phone rang more than ten times. 'I'm sure he'll turn up soon, Mr Foster. Can I get you anything?'

'Oh. Yeah, please. A glass of water please. I'm *melting* out here.'

Becky beamed at him. 'Coming right up!'

Peter's PDA was sat on the garden table in front of him. He picked it up, pressed the Spidernet icon and spoke: 'Ralph Jensen. Wiki.'

In a few seconds he was looking at a picture of his new friend and reading pretty much the same history he had learned the night before. Ralph was Swedish, alternately ostracised and hallowed, sometimes worshipped and idolised, but also heavily criticised for peddling his beliefs. It seemed, Peter thought, that his friend courted and enjoyed controversy. He also wondered whether an apparently intelligent man could be so wrong about something. Maybe this bullshit wasn't bullshit after all.

An alert flashed up on the top right of the PDA: 'New Messages.' Peter tapped the alert and the screen refreshed to show a list of old, greyed out messages and two new, darker entries. He tapped the top one, which read *Missing you*. The message opened. It read:

Hi daddy. When are you coming back from England? Mom says you went for six months. Please come home soon. Mommy says we can stay with you for a whole week! Love Molly.

Peter stared at the message and closed it. He tapped the second entry, which read *Subscription expiring – hurry!* The message read:

You are receiving this message because your subscription to Enforcer runs out in

7 days. If you wish to continue, please click here to confirm.

Peter looked up and back at the bar. There were a few bodies moving about in the bar now. He clicked the link on the PDA. A new screen came up. *Please enter your details here.* The user name field was already filled out, and the password field blank. The user name read *Paul Motta.* He tapped in his password, *angel0m0tta,* and clicked *Submit.* The screen refreshed: *Thank you for your continued custom. You will be billed according to the particulars of your subscription.*

~~~

At 10.02, Ralph made a discovery that just under an hour ago he had told his new American friend would not happen today. Not here. Ralph had been wrong but did not have the time to ponder this revelation. He had followed Penny the mad barking dog into the kitchen. As he rounded the central breakfast bar, he saw Polly's body, face down in a large pool of blood. The sun peeked through a tiny gap in the curtains and shot a single ray of light onto the blood, giving it a serene glow.

In the back of Polly's head was a large hole, dark red and with a caked-on rivulet of thick blood leading down onto her cheek, and meeting the pool on the floor. The house was silent – and Ralph felt this silence. He stepped around the corpse and walked on through to the bottom of the staircase, standing in a hallway leading out towards the front of the house. Penny let out a single, short bark. It was the sort of sudden event that would make a man jump, but Ralph did not. He looked back at Penny, who was facing the guest room at the other side of the kitchen.

Ralph walked back and around Polly's corpse, looking down at it briefly and feeling something, some emotion that he didn't consciously register, and met up with Penny. The guest room door was ajar, but as he nudged it open he could see another body. Jim was on the bed, face up. His head also had a large, round and red hole in it, just above his left eye. The head rested awkwardly on the edge of the pillow beneath it, and his left arm hung off the side of the bed, blood trickling along it and down out of Ralph's line of sight.

Thud. A noise came from above the guest room. Ralph looked up at the ceiling, back at the body, and left the room. He stood in the kitchen, facing the archway leading to the stairs. Another sound above. Footsteps heading towards them. He walked casually over to the breakfast bar and selected the longest looking kitchen knife from a rack. Edging back into the guest room, he set the knife down against his right leg and closed the door gently with his left hand, leaving a tiny gap that he could see through. He couldn't see the archway or stairs but most of the breakfast bar was visible, and just to the right he could see one of Polly's lifeless legs.

He looked down to see that Penny wasn't with him. Just outside the door, he saw the dog brush past and walk softly over to Polly. It sniffed her foot and moved out of sight.

Ralph heard footsteps on the stairs. His right hand tightened around the knife handle and the blade twitched upwards. He thought he should have felt nervous, or just *something*, but he felt as calm as he had an hour ago.

A figure appeared in Ralph's sliver of the scene. Its back was turned. Ralph edged the door an inch further, widening his view far enough to see through to the archway. Another figure stood in it, a ray of light casting a bright glow on the face. It was the face of a pig. The light bounced off its snout. Its eyes looked dead. Black holes, windows to nothing. Ralph wanted to draw back but didn't. He realised the pigman was wearing some kind of uniform.

The first figure turned and Ralph saw its face too was that of a pig. His right fist tightened further. The two figures rounded the breakfast bar to where Polly's body lay, and out of Ralph's sight. He heard some muffled talk, but could not discern the words or language.

Ralph dared another inch, and as his shoulder pressed lightly against the door, it thumped back against him, sending him reeling backwards against the edge of the bed. Pigman 1 stormed in at speed, shooting a gloved hand out to snap around Ralph's neck, picking him up and slamming his body against the guest room wall. The glass frame around a painting – one of Jim's early watercolour efforts depicting a small boat drifting out at Lymehead Harbour – shattered and fell to the floor, two or three shards getting caught between Ralph's jacket and the wall, and another spiking out into his neck.

Ralph grunted and the blur of the event ceased. Pigman 2 entered the guest room, a black pistol pointed at Ralph's head. Pigman 1 held Ralph against the wall with a disconcerting lack of effort. His grip loosened around Ralph's neck and he let go completely, then used his left and then both hands to rest Ralph back to standing. Pigman 1 backed off by a foot. Pigman 2 lowered his pistol, turned and left the room.

Ralph and Pigman 1 stared into each other's eyes. For Ralph, the view was of something deeply disturbing but he felt indifference – a conflict whirring in his mind. His stomach lurched but he did not notice it. Pigman 1's eyes were pure black and deeper than any head could accommodate. It was like staring into an abyss.

Pigman 1's view was almost exactly the same. Ralph's pig face bore no resemblance to his human one – it was in all probability a facsimile of his attacker's visage. His eyes, too, were dark and deep. Roads to nowhere.

Ralph dropped the knife to the floor. It landed on a large shard of glass, splitting it into three, before resting against the wall. From around the corner, he heard a gunshot and the tiny yelp of a dog drawing its last breath. Pigman 1 left the room and again Ralph heard muffled voices. He glanced at Jim's body and followed his pig friends into the kitchen. Pigman 2 looked at him with dead eyes. Pigman 1 knelt down over Polly's corpse. He was scraping something off the floor.

Ralph moved over to stand at Polly's feet. Pigman 1's gloves were dark red and dripping. He raised his hand to his mouth and dabbed the end of the glove on his lips. He stood up and turned to face Ralph, who was still held in the hypnotic gaze of Pigman 2.

Pigman 2 spoke, barely audible as if speaking through a thick cushion, his mouth still: 'Come.' He pointed to the kitchen door, still open and red from Penny's frothing mouth. Ralph now saw Pigman 1 as he turned, noting indifferently that his face was daubed in red prints.

'Why do we need the blood?' Ralph spoke but didn't *feel* himself do it. Looking down at the pool, now smudged and without its serene glow, he understood. As his gaze drew back to the exit, a picture frame just outside the guest room showed his reflection. He felt nothing. He walked to the picture frame and stared into it, bypassing the painting within – another one of Jim's originals, but that didn't matter – and using the reflective glare to admire his new mask.

Pigman 1 spoke again, 'Come.' He brushed against Ralph, who absently supposed he was probably Pigman 3 now, and left the house.

Pigman 2 followed behind and Ralph exited back out into the glorious sunshine, atop a hill overlooking a beautiful valley, a picture postcard, a view to die for – literally.

'Where are we going?' Again, Ralph's new face was motionless and he didn't feel any sensation of speaking.

His two new porcine brethren spoke together. 'Home.'

~ ~ ~

At 12.20, Paul decided not to wait any longer and asked Becky to give Ralph a message if he turned up. He headed out through the garden gate, between a row of tall trees and found himself on a dusty path that led up a gentle incline towards a plateau, itself shielded to one side by a forest. Looking out to his right he could see the rear of a line of properties with long gardens, a smattering of willow trees and just beyond them a pretty lake. He thought he might have a look over there on his way back.

He reached the top of the hill and took a moment to look back down at the village, registering its postcard qualities. He took his PDA out, flicked a switch at the back and held it up. Another click and the scene was immortalised. *I'll send that to Molly*, he thought. Before he could do so, excited voices behind him drew his attention.

The hilltop was a hive of activity. Marquees, smaller tents, banners and bunting filled the view. Paul walked over to a gap in the bunting, covered over with a gazebo with a large paper sign that simply said *Entrance*.

'Competing or capitulating?' A small woman in her fifties, wearing a flower print dress and a wicker hat, with round spectacles resting on the end of her nose, smiled up at Paul, offering a ticket in one hand and reaching the other out, palm up.

'How much?' Paul enquired. 'I'm just here to soak it all up!'

'Twenty, please.' He reached into his pocket, pulled out a twenty-pound note and handed it to her. Paul thought it was very quaint that England still used physical money. The United States had given up on it years ago.

'Thanking you muchly, sir. The show kicks off in about an hour, but you can find plenty to do before that. Have a great day!'

Paul did as he was told and ventured inwards. Off to his left was a large marquee with several stalls in it, and in a line heading further out maybe five or six more, smaller stalls. In front of the marquee by about fifteen feet was a barbecue, tended by three men in aprons, another elderly looking lady cutting bread rolls in half with a short knife, and a stack of boxes with pen scribbles he couldn't make out.

Off to the right was what looked like a staging area. There were maybe ten 'flying machines' – most looked like elaborately coloured heaps of crumpled plastic and cloth, one appearing more resplendent as something resembling a hang-glider. *That's the winner then*, Paul thought. Next to the staging area, cut off from the sweeping valley below by a long but not very thick rope, was a group of around forty chairs. Some were taken already, their temporary inhabitants watching the men at the barbecue intently. A man sat alone at the far end of the front row of seats, wearing a thick cap that together with a shadow obscured his face. He was leant forward, elbows on knees and fists resting under his chin.

Paul turned to look back through the gazebo entrance to see if his friend had caught up. He had not. It occurred to him that perhaps Ralph had seen through his thin disguise – using a false name had been more of a flighty than a professional decision but all part of getting away from his troubles. Ralph was intelligent, evidently. Their jobs were not all that different; perhaps Ralph, professing to be in tune with nature and spirituality, was simply a psychic detective, replacing Paul's scientific approach with one so much more fanciful but maybe just as effective. He didn't really know. That kind of thing was beyond his comprehension, or maybe just beyond what he felt comfortable comprehending.

In any case, he was not there. He probably just got caught up with his other friend; his real, local friend. They had been due to do some kind of work. It didn't matter. The combination of searing sun and the previous evening's alcoholic veil wearing off began to show internally as Paul gravitated towards the seating area. He veered off towards the safety rope and saw, around two hundred yards away at the bottom of the valley, some men marking out an area with small red flags.

He turned back to the seats and saw the man in the cap had gone. He surveyed the area, over to the barbecue, the marquee and stalls, and back at the gazebo, but he wasn't there anymore. Paul had only looked down the hill for about five seconds, a glance at best. *I'm seeing things.*

'I know you.'

Paul jumped. The voice came from behind him. 'Uh...'

He turned to see the man in the cap, his face now free of shadow. It was weathered, but kind.

'I saw ya in the bar last night. With that old feller. You're American, right? Me too.'

'Oh, well, pleased to meet you.' Paul reached out his hand. The man shook it limply with two fingers and a thumb. Paul *loathed* wet handshakes.

'Likewise. You a policeman? You look like a policeman.'

'Yeah. Yeah I am, actually.' Paul smiled uneasily. He didn't think he looked like anything in particular. 'Up in the Windy City. And you?'

'This and that, here and there.'

'So...are you part of the air show?'

'Nope. Just passing through.'

Paul wondered how this guy, or anyone for that matter, would be *passing through* an air show in southern England. Still, he supposed he was passing through too, albeit stopping for as long as he could until feeling the pull to get home.

'Passing through, huh? Well, it was nice to meet you. See you around.' Paul smiled as sincerely as he could manage.

'Yep, surely will. I'd bet on it.'

The man's eyes widened and for a tiny moment fixed harshly on Paul's. It felt like a jolt, like a sharp burst of air had hit his face.

Paul turned back to the seats and noticed he could smell meat cooking. He glanced over at the barbecue and saw two of the men spraying water at it, while the other, who now had a bright red face, was moving the boxes out of the flames' reach. The elderly lady with them was laughing.

He wanted to sit away from the strange man in the cap. He had proved to be quite an oddity. Not necessarily in appearance, but his manner was unsettling. There were enough weirdoes back home, and he didn't intend to consort with them on his time off. The people who had been watching the barbecue intently were still doing so and now chuckling about it, looking excitedly around at each other. Paul sat in front of them, tipped his head back and took in the beautiful vista of green and blue, a wisp of cloud streaking across the middle of his personal skybox.

Paul felt the curtain of fatigue draw over him and within a few minutes he had fallen into a light doze, warm and comfortable, the heat easing him away. He slept for forty-eight minutes and was awoken by the cheering of those now sat around him. His head lurched slightly forward as his eyes were greeted with a bright flash of sunshine. He raised a hand to shield the glare and was surprised to find a couple of hundred or more people crammed into the area, some holding drinks they had brought up from the inn, others munching on food from the barbecue. All of a sudden he felt very hungry.

As he got up and began to calculate his chances of making it through to the barbecue area, which would involve saying 'excuse me' to fifty people or more, a loudspeaker burst into life, apparently aimed straight at his ear drum. With a loud squeal of feedback and then a grainy hiss to introduce him, a man's voice boomed: *Welcome one and all! Ladies, gentlemen and furry friends, we welcome you to the finest air show of all time, a jamboree of flight and fancy. Please make way for our contestants!*

Paul looked back towards where he had been sitting and saw the area was now filled with flying contraptions of various shapes and sizes. The seating area was full too – and his seat had been taken just seconds after he vacated it. A man in his twenties – with a beard that made him look like a druid, Paul thought – sucking on a large plastic cup of beer, now leaving Paul in limbo: would he stay put, leave, push through the crowd in the hope of finding some food...

Shit. A pleasant afternoon had suddenly, or at least as suddenly as going to sleep and waking up a while later, turned into a hassle. *Barbecue. I'm starving.* Paul began the hunt for food and, as expected, did not enjoy the only option he had of nudging, tapping shoulders, smiling and requesting. A good minute later, he found himself the other side of the crowd, now among a smaller group huddled around the barbecue where – *thankfully* – burgers were still being prepared.

Paul bought a cheeseburger. As he bit into it, he felt the disappointing familiarity of stale bread encasing some limp meat and greasy, inexplicably oily onions. This mundane, unpleasant formula was topped off with a cocktail of ketchup and mustard, rounding the flavour off into the realms of *disgusting* but yet the mind had a habit of processing it into something far more desirable than it was. Every man, woman and child, and dog for that matter, who deliberately made the decision to eat such an abomination knew exactly what they

114

were getting, but they would do it anyway. There would be a wince of discovery on the first taste, but the rest would be in the stomach within seconds. Some brave souls might even venture forth for a second course.

Paul thought about this longer than he had ever intended to. As he chomped on the last mouthful, a dribble of ketchup shot from his tongue and onto the white blouse of a lady with her back to him. It hit her right on the spine and left a red dot about the size of a pimple. She didn't notice. Paul stared at it and thought it was getting bigger. His eyes blurred around the dot and it began to grow, like a fresh bullet wound seeping plasma.

His macabre daydream was cut short with another squeal, hiss and announcement: *Give a big hand and welcome to our first contender – Mr...Mr Jason White! Remember folks, the rules are simple. Man and machine must both land together and the winner, taking away our grand prize today of ten thousand pounds, will be whoever makes it furthest. So, Mr...White! Are you ready?*

A small cheer sounded from the crowd and Paul guessed this meant Mr White was indeed ready. *Does this interest me?* he thought. The woman with the tiny blood stain had moved into the crowd, which had fanned out a little to allow everyone a chance to see. *Shall I just go back to the hotel?* A loud cheer erupted from the crowd. The hot sun on his head made Paul feel unpleasantly warm.

The loudspeaker boomed again: *Ready, on three! One...two...three!* The crowd cheered again, this time longer and louder. Paul looked up a little and instinctively closed his eyes to shield the bright sun, which had now scared any and all clouds away. His head felt heavier and he let it drop, opening his eyes again to see the grass beneath him. The crowd roared louder. *Fuck this.*

The roars turned to screams. Paul was pushed off his feet and fell to the ground with a thump, landing awkwardly on his right arm, his shoulder crunching into the earth and his head thudding in after it. A large boot missed his nose by about half an inch as he managed to roll back and over, rising to a squat position to see a hoard of terrified bodies running past him to the entrance gazebo.

'Hey!' Paul tried to catch the attention of a man in his fifties, who kept turning his head back to make sure whatever it was had not caught him up. 'Hey, sir!' The man didn't stop but called: 'Just get out of here!'

Paul rose to his feet and found a path through the last remaining runners. The seating area was now empty; the flying machines stood where they had before; four or five people stood looking down the hill. Paul called to them. 'What the hell's going on here?'

'See for yourself.' A young woman was pointing a camera down at forty-five degrees, capturing the drama below. She had a look of grim fascination on her face. Paul saw her hands were trembling.

Resting his hands on a flimsy rope of bunting, giving way slightly before he righted himself, Paul surveyed the area, his eyes darting from point to point, registering each element and assigning a memory to it. This was what he did best, a detective through and through: reducing the event to a series of incidents and accidents, understanding the science of the scene.

Jason White was lying, dead, at the foot of the hill, roughly central. His flying contraption was off about ten feet to his left. A figure stood facing away, arms slack, its right hand holding a gun. Jason's head was missing most of its left side. There were five or six bullet wounds in his chest.

Paul went for his gun. *Shit*. He wasn't armed. He looked at his fellow observers and spoke firmly: 'Get out of here. I am a police officer. Back away and get out of here, now.'

The girl with the camera began backing away, closing up the lens as she did and turned around into a jog. The others followed her, looking back with mixed expressions of worry and horror. One man stumbled backwards, scrambled back up to his feet and moaned like a child having a nightmare. The girl dropped her camera, its viewer snapping off at the hinge. She didn't try to pick it up.

Paul was now alone. A hundred yards down the hill, the figure turned. He could see it was a man, but he couldn't make out his features. *Is that blood?* Dark patches covered most of the man's face. Paul's detective brain completed the scenario: a man with a gun had appeared from the woods and shot – with a silenced pistol – Jason White as he landed, at close range. He would find out *why* later.

Paul knew he had to run too. With nothing to defend himself, there was not a chance he could take on the gunman. The figure turned again, walked towards and stepped on the body as if he hadn't seen it, picking up pace into a jog and then a sprint, disappearing into the wooded area beyond.

'Damn!' Paul hooked the bunting up and slid below it, hurrying down the hill towards the murder scene, giving a chase which he knew was foolish. What would he do if he caught up to this man?

The gradient of the hill kept Paul in an unsteady descent but as he reached the bottom, he too quickened into a sprint and headed for the woods. The sun disappeared behind the canopy, a few rays shooting through and casting the scene in a dark brown hue. He stopped and threw his back up against a tree which shielded most of his body. Swinging his head out sharply, he saw the figure about eighty yards away, now heading slightly uphill.

Paul swung his body out too and sprinted through the woods, jumping with adrenaline-enhanced agility and managing to gain ground on his mark. He leapt a fallen branch and into a narrow and moist ditch. A bullet missed his arm by the tiniest sliver and thumped into a tree just behind him. He hunched down into the ditch and waited, listening intently for a location.

Another two bullets shot overhead and he jumped out to his left, coming out of the ditch and back around to lean against a thick trunk. Another bullet shot past, followed by a sharp pneumatic sound. *Reloading.* Paul darted back out to the right of the tree and kept as low as he could while scampering further uphill. Forty or so yards away, the figure was on the move again, the hill steepening and not much further ahead breaking out from the woods like light at the end of a tunnel.

Paul quickened his pace, gaining ground and closing the gap to less than thirty feet. The figure appeared to be tiring. He shouted: 'Drop your weapon!' The figure turned hastily and let off another round, missing Paul by a clear metre. 'Put it down! Stop!'

This time it did stop. It turned to face Paul and raised its weapon again, pointing directly at him. Paul had ventured just far enough out of cover to be a sitting duck. The figure's face was steeped in shadow, its features still mostly obscured by its victim's blood.

Paul slowly stood up straight and put his hands up, staring into the gun barrel. The figure stepped forward, a ray of sun at last revealing his face. The blood around his mouth cast a dull shiny reflection. The figure was wearing a black suit – Paul recognised it now as a police combat suit, not standard issue. His eyes flicked back to the gun and particularly the hand clenched around it. The figure's finger tensed and twitched towards the trigger.

'Please...' Paul said, soft and trembling. It was not the first time he had been in this situation, but it was possibly the last. 'Please. I am unarmed.'

The figure didn't speak. His hand squeezed into the trigger, stopping just shy of the point of no return as a loud thunderclap sounded behind him. He turned his head slowly, deliberately, and then snapped back at Paul, hands still raised but a flicker of confidence in his eyes.

Paul sprang backwards and to the ground, his arms outstretched and feet up as a bullet whizzed past him and hit a tree far behind. A second bullet fired less than a second later caught the tip of his left shoulder. Although he did not realise, his jump had put about two degrees of uncertainty between his assailant and a comfortable shooting trajectory.

Play dead. I'm dead. Paul lay lifeless. His eyes were open wide but he couldn't see anything but the trees snaking up to the heavens all around him. He concentrated on slowing his breathing. The crunch of feet on twigs and earth came towards him. Another thunderclap came from the distance. The crunchy footsteps stopped again. Paul's breathing slowed to an almost imperceptible pace, or at least it seemed that way to him. It was like a storm had rampaged through the woods and then just stopped, leaving no trace. There were no birds tweeting; no planes flying overhead. Almost total silence. Then another *clap!*

Paul opened his eyes wider, trying to create a believable face of death. He let his jaw slacken and tightened it into a pose. The pain in his shoulder grew more intense. A bug or ant crawled over his right arm. The footsteps seemed to become more distant. *He's leaving. I can't get up. Can I get up? Wait a bit longer...what if he's not alone? He would have been here by now.*

Slowly as he could, Paul raised his head. He angled it up just far enough to see a blurry nose and top lip puncturing the horizon and then a little further to bring his line of sight level with the ground sloping upwards. The figure was gone. Paul pushed his hands into the earth, sending a sharp pain through his shoulder and arm, back down into his hand, but managed to get upright. Before standing, he stopped to make sure he was free.

As he stood up, he looked down at his shoulder. A shallow scratch had already caked over with a trickle of blood, his shirt ripped neatly. He put his index finger in the hole, pulled the shirt up a couple of inches and was satisfied that he wasn't about to need a blood transfusion.

Clap! That sound again. Paul started forward and made his way slowly past where the shooter had just been, and then up to where the woods tapered off. He crouched down just inside the tree line and looked left and right for signs of his attacker. A minute or two later, he ventured out and found himself looking up a hill of fields, towards a house in the distance and essentially no sign of human life apart from his own. *Shit.*

Thirteen – Home truths

When Joe came to, he was unsure of his surroundings. No one could have blamed him for feeling a little out of sorts – having been whisked from pillar to post ever since settling down on a comfy sofa that afternoon. His neck and back were stiff. His legs felt numb. As his eyes adjusted to the night sky and trees surrounding him, he realised that at least this time, he had stayed put.

'Finally awake then?' He looked to his right and saw Ged, up on his knees and scraping a stick the size of a pencil into the earth.

'Uh...yeah. I guess so. What time is it, and...what's happening?'

'Well sonny, the good news is the *poo-lease* have buggered off. I suppose there isn't any bad news. We need a plan.'

'A plan.' Joe exhaled loudly. Ged's dog, who was curled up between them, looked up at Joe and snarled. 'What kind of plan? I don't even know what's going on here.'

'No, I guess you don't. I guess you *don't*.' Ged set his stick down on the ground. 'Okay. Let's say you're Mr Ignorant. That's kind of my concern, you see. When I whipped you out, you see...I've been watching you. So have they. And the police. Shit, dude, *everyone's* been watching you!'

'Why? What's so special about me? That shit you showed me...what the fuck *was* that?' Joe felt his pulse quickening. 'You say I delivered... what, bombs or something and had something to do with that fire? I don't get that. That isn't me. Whatever you think I've done, I haven't.'

'Oh yes you have, feller. No doubt about that, but the fact you don't know shit about it means we just might be able to make this work. If you really are just a meat puppet, we can try to cut those strings.'

'A...a meat puppet? Are you serious?' Joe's look of bewildered frustration intensified. 'Just how the fuck can I be a meat puppet?'

'Calm down, Joe. Just calm down a second. We're safe here. Nowhere else just now. Right here. I'll tell ya some stuff.'

'Great.' Joe's look turned more angry than frustrated. 'More mumbo jumbo?'

'Don't be fuckin' insolent. You've got a lot to learn and we don't have much time for you to learn it all. Okay? Just shut up and listen.'

Joe nodded. Whistle snarled at him again.

'You got a lot of memories of being a kid?'

'No, not really. This and that. I had a big head injury years back. I remember...some stuff. My parents...who died when I was young, thirteen or fourteen I guess. Lived with my uncle and aunt after that, a foster home outside Chicago. Joined the police out of school. Not much more to tell.'

'Ah, but there is.'

'Like what? You know something I don't?'

Ged chuckled, grimly, then drew nearer to Joe's face and grinned: 'I know all about you, Joe. You're one of us. But you don't know you're one of us. But don't worry about that – it's normal, kinda.'

'Right – yeah...this is all so very *normal*. Would you care to explain, Mr Normal, what the fuck you are on about?'

Ged's face darkened. 'I told you not to be insolent. Just shut up talking and listen. Your parents. They drowned, right? Boating accident. Did you know you caused that accident?'

Joe's jaw dropped. He looked angry and shocked. All the muscles in his arms tightened.

'That's how we find you. That's how *they* find you.'

'Who are *they*?'

'Thousands of years ago...' He hesitated, seemingly trying to find the right words. 'There's a place. There's a *core*. What is in that core, nobody can define. Men can feel it but they can't get into it. It's an invitation only affair, you see. You got your invitation same way I did.'

'And how was that?' Joe asked, sarcastically.

'Just shut up. Listen and understand. Your parents, and you...you had a good thing going. People do. Families are where it's at, you know. But for some people, there's a turning point. There's a pivot, where something happens and it's like a switch is flicked – it turns you off in one way and on in another. Nod if you follow.'

Joe shook his head.

'Right. If you opened your mind and stopped being so damned awkward...listen. You didn't kill your parents but you did cause their deaths. And what happened right after is when your switch was flicked. That switch goes up, or down, and someone knows about it. You become a candidate.'

'A candidate for what?'

'You're recruited. You were recruited, Joe. Just like me, just like thousands of others in thousands of years. Think about it – rapists, murderers, arsonists, paedophiles...where do you think these guys come from?'

Joe shrugged. 'You're gonna tell me, right?' Whistle snarled again. Joe didn't notice this time.

'Do you remember how you felt after the accident?'

'No, I...I don't remember much of that at all.'

'That's because it's not your memory any more. I'll try to put this as simple as shit: you didn't show any remorse about what you did. There was something dark around that day. Sometimes the dark stuff is just there. You feel it but you can't do shit about it. That dark turned you. It crept into that consciousness and it re-wired your brain. It seeped into your heart and into your soul and it changed who you are. Who you were.'

'I don't remember the accident.'

'You never will. Maybe you'll dream about it. Maybe not. It doesn't matter. Once you've turned, that's it. You can fight it, but we – *they* – don't let you. Now this core I talked about. That core is like a giant ball of darkness. Think of it like a giant spider, and that spider is shooting webs out all over the place, catching the darkness and pulling it back in. But the spider is hungry...'

Joe felt enveloped in dread.

'...and so you have to feed that spider. The hungrier it gets, the more desperately it shoots out those webs.'

'I still...this is crazy.' Joe's voice was low and trembling. He felt suddenly cold. His hands and feet began to tingle.

'Yeah, it is crazy. But it's real Joe. This crazy shit is *real*. Just listen. Once you're turned, that spider brings you in. It gives you a job to do and to make you do that job properly, it only gives you what you need. That's why you don't remember. If you don't feel guilty, you don't look guilty. Get it?'

'Uh-huh.' Joe was breathing much faster now. His forehead was sweating.

'You get your job and you do it and you go back to that spider and you feed him. He feeds on your memory. He eats it out of your soul, he drinks the dread from your eyes...he sucks up all the darkness out of you. That's what happened up at that farm six months ago, Joe.'

I'm having a heart attack.

'But there's more. You see, some places are darker than others.

There are lines all over the world, Joe. That's how we get about. They used to be called ley lines. Some folks had them as mystical but really, well...they're our roads. Our *pathways*. The spider's web.'

I'm having a fucking heart attack. Shit. Shit.

'Are you even listening to me?'

Joe's eyes closed and he fell heavily on top of Whistle. The dog yelped and jumped out from underneath just before he was squashed. Joe's head hit the ground. Ged saw he looked as pale as the moonlight, paler still in it, and his breathing was fast and shallow.

'Goddamn this. Wake up, Joe. We don't have time. Just fuckin' wake up. You have to hear what I gotta say.'

Joe opened his eyes. The eyelids were flickering. The whites of his eyes were dull. He moaned, softly: 'Help me.'

'You're fine, boy. Just in shock. Really, come on. Snap out of this. Get up.'

Joe didn't get up, but he managed to slow and deepen his breathing.

'Get back to the spider.'

Joe's mind conjured up a giant ball of black smoke sitting above a fiery abyss with winding, hairy legs shooting out of it in a thousand directions. He opened his eyes again to clear the image, but found them close straight away. In the centre of the black ball, a huge eye opened and fixed his gaze. The eye began melting away, seeping back into the smoky ball. Joe felt his own eyes sting. Ged placed a hand on his forehead.

'You can travel down those lines too, Joe. You just don't know it right now. You just need the memory back. You need to go back to the waiting room.'

An image of a white and red ballroom full of well-dressed pigs flashed into Joe's mind. He opened his eyes again and managed to look up at Ged, almost gratefully. Whistle was up on his hind legs growling at Joe. 'Shut up, boy,' Ged told the dog.

'What do you want from me?' Joe's voice was croaky, unsteady. 'If all this...if all of this is true, what's your story?'

'I was like you, Joe. Just like you. Whistling my way through life and had no idea what I was. But then I saw it. I was in the belly. But they don't know I saw it. I'm like you but my eyes are open.'

Joe's breathing was almost back to normal. 'You were...in the belly? The spider?'

'That's right. You know...everything it drinks goes into a pot, let's call it a pot. All that shit just swirls around, mixing together. I saw it all. I guess no one is supposed to see any of it. Maybe I'm wrong, but I ain't special. There's no peckin' order I'm aware of.'

'How do you get in?'

'You don't. It's not a *spider* at all – you get that. But it is a great mass of darkness. You cross over and you go into the waiting room. Usually they send someone out to bring you in. That's what you got up at that farm.'

'So is it...are Tom and Frank like us?'

'They weren't before. You could think of it as some kinda recruitment drive. You bring your friends along for the ride and they end up fully paid members of the club.'

'So...I. I'm still confused. What do you want from me? Why have you pulled me up here?'

'Because sonny, the cracks are showing. I keep an eye on this town. I sit in my shack and I take it all in. I recognised you and your boys. We're not all in the waiting room at the same time, but I seen you in there before. Six months ago. Now not a lot's happened between then and now and you ain't been back since. I reckon you did a big job and it's time for a little rest and relaxation and they're lying you low, or maybe there's somethin' else going on.'

'So what else...what else have I been *used* for?'

'All sorts. Only *they* know – they take the memories away. But they can't get at your dreams. They come from somewhere else. If you got some really nasty dreams, you can bet they have a root or two in reality.'

The kid. Joe's mind filled with the image, the broken memory, the one he had tried to suppress but also that he could never grasp – fragmented and uncertain.

'I remember some things,' he said, eyes still closed and clutching at the fragments. He saw a small pile of white powder on a desk, and he could almost hear shouting and screaming behind him.

'If you do, the cracks are really showing, opening up, whatever. Maybe you've become a liability. Problem is, so have I. Coming after you, they're gonna be coming after me. I couldn't let the police get you. There's a certain balance we have to keep. And these people are *everywhere.*'

124

'Is that why there's never any crime down here?'

'That explains why you are here, I guess. Sure, they're trying to keep you out of harm's way. You must be an asset. Plenty more before you, before me, have been turned back to dust.'

'This is all still so...I don't know how to think of it. Real or unreal, what's next? You said we need a plan?'

'Yes, we do.'

Fourteen – The hunt

Paul Motta sat in a large leather armchair facing a desk in his new incident room, otherwise known as the Coldharbour police station briefing room.

Chief Silas Bangay sat on another armchair opposite Paul, who was looking down at a PDA. 'So, Mr Motta. You gonna tell me what the hell is going on here?'

Paul looked up briefly and back at the PDA. 'Sir, I have here the PDA of our chief suspect, Joe Gullidge. It was found in the home of one Ged Hollins. I've got a team combing his shack right now. In the meantime, this is our evidence.'

'So why have you called me out here, Paul?'

'All hands on deck, chief!' Paul looked up and beamed an uneasy grin at his superior.

'Don't give me that shit, son.' The chief looked annoyed. 'I've got the Mayor breathing down my neck, the whole commercial construction fraternity nipping at my heels and, well, I ain't got a lot of time for cross country jaunts.'

'Chief.' Paul's grin had turned upside down. 'I really do need your help. We don't have enough men for the manhunt.'

'Are you sure this guy is...*the guy*?'

'As damn sure as I've ever been about anything, chief. Listen...' He put the PDA down gently on the desk. 'I know this man. By which I mean I *encountered* this man before. We both worked in Chicago, but he moved on before I got there. When I was in England – that's where I took my R&R – he shot at me. Took a tiny lump out of my shoulder.' He pointed to where six months ago a bullet had been fired in the forest and gouged a small groove into his flesh.

Chief Bangay looked puzzled. 'Go on.'

'Gullidge came and went as if he was never there, chief. In England I searched that whole forest. A family was murdered and he was there. Now when I came to Shenbury at your request, I saw something familiar in those files, but when he shot at me in England I didn't register his face properly. It was all a rush, see. But when I saw that photo in the station, maybe for the tenth time, it clicked. Then the evidence came in and…'

'And you found him. Okay, Paul. What the hell was he doing in

England? You think he murdered a family?'

'Shit. I would say I am about ninety per cent sure on that. I saw him murder someone else, right in front of me. That's why I went in pursuit and that's why I got shot.'

Bangay frowned and nodded. 'Okay. So what's on his PDA?'

'Not a lot. Some messages from his girlfriend and some others from an unknown number. An unregistered number. Illegal then. I'm betting it's Ged Hollins. One of them tells him to *stop digging*.'

'So what's your take on this?'

'I don't have a take on this. I have some evidence and first-hand experience that this man is a murderer. Right now he's somewhere in this town. We've got roadblocks at every exit. The docks are shut down. I've got officers outside of the woods leading up to his house. I want this man in custody. I want him alive.'

Bangay nodded again. 'Right. Okay. You can have my guys. They're setting up now out front. Just catch this motherfucker, okay?'

Paul nodded. 'There is no doubt in my mind. I *will* catch this motherfucker.'

Bangay stood up. Paul followed suit.

'What about the girl?'

Paul picked up the PDA and slipped it into a pouch, which he put in his inside jacket pocket. 'Louise. I don't know much about her. She's not at the house. She is not currently a priority. Chances are she has no idea who her boyfriend is, but we'll worry about that later.'

Bangay left the room, walking up the corridor to the station entrance, leaning on the double doors and pushing out into the cool evening air. Paul followed. A group of six special officers was gathered around the open back doors of a large black van. Four of them were wearing combat suits with visors up and rifles attached to their backs. The other two were pulling their suits on. Beyond the van was Paul's police cruiser. Otherwise, the car lot was empty.

'Gentlemen!' Paul managed to get his new task force's attention. 'We are looking for Officer Joe Gullidge. It is essential that we take this man alive. Exercise caution. Fire only to wound. We are also looking for his accomplice, Ged Hollins, whose mug has been uploaded to your PDAs. Check the intel, follow protocol and bring me these men ASAP.'

He turned to face Chief Bangay. 'Thanks.'

'No problem.' Bangay approached his men. 'Right fellas. We need a smooth op here. You report to Officer Motta and he reports to me. We are monitoring all com, and we want your visor feeds *on*. The op is on. We believe the suspect is hiding out in the woods to the north. Everything you need to know is in your visor feeds. Now go...go-go!'

The van's doors closed as the last man jumped in. It pulled away slowly, turning up towards the main Coldharbour street. One of its passengers, Sergeant Rogan Stevens, flipped his visor down and read the intel.

Insertion Point was marked on his AR map with an *X*. A light blue arrow at the top centre of the visor pointed a little north-west. As the van turned right, the arrow swung left. *OPS: NON-LETHAL* remained in the top right corner.

Officer Stevens blinked his left eye twice. Images of Gullidge and Hollins overlaid the map. He blinked his right eye twice and the images were replaced with *IR Diagnostics*. Five green bars were full, confirming he was combat-ready.

'Okay, folks. We are running NV, so switch up now.' Stevens was leading the ground operation. 'We'll maintain arrow formation. Weapons up. Slow speed. No cover.'

'No cover, Sarge?' Special Officer Cole Sefton looked over at Stevens.

'That's right. We are in forest, medium density. Rely on your suits. We don't break the line. We don't get split up. This is a team op. Stay close, stay ready. Don't fuck up.'

'Sarge.' Sefton nodded. Sat opposite him, Special Officer Tony Lombardi shook his head comically. Sefton responded with his middle finger and an air kiss.

The van slowed down, pulled around in a semi-circle and came to a halt. Stevens got up, nudged the doors open and jumped down. Lombardi followed, with Sefton behind; Special Officers Robert Cliffham, Jonas Hedges and Eric Balthazar came after.

'Release the dogs.' Stevens gestured to Cliffham, who opened a large black metal case and removed two thick discs, setting them down on the ground, and a small tablet. He closed the case and pressed his palm against the tablet. A three-note tune played as the tablet screen came to life. Simultaneously the discs shook gently on the ground, launched slowly upwards and hovered at about six feet.

'Deploying now.' Cliffham pressed the two areas on the tablet that said *Cover* and slipped it into his breast pocket. He folded the flap over. The discs climbed to about seventy feet and stopped. 'Deployed.'

'Okay team. We are go. Everyone check systems.'

Stevens led the line from the right centre, Cliffham to his left. As they entered the woods, Cliffham glanced upwards to see the drones disappear above the tree line. They were a good ten feet above the canopy.

The line proceeded slowly, Stevens setting and maintaining the pace. 'Eyes everywhere, team. *Everywhere.* Be ready.'

~~~

'Ah shit.' Ged pointed out to the south-east where just above the tree line he saw two discs with thin neon lines – he would have seen the drones anyway against the backdrop of an almost full moon. 'Time for us to move. You'd better be strong enough.'

'I still don't get how...'

'You will. It's in you. Listen. They've found us. We don't have time. We need to go. Now.'

'But you've taken me before. Why can't you take me this time?'

'Son, I'm all knacked-up here. It ain't easy work, shooting around with a passenger.' Ged looked exasperated. 'If you wanna stay here and get shot up, you go for it. If you'd rather not get shot up, quit bein' a pussy.'

'Okay, okay.' Joe closed his eyes and let his mind go back to the most recent memory flood Ged had given him. It was like driving in a snow blizzard – white light shooting at his eyes and probably what flying a spaceship at light speed felt like. It made him feel instantly dizzy. He also felt he knew *how* to do it.

Louise. Louise! The face of his absent lover appeared suddenly, obscuring his mind's determination to carry out the instinctive urge to escape. 'Louise,' he said, looking painfully over to Ged.

'We don't have time for your fuckin' woman. You gotta go. Now!'

Joe's mind filled with thoughts of his quandary. 'I'll turn myself in.'

'No you fuckin' won't, dipshit. They'll shoot you. You wanna die?'

'Why the fuck would they shoot me?' Joe felt a surge of angry indignance.

'You...you are gonna get us both killed!' Ged's face was full of sweaty fury.

'No! Bullshit. We don't just careen around the place killing people, Ged.' He raised his arms up to a shrug. 'I'm staying here.'

'You can't stay here, you little prick!' Ged advanced on Joe, aiming to put a hand round his throat. Joe ducked it to the left and retorted with a swift but solid jab to Ged's stomach. Ged recoiled and fell back slightly but got back up straight faster than Joe thought he should have. Whistle leapt up, looking primed to pounce.

Joe kept his guard, hopping gently from foot to foot. 'Why's it so important to you, Ged? Huh? What do you need me for?'

Ged's fury turned to pure aggression. 'I told you!'

'You didn't tell me shit, old man. Cracks are showing, yadda-yadda-yadda. Well I'm not sure I believe all this shit and I'm not going anywhere until I know who the fuck you are, why you are so interested in me and where Louise is.'

Ged looked back over his shoulder. The drones were closer now, maybe thirty feet away. From this vantage point, he could see across the tree line of the bulk of the forest down below; in front of him and behind Joe the forest cresting up and out into more level and dense woodland. He dropped quickly to a squat, grabbed hold of his faithful dog's collar and both disappeared.

Joe stared at the space previously occupied by his – his what? *Tormentor? Mentor? Demented old bastard who had more secrets than answers.* 'What the fuck?' he whispered to no one. He now saw what Ged had seen: drones approaching. *Special ops*, he thought. *Maybe they* will *try to kill me.* It occurred to him that he no idea what he might have done, according to Ged's account, and no idea how much the police knew about his history. A hell of a lot more than *he* knew, apparently.

A single shot rang out in the forest below. It was *close*. Then another shot. *I do need to get out of here. Now.* With one last glance at the drones, which were no more than twenty feet off his position, Joe closed his eyes tight and imagined himself entering a vein. He pictured an arm – wider than it would have been in reality but he was new to this, today.

The arm folded open and a river of blood splashed up against the skinned bank, spilling over the sides and running out and over to cover the arm. He saw his feet and legs step into the river and felt a dizzy rush as the world disappeared around him.

'Do you see him? Does anyone have eyes on the mark?' Rogan Stevens scanned the rising horizon. Cole Sefton lay behind him, slumped against a tree, clutching his chest. Blood spilled out through the gaps between his fingers. The line was one down; the rest intact but panicked.

'Sir – what the *fuck* was that?' Jonas Hedges called.

'Quiet, keep eyes all around,' his superior responded. 'Eric. Break off. Take care of Cole.'

'Sir.' Officer Balthazar edged backwards and crouched down next to Sefton. He tapped the top left of his visor and a LIFE SIGNS display appeared.

The four-strong line proceeded. A slashing-rushing sound shot behind the line, Eric Balthazar screaming in the split second it took for a blade to swipe across his chest, a thick red jet shooting from the wound and just missing the back of Jonas Hedges' legs but hitting the leaves and sticks on the ground.

The line stopped and swung, awkwardly sending each of its components reeling, breaking the pattern. Stevens stumbled down roughly onto his right knee, looking back to see two of his men down – Eric Balthazar dead and Cole Sefton still trying to plug his wound.

'Fall back! This is a One Zero! Fall back. Now team.' Stevens grabbed Sefton by the thick collar of his suit and yanked him upwards. Hedges did the same on Balthazar. 'Leave him. Move!'

'But sir!'

'But *nothing*! Fucking move out now, officer! Now!'

Stevens hooked an arm around Sefton and ran forward, jerking unnaturally and stumbling against a tree. Sefton's head smacked against his chest, hard. 'Stay with me, Cole. Stay with me.' He repeated these words right up until he and Sefton emerged from the woods, falling forwards with a lunge towards the ops van. He set Sefton against the side of the van as gently as he could given the circumstances, rounded back towards the forest line and aimed his gun back up.

'Hedges, report!' He shouted through a croak. 'Lombardi! Cliffham!' His voice felt like it didn't carry at all; as if he was just shouting into a thick fog.

He pressed a finger to his ear. 'Chief, are you seeing all this? Chief?'

Chief Bangay had seen everything that Stevens had seen, which wasn't much to speak of apart from the sight of two officers down and then a panicked dash back to the ops staging area. He had been barking into the com unit repeatedly but, amidst the chaos, he hadn't been heard.

'Goddammit!' The voice of Paul Motta came through with a sharp crack. 'Report. What is happening out there.'

'Sir! Sir, we hit an ambush. We didn't see him. Sefton's...'

Motta interrupted with urgency: 'Was it Gullidge?'

'Sir, we...we didn't see who it was. Balthazar is...'

'Bangay – off com, now.' Paul pulled out his earpiece and threw it to the ground. It bounced a little and disappeared under the desk. Bangay left his earpiece in and stood up to face Paul. 'I said off com, dammit.'

'I'm not leaving my men – we're in the middle of ops here, Paul.'

'The op is fucked!' Paul kicked out at a trash can, knocking it with a thud against the desk. 'He's got away again. He's killed more...more of my men! What part of the op is still going?'

'Calm down, Paul. I'm going. You coming?'

'Fuck!'

'Yeah, very good Paul. Very good.'

Bangay turned on his heels and rushed out through the double doors. 'Stevens, report. Do you have a visual on the suspect?'

'Sir, no sir. Lombardi and Hedges are out. We lost Balthazar, sir. We lost him. I'm going back in.'

'Stand down, officer.' Bangay's voice was calm. 'I am coming to your zone. You will stand down until I get there. Stay weapons ready.'

'Sir!'

~~~

Seconds after delivering a lethal blow to Eric Balthazar, Ged and his trusty canine companion appeared back in the clearing. Joe Gullidge was not there.

'Oh shit. Shit. No!' Ged kicked Whistle in the head. The dog smacked hard against a thick tree, yelping on impact. 'I don't fuckin' believe this!' Ged's arms raised to the sky, his hands clenched into fists. 'This is not happening!'

A second later he and his dog had left the clearing. Four seconds later Ged stood in the midst of a huge flame; like a raging storm covering everything in its path. There was no space, no clearing – just fire. Ged felt no discomfort here. It was his home.

Another figure appeared and approached Ged. Silvery, sharp stabs – the vocal equivalent of a lizard's tongue snapping at flies – sounded between and all around them.

Where is he?

The plan failed. He is not here.

Is he active?

Yes.

We have to get him back. This is unacceptable.

I know.

You will be punished for this failure.

I know.

~ ~ ~

Mayor Ernest Tifton walked back into his makeshift library. Peter Johannsen, local publisher *extraordinaire*, looked out onto the caravan park through the large window at the scenic end of the unit. The mayor's caravan was the biggest in the park, forty by forty-five feet. It was up on a raised mound and had fewer close neighbours than any other. Peter could see from this vantage point right out to the warehouse slums in the distance. It was dark but a series of floodlights powered by the same generator which ran electricity to the caravans lit the view all the way down as far as he could see. The new town's residents had petitioned for twenty-four hour lighting.

Peter heard the door close behind him and turned to face Mayor Tifton, who had stopped next to a small round table and was filling a short tumbler with whiskey.

'So?' Peter enquired.

The mayor hesitated. 'He's active and we don't have him. You want a drink?'

'Shit!' Peter's hands clenched into fists. 'How did this happen?'

'Ged, the old bastard. He fucked up. Gave him too much too soon.'

'I told y…'

'You told me nothing, son. Nothing. You will not…Just sit down

133

and calm down. Ged was handling it. He didn't handle it. We have something of an unpredictable player in a game where the rules have changed. That's all.'

Peter sat down but was still furious. 'There isn't time to be messing around with this. No damn time at all.'

'Calm down, Peter. This isn't your problem. You have your job, so do it. I will make sure everyone else does theirs and I will do mine.'

'Y...yes, okay. *Okay*. But he's active. Surely that's...'

'Surely *that's not your problem*, Peter.' The delivery was firm, slow and deliberately sinister. 'Do you want me to be frustrated?'

Peter didn't react. He stared back out the window.

'Right. Right now, Peter, you are frustrating me. We all have our roles to play and right now you are not playing yours. So go take care of whatever you have to take care of. *Now*.'

Peter looked back at Mayor Tifton, who was finishing off his double whiskey like it was water. It might as well have been – he couldn't taste it anyway. Peter looked an uneasy combination of frightened and irritated.

'*Now*, Peter. Just calm down. Gullidge has no idea what's going on. He doesn't know. Just *calm down*. We're okay, okay?'

Peter left, closing the caravan door gently behind him. Mayor Tifton strode across to the large window and surveyed his kingdom. He was rubbing his hands together. As he looked down to acknowledge this, a broad smile burst across his face.

Fifteen – Friends reunited

Joe tried to open his eyes to nothing. He was nowhere; just not there, without any feeling, any sensation, and on those terms unable to move. His mind was there – in a deep black void. No eyes to open, no head to turn and no glimmer of light to not turn it towards.

What do I do? Am I dead?...Louise...I need to see Louise...

Nothing happened.

How do I get out of here?

This thought held – it echoed, intensifying until he interrupted it.

Louise!

More than the word this time, he saw Louise – her face. It unsettled him more to see she was glassy-eyed, expressionless. A floating apparition or avatar, but not *her*. But something was happening. Up until this point he had felt no physical sensation but now some solidity was returning to his mind; around it. The image of Louise rushed at his mind's eye and he felt a huge jolt in the centre, throwing him with full physicality up and then down with extreme force and yet no impact on landing – he knew he had stopped and this took him to the conclusion that he had landed.

This time his eyes did open. A stark, brilliant bright light immediately forced his eyes closed, his head stuttering back over his shoulder as if a punch had come out of nowhere. He instinctively put a hand over his eyes to shield and cautiously opened a crack between the fingers. The sliver of light came like a crossbow bolt. It *hurt*.

Joe.

The voice was soft, dull.

Joe.

He opened the crack again and saw a figure jutting out of the light; somewhere deep within it but also right at the front, like a projection.

Is that you, Lou?

Joe's voice came out soft and dull too, as if there was no air in this place – if it could be called a place.

Joe.

Joe stopped. A metaphorical punch in the face by a bright light had been followed by a gut punch. His stomach turned in a knot. It *really hurt*.

'Joe. Get up. Stand up, Joe. I'm scared.'

'What…'

A hand grasped around his arm and pulled it up, his body following without effort as if something had pushed him from underneath too. It felt a little like the upward bounce from a trampoline.

Joe's eyes opened to see Louise's worried face. He tried to smile but it looked more like an expression of pain; although he felt none. In fact he felt nothing.

He was in a white room – so white that there was no seam; no place where the floor met the walls. He couldn't see walls exactly but he *sensed* it was a room all the same. No doors; no light on the ceiling; no furniture. Just Louise. She was wearing a white dress. No, not a dress. Just white. Louise was white.

I'm dead, Joe thought. *This is it. I'm actually dead.*

'Are we dead, Joe?' This time Louise's voice was normal – it was *in* the room.

'I don't think so. Where are we?'

'I don't know. I got here when you did. You brought me here.'

'How did I bring you here?' He paused. 'How did I bring *us* here?'

'Something happened, Joe.' Louise frowned. 'I was waiting for you to come home from the doc. There was a knock at the door.' She bent forward and fell into Joe's arms. She closed her eyes. Joe closed his too.

Just as a few hours before he had witnessed events through a remote pair of eyes, now he saw through Louise's. *Can you see this, Joe? I feel like you can see it.*

Yes.

She approached the door and called, 'Is that you, honey? Forget your key again?' There was a muffled response from the other side of the door. Louise's hand found the catch and pulled it aside, the door opening out.

'Who are you?'

'Ma'am. I'm Special Officer Paul Motta. We are looking for Officer Joe Gullidge. Is he here?'

'Oh, no. No, sorry. He's out.'

'I'm going to have to come in, miss.' The man turned and gestured to his colleagues who stepped up and into the apartment, brushing past Louise. Her gaze followed them as they went about their business of checking rooms. They were both armed and ready. She turned back to Special Officer Paul Motta, who shrugged and half-smiled.

136

'I'm sorry, ma'am. He's gone AWOL and we need to speak with him urgently.' Motta gestured for Louise to step out of the apartment. She did and he walked inside.

Louise opened her eyes. The vision broke, their eyes opening gently to reality – if this could be called any kind of reality.

'I saw Frank. He was waving at me from the woods.'

'Let me see, Lou.'

Their eyes closed again. Louise caught sight of two figures; one was Frank. She turned back to see no one watching her from within the apartment and jogged briskly over the sixty or so yards to the tree line, looking back over her shoulder once. 'Frank, where's Joe? The police...'

'Shh.' Frank raised a finger to his lips, then whispered: 'They're after all of us. It's Joe. Have you seen him?'

'No, no. I don't understand, Frank. Why are they looking for Joe?'

'The fire – they say he started the fire.'

'What?' Frank pulled her arm gently to round behind the tree. A man she didn't recognise stood behind Frank, staring back at the apartment. He didn't pay her any attention. 'Joe didn't start any fire.'

'Where is he, Lou? You gotta tell me.'

'He went to the doc, hours ago. I haven't seen him since then. Frank...this must be wrong. Why would Joe...'

'Miss?' Paul Motta called from outside the apartment. 'Miss?' This time louder.

'Louise – you gotta come with us.'

'I don't know...who's that?'

The stranger turned to face Louise. He was weathered, she thought. But he looked kind. He reached out and put his palm on her forehead.

The vision broke again, forcing their eyes open this time.

'Where did he take you?'

'Nowhere! This is it – I'm here. With you.'

'Okay. So... so what do we do now?'

'Joe, what's going on?'

'I'm not sure, Lou. This morning everything was normal. Now nothing is.' He spread his hands and looked intently at the white floor. 'I've been given a...a power. I can move around...these lines or something. That old fart Ged, the shack tramp with the dog, he showed me this. He showed me...I saw myself doing stuff I don't remember. He gave me some memories. I dunno...'

'Honey...'

'I know. This is all really, really confusing. And not good. Not good at all.'

'Can you get us out of here?' Louise looked around. Just white, stretching forever.

'I guess so.'

Joe focused on an area in the distance. It seemed to fold up and rush towards him. A door appeared behind Louise. It was an outline, a thin mark on an otherwise blank white sheet. He looked down to where a handle might be. One appeared in an instant. Louise's mouth dropped open as if her jaw had been removed. She looked back at Joe, who shrugged.

'There. How about that?'

'That'll do.'

'Where do we go then?'

'Should we just try the door?'

'Lou, I don't know. I don't know about any of this.'

~ ~ ~

'This is the most fucked up case I ever worked,' Chief Bangay said, glancing across at his passenger.

'Likewise.' Paul Motta was staring out his window, watching the rush of trees fly past, punctuated by an occasional clearing or layby. The headlights flickered over the trees in such a way that made the world go by in slow motion. They passed a sign which read *Welcome to Shenbury. A friendly neighbourhood.*

A dead neighbourhood, Paul thought.

'There's nothing more to do out at Coldharbour, son. We've looked everywhere. It's time to regroup. We'll get some focus back.'

Paul said nothing for a few seconds. 'Yeah...focus.'

'Lost a couple of good men today. My men, Paul. No one's pointing any fingers here but we're gonna have to take stock tomorrow. For now, I need some sleep. Hell, you need more sleep than anyone. You look like shit.'

'I feel like shit,' Paul said, slapping a hand to his forehead and massaging the thumb and forefinger around his temples. 'And chief, you look like shit too.'

Silas laughed. 'I've spent six months of my entire existence out here, chasing ghosts. I've seen more bodies than the average morgue sees in a year and I've bagged up more evidence and artefacts that have no significance bar a catalogue number than I care to remember. Of all the fires I've worked, this one's the fucking worst. But at least we got some leads, huh.'

'Yeah, well we have one lead...and that lead led us into a dead end. Again.'

'You gotta stop being so negative, Motta.'

'Sorry, chief. I can't think of any reason not to be.' He now had both hands massaging his temples. The front of his head burned with dull pain.

'We'll get him. Don't worry about that. We have to get him.'

~ ~ ~

'What happened? I've heard Ged's tale of failure.' Mayor Tifton was sat at his desk in a leather swivel chair, rocking from side to side but keeping his focus on a mirror hanging on the wall opposite. His physical eyes met his reflected eyes.

The voice on the other end of the phone: 'We lost him too. That bastard attacked us.'

'He was buying time.'

'He's bought a fuckin' trip to oblivion, E.'

'This whole thing's getting out of hand. We'll have to let him out.'

'Yeah, great idea. Let's have two of them running around.'

'That won't be a problem. Ours is ours. He's turned. Hell, I turned the little ant.'

'Okay, okay. Back to the farm then?'

'He's not at the farm. Besides, I don't want to be seen out there.'

'Right. Where is he then?'

'We brought him close. We'll have to do it tonight. Come here as soon as you can.' The Mayor paused. 'Make sure *no one sees you*. We cannot afford to draw attention to ourselves.'

~ ~ ~

Paul came out of the shower and got dressed. He took his PDA from the locker and noted the time. It was 11:52. Chief Bangay poked his head into the room. 'That's it for me, Motta. I'm switching off. Gotta lock up.' Their temporary – well, for six months and counting in Silas' case – accommodation was out the back of the investigation centre. He had his own room, as did Paul, but the other officers shared a dormitory.

'Lights out, huh?' Paul produced a genuine look of dissatisfaction.

Silas shrugged. 'I want to lock the place down for the night. Today has not been a good day.'

Paul shook his head and pursed his lips together. 'I need a walk. Need to clear my head.'

'Not sure that's the best idea.'

Paul gathered his jacket and picked up his holster. 'Sorry chief. Way past your bedtime, huh?'

'So my mummy says!' Silas raised his eyebrows. Under better circumstances they might have been smiling through this whimsical exchange, Paul thought.

Paul walked past Silas, headed down the long corridor past several closed doors which prevented unauthorised access to various forensics laboratories and the armoury, out into the lobby and then, as the chief bolted the door behind them, out into a small car park. The SWAT and operations vans were parked up alongside Bangay's cruiser.

Paul strapped the holster back over his shoulder and slung his jacket on. The moon was brighter than usual, he thought. Zipping his jacket up, he headed out of the car park and around to the right of the building, looking back as Silas' footsteps stopped.

'What's up, chief?'

'Ah shit. I forgot something. I'll see ya.'

Silas turned and headed back to the HQ door. Paul pressed on a few feet and punched in the entry code with a weight in his arm. He missed the final digit and hit the 7 by mistake. *Fuck it.* His second attempt granted access. As the door closed, he reached down for his PDA but didn't find it. *Oh…shit.*

He turned back and caught the door just before it snapped shut. *I'm not leaving it in the showers.* He exhaled with deliberate force and pushed the door back open. As he rounded to the left, he noticed the lights were still off in the lobby. He got nearer to the door and saw it was still bolted.

'Fuck!' Paul kicked out at the door. *Where did Bangay go?*

140

He turned to look at the ops van and walked over, certain that whatever the chief had forgotten was not in the HQ but in one of the vehicles. Silas wasn't there. *I don't believe this. I don't...*

Just calm down, calm down. He's around here somewhere.

'Silas?' he called, loud from his diaphragm. No response. There was nothing else around. Paul reasoned that he must have decided to head out to the new town. There was a twenty-four hour store there.

'Great. Guess I'll take that walk after all.'

He felt mildly foolish talking to himself with the moon casting down a spotlight; like a theatre show about someone who forgot his PDA that no one would ever want to watch.

Will he ever find his PDA? Does anyone give a fuck?

~~~

Joe grabbed the handle with his left hand – Louise was holding tightly onto his right – and pushed the white door open. Immediately they were plunged into darkness.

Joe?

As if the air had been sucked out of the room, her voice was muffled and far away. It wasn't spoken; a thought.

It's okay. I've been here before. Hold on.

I'm not letting go for anything. Please hurry!

Joe focused his mind just as he had before. This time it came easier. But he didn't want to return to *The White Nothing*.

We'll go home.

No, they have people there.

What about Frank? Seems he knows more than us.

Okay, just do whatever you're doing quickly. Please.

Frank...

The same sensation of being picked up, thrown a great distance and dropped – like a catapult with a guaranteed soft landing – was over in a flash.

As suddenly as the white had disappeared into dark, the familiar world came back to Joe and Louise. They were standing on uneven stones. Water – waves – could be heard nearby. A beach?

'Where are we, Joe? Oh, and that was *awesome*.' Louise was still clenching Joe's hand. 'Horrible...scary...nasty – but awesome.'

141

'Ease up on that grip, honey. And yes, it is *awe…some*. Weird and wonderful. A real *mind…*'

'Joe?' Frank's voice called from behind them.

They turned to see two figures illuminated by bright moonlight, standing a few feet from where water lapped gently against the stones.

'So you found each other – excellent. Joe – this is Nel.' He gestured to his companion, who stepped forward and waved.

'Hey, Joe,' he said; then looking to Louise, 'Hi again.'

'Hi.' Louise was quiet, cautious. She tugged at Joe's hand.

'Frank,' Joe said. 'You got any idea what's happening today?'

'A little, sure. But that's Nel's department. We're in a good spot, here. Difficult to be found.'

'Er…' Joe smiled. '*We* found you! So this good spot we're in. Where exactly is it?'

Nel stepped forward again. 'Safe. We're a-ways out of Shenbury. That's where the action is. Hawks Farm is about five miles back inland…' He stopped, turned his head and pointed: '…that way.'

'And who are you, Nel?'

'I'm sort of an observer, you could say. The way I like to think of it is there are good people and there are bad people, and I am neither.'

'What do you observe?' Louise asked.

'This and that. Just recently, it's been you folks. You folks are real interesting!' Nel smiled and turned back to Frank. 'Shall we find somethin' comfortable to sit on?' He twisted on his heels awkwardly, the uneven stones preventing sure-footing, and started off towards a grassy mound poking out of the stony beach, about forty yards off. Frank followed, waving to Joe and Louise to join him.

'Frank – where did you get this guy?'

'Just listen to what he has to say, Joe. It's a bit crackpot but today, well, my life went *one hundred per cent* crackpot.'

Once all four were seated, the four of them unknowingly sitting at the main points of a compass, Nel fixed his stare on Joe.

'Son, you're in a real pickle. A real shitty pickle.'

Sixteen – Travellers

Chief Bangay made it to Mayor Tifton's caravan just before quarter past midnight. The door swung open before he could raise his hand to knock.

'Good. Let's go.'

'I'm getting a bit fed up of this walking,' Silas said.

'We don't have a choice there, so quit complaining. We're nearly there with the restoration, so it won't be long now.'

'I haven't been down here before. How far is it?'

'Shit, S. Care to stop just long enough to forget how old your shell is? We'll all have new ones soon.'

'Fine. But I *am* tired. Chasing ghosts isn't a lot of fun when your body nearly is one.'

Having put some distance between themselves and the caravan park, the two men made their way down into an area of dense forest that trailed for twenty or so miles in most directions. This forest had survived the fire purely due to geographical fortune, but it was a fortune that had been calculated quite precisely by those who had been behind this grand plan.

~~~

'Shh. Did you hear that?'

Tereza fell backwards off the log, laughing although or because she had just cracked her elbow awkwardly on a jagged branch resting on the ground. 'Hear what?' She carried on laughing.

'Seriously,' Alex said. 'Shh. There's some people over there. Here.' He passed the joint to Che, who was grinning at Tereza. 'Turn the lantern off.'

'Huh?' Che turned around to match Alex's gaze and saw what looked like a torchlight heading their way, flickering over the trees. He leant over to the lantern and flicked it off. The flame died down, puffed with a pirouette and disappeared. The torchlight intensified in the new darkness.

'Shit, Alex. Did you tell anybody we're coming out here?' Tereza stopped laughing. Years of mild drug abuse had sharpened her senses to snap back to default paranoia.

Che stood up, his right knee cracking and too solid for comfort. 'No. We've been here for ages anyway. No one would come out looking.'

'Let's just get out of here,' Tereza said.

'Right, yeah.' He took a big drag on the joint and dropped it to the floor, crushing the remains under his foot. Alex bent down and picked up the lantern. Tereza grabbed her bag from the foot of a tree and slung it over her shoulder.

'Which way?' asked Alex. 'We'll have to round back deeper a bit and...'

'Wait.' Che held his hand up and pointed towards the torchlight. It had stopped moving and was now mostly facing away from them. It then flicked back in their direction – all three instinctively hunched down to avoid its glare – and then away again, going round in an arc before stopping and aiming down. Che and Alex stood up cautiously, aiming for a better view.

'They're looking for something, all right,' Alex whispered. 'Just not us.' He edged forward and stood to lean against a tree. He leaned over far enough to see a little better. The torch was resting on the ground, pointing just slightly up to cast light on two trees. He pulled back sharply. 'They've gone.'

'Huh?' said Tereza. 'Gone where?'

'Shh, quiet,' Che said. 'Listen.'

'To what?' Tereza's whisper was barely audible.

'Nothing. There's nothing.'

The three friends, their senses artificially heightened from smoking a heady concoction of THC paper wrapped around meth-soaked marijuana, stood as still as possible, straining to hear something – *anything*.

'This is too weird, man. Let's just run – just run straight back there, go around and back out the other side of the railway.' Tereza's voice was shaky.

'I'm going to have a look,' Che said. 'Whoever was holding it has gone. It's dark enough to hide.'

'Fuck that,' said Alex. 'Seriously man, my heart isn't gonna take any tension tonight. Let's just scoot back to slumsville.'

'No,' said Che. 'I'm in the mood. You guys wait here then.'

'Che!' Tereza managed to whisper-shout. 'Che...Che.'

He rounded the tree and stepped slowly and deliberately towards the torchlight, turning round to give a cheeky thumbs-up to his *douchebag* friends. As he drew nearer he saw the torchlight flicker gently and his heart jumped in his chest. He stopped in his tracks to hear Tereza gasp.

Pressing on, Che reached a small clearing, a circle that could have been made by a giant cookie cutter from the sky. It looked too perfectly circular to be an accident of nature. The moonlight managed to cut through this hole in the tree canopy too, almost creating a spotlight. He heard the crunch of forest underfoot and one hand closed around his mouth, another across his arms and both dragged him backwards. A figure much stronger threw Che down against a tree, pressing a hand against his mouth and using the other to press a finger to its own lips.

'Shh – don't say a word. Quiet.'

Che nodded as fast as he could. The figure took his hand away slowly.

'If you make a noise, you will give away our position. Do not make a noise. Understand?'

Che nodded again, his eyes wide open and scared.

'Good. I am not afraid to use this. My name is Paul Motta. I am a police officer.'

Paul unholstered his weapon. He walked forward far enough that he knew he could be seen and raised a hand as he looked over at Che's friends – although he couldn't see them. Tereza and Alex both saw this and looked at each other, bearing the faces of frightened children.

The torchlight shone a wide arc on a wall of nothing. Two trees in the circle had some kind of invisible wall that reflected the light – or rather stopped it dead. Paul felt his pulse quickening. *What is this?* A weird day was getting exponentially weirder by the hour.

The light flickered again, stopping Paul dead. He pointed his gun straight at the arc then walked in and reached a 'wall'. Gun in his right hand, he reached his left out to touch the wall. His hand did not stop. A horrible feeling came over him. A feeling of being drained of all warmth. He became aware of every sensation in his body. Pain in both feet, aches in his arms and his headache much worse than an hour ago.

He edged closer and now had most of his left arm stuck through the wall. The torchlight was mostly obscured by his body but now a sliver shot up his arm as if he was directing the light into a black hole.

In for a penny, in for a pound. He remembered this curious English phrase and repeated it over and over, edging further in. He didn't realise that he had crossed over entirely until he found himself in total darkness. He turned around to look both ways but saw nothing; a muffled noise seemed to come from straight ahead. He reached out and touched nothing; no walls, no indication of which way to stumble. The floor, however, had become smooth; perhaps even like marble. Turning fully around, he could not see where he had come from.

Re-orientating to find the noise again, he crept onward and as he did, a warm light graduated into the darkness. Similar to coming out of a tunnel, but with no tunnel. It was more like colour being blown back into the darkness. All he could hear was his heavy breathing and a sound – something musical?

Black and white gave way to full colour as he came to something like a curtain; the piano sound was louder now. Right in front of him was a fine mesh. He looked up but didn't see where it began, and looking down it gave no indication of stopping. He put his hand through the mesh – it didn't move; his hand slipped through with no resistance. The same feeling of life being sucked out. *Horrible.*

The rest of his body followed and as his eyes crossed the mesh, he found himself in a large red and white room, pointing a gun at nothing in particular. His headache vanished in an instant. Aches and pains disappeared. The sensation reminded him of a morphine injection – the rush of heavy fog clamping around the brain.

He turned around to see the darkness but it was gone. The room had opened up, as if the perspective had changed. In the far corner sat a piano. At the piano were three figures. One was sat down, playing the instrument. The sound was slow, an unrecognisable melody in which every note seemed to resonate through Paul's mind; like bells ringing in a tower.

One of the other figures turned to face him. It had the face of a pig. There was no expression on the face but Paul felt warmth drain back into him. It was a comfort. The other figure turned and both started walking towards him. The figure at the piano carried on playing but turned its head to see Paul.

The two figures' footsteps were silent. Paul stood rooted to the spot. He didn't feel any need to move. The figures reached him at the same time, the one on the left putting his arm around Paul's shoulders and leading him back towards the piano. The second figure stood facing the same direction it had walked. Its head cocked slightly left and right, as if it had spotted something. It then turned and walked back towards the others.

As all three pigs made it back to the piano, Alex Fratelli stood with his nose one inch from a mesh wall and gasped, his heart thumping against his chest; his eyes stinging; his legs barely holding him up.

He turned his head to look back, hoping to see a way out. There was nothing; not even a faint glow. Just black. Darkness. The piano stopped, urging Alex's gaze back to the room. The figures were all gone. His heart was thumping harder now, faster too. His mouth was dry and his eyes strained now to see anything.

Alex edged forward through the mesh. As soon as he reached the other side a rush similar to opiates came over him. It wasn't gradual – an instant change of state. His heart rate slowed immediately, but he didn't notice.

The room was now empty of figures and sounds, yet there seemed to be a strange low hum – like an engine resting in neutral; there was nothing in view that would explain it anyway. To the left, beyond the piano, stood a single white door. To the right, much further away, a set of double doors, also white. Alex turned to find himself trapped in this room. His entryway was now a solid wall.

He started towards the piano in slow strides, as if underwater. It reminded him of how astronauts walked across the surface of the Moon. His whole body was pleasantly warm. He reached out to touch the piano – to see if it was real, he supposed – and saw that his hand was gloved. Looking down at his other hand, it too was covered in white satin. It was a struggle to care about this detail. He sat down at the piano and began to play, looking up briefly to catch his reflection in the shiny face of the case. The face of a pig, expressionless, looked back at him. Inside he grinned and his eyes closed softly, his fingers softly dancing over the keys and playing a tune that made him feel like the happiest guy alive.

~~~

Joe and Louise had been listening incredulously to their new companion. He had rescued Frank just as a masked group of men bearing arms had broken his apartment's door down. Nel had appeared from nowhere, put his hand around Frank's wrist and pulled him from danger into safety – in a horribly unsettling manoeuvre that had now become familiar to Joe and Louise.

Tom was a problem, Nel said. He couldn't find him – anywhere. He had gone on to explain that he had first seen Joe a while back, the night of the fire. Nel liked to see the world and he also liked to follow people around. If he saw something that interested him, he would follow it or him or her, whatever or whomever it might be. He was a traveller.

Joe asked if what Ged had told him was true. He asked if Ged was friend or foe. Nel said Ged was nobody's friend, although some of what he had told Joe was true. Joe did start the fire. He had taken several packages of high explosive to a warehouse in the department store and helped a group of men prime them. Those men had then fanned out across the town, each one carrying explosives strapped to their torsos. It had been a delicately plotted plan – a mass suicide of sorts, although those men who had taken part were not like real men.

Nel had watched Joe – and he later followed him and his two friends at Hawks Farm. He knew what the farm was. Nel could come and go as he pleased, of course. Nel was 'gifted'. Joe asked how it was that Nel was able to wander the corridors of evil. Nel replied that the corridors were not evil, but some others who walked in them were.

Joe asked about the fire – why did he participate in what was essentially a meaningless terrorist act in his home town? It wasn't meaningless at all, Nel said. Everything had a meaning. He just wasn't privy to the reasons for everything – how could he be? However, after the events that night at Hawks Farm, Nel had witnessed other pieces of the jigsaw coming together, and he had decided he should follow Joe for a little longer. He had realised that Joe was not himself.

'Why should we trust you?' asked Louise. She had been quiet all through this enlightening exchange, as had Frank. In fact, Frank's body language said he would rather have been anywhere else. 'Why didn't you do something? You could have stopped the fire.'

'Quite the contrary, dear,' Nel said, without the condescending tone those words might have come with. 'I don't stop things and I don't start things.'

'Then what are you doing here, with us?' she interrupted.

148

'Calm down,' Frank said, surprising everyone. 'We trust him because this is some crazy shit and he saved our lives.' He looked at Joe. 'I don't know how or why you can do those things – that travelling. I can't do it. If you and Nel have the same...gifts, then you guys are peas in a pod, right?'

Joe nodded slowly. 'Okay. So...Nel, I trust you, okay? I trusted Ged and look where that got me. Speaking of which, who is Ged – really?'

'Think of it like an airline,' Nel smiled. 'We're all headed to the same place but how we get there is a little different. Louise – no offence intended. You're in economy. That's just fine back there. You sit in your seat, you can walk about a bit when they let you, you can take a shit or watch something on TV, you can sleep, they feed you something, and it's not the most comfortable ride but hey, if you land safely at the end, you did okay.'

Louise managed a sarcastic smile.

'Frank here...Frank is in business class. Bigger and more comfortable seats, which you can recline and you get a bigger plate to eat your food off, and some nicer shit to drink, and the TV is bigger, and the ladies who serve you smile that little bit wider and show you a little more cleavage. You're nearer the front but you're still not quite at the top.'

Joe interrupted: 'So you're the pilot?'

Nel laughed sincerely. 'No, no my friend. I can see why you want to say that, but...no. You, Joe. You're the pilot.' He pointed at Joe with a bent finger. 'You're the one leading the way here. I'm just a guy back on the ground, watching your plane flying overhead, wondering where you're going. Up there in the cockpit is you. We're all just along for the ride.'

'I don't really get this Nel. Why am I so fucking important?' Joe's hands were up against his cheeks, his fingers massaging his temples.

'Ged, your friend. He's the guy sitting in the control tower, manipulating where you take off and land, how fast and how slow. But that's just the thing, Joe. You're still in control of the plane. And your friends here are passengers on that plane. You want to know why you're so important? I've been watching people come and go since before Jesus Christ walked on the water. I watched him, I watched the first Superbowl, I watched all sorts of stuff. I watched you put a bullet in some kid in England.'

'Hey...what?' Frank looked at Nel and then Joe. 'Joe?'

149

'I haven't been to England.' Joe stopped rubbing his temples for long enough to look Nel in the eye and shrug his shoulders, as if to say, *What now?*

'No, that's right, *you* haven't. But I saw *you* there.'

'Okay, okay. I get it.' Joe didn't really get it. 'So some of what Ged told me was true. At some point in my life I flicked a switch and became someone else. It's all bullshit to me but I don't know that anything is pretty believable right now.'

'Sure, Joe. To you guys this stuff is beyond the beyond, but to me it's routine. Yes, at some point something happened to you. That's in your memory somewhere.'

'It isn't.' Joe shook his head more than was necessary. 'It isn't.'

'Well then, that brings us a little closer to finding out what's what.'

'Ged said I wasn't who I thought I was.'

'Okay. He's right about that. Hawks is not your run of the mill farm, guys. It's a gateway. It's the only gateway, actually. The way Ged explained it to you, it's like a spider with legs shooting out around the globe, huh?'

Nel looked at Louise. 'It's not a spider. That's a bad analogy. Ged isn't the brightest of sparks. Shit, he isn't even a spark. It's more like a heart, with veins coming out – that's far simpler and much more accurate!' He let out a chuckle and Louise flashed him a disapproving look. What was there to laugh about?

'This heart needs all that blood to function. But this blood ain't red, it's black. And we, you and me Joe, we can be in that blood and we can go up and down and around whenever we damn please. It's pretty cool if you ask me.'

'So this heart...do the veins go *anywhere*?' Louise was doing the asking now. Joe was still head-in-hands, staring about a mile beyond the ground.

'Oh these veins go everywhere, darlin'. All over. Just about to every single house or church on this lovely planet! Ask Joe to take you for a ride.' Nel smiled broadly again.

'But he can't just take you along all the time, see. Everything needs juice. If there's no fuel in the plane, it doesn't fly.'

Joe snapped back into the conversation. 'So that's why Ged was shooting around with me for a while but then needed me to do the flying?'

'Yep, that's right.' Nel nodded briskly. 'He was your co-pilot for that one.'

'How?' Frank popped in. 'How do you get the juice?'

'It's there just like with everybody else. Ged's old. He's really old. He can't just go popping about all over the place whenever he likes. But *you*, Joe, I bet *you* can.' He pointed with his bent finger again. 'Young man like you, keeps good care of himself...'

'Right!' Joe stood up, quickly. 'Right then. I think I get this now, or as much as I need to anyway. Nel – have you been to the heart? Have I been to the heart?'

'Sure, sure. I didn't see you in there but I saw you *go* in there. That's what you were doing at the farm. You guys and your friend.'

'Tom,' Frank said.

'Sure, Tom. And if I can't find him, he's already there.'

'In the heart?' Louise asked.

'Yep. You see, everything's for a reason. All of this. Us being here now. It's all part of the plan.'

'What plan? Whose plan?' Louise looked desperate for an answer.

'Call it whatever you want. God, the creator, the games master, the whatever.'

'I don't believe in *God*,' Joe said.

'Joe,' Nel laughed, 'you don't believe or disbelieve in anything. What makes you think you don't believe in God? You don't have any memory of your life really. You're not whole. You're an echo. You're a remnant of yourself from another time. You only remember whatever you remembered at the time you became your echo.'

Louise looked worriedly up at Joe. She stood too and grabbed his hand in both of hers. 'I don't get any of this. Why are *you* here?' Her expression pleaded with Nel.

'I told you. I watch things. But this time I thought I might get involved a little, as I don't like the idea of what's coming.'

'And that is...?' Joe asked.

'I don't know. Big fires like that are usually followed by worse, much worse. They have a clean-out every now and then. The veins have too much noise in them.'

'We're...we're just noise to you?'

'No, Louise, that's the wrong way to put it. I mean...Hawks is right at the centre, and your little town of Shenbury is where all those folks live. All those folks in air traffic control, the middle management and the head of the airline. That's their offices!' Nel was clearly enjoying himself and this mundane analogy. 'That fire – the one they got you to start for them – that fire is part of their plan. You scorch the earth, you spill blood all over it, and you spread pure evil over the top. That becomes their ground. They earned it. They killed for it.'

'Why? Who are these people?' Joe said, noticing that Frank had been staring into space for too long.

'They aren't people, Joe. I never have found a good way to describe them. Not demons, no. Not ghosts...'

'But you're one of them,' Louise said, almost snarling.

'Hold on, sweetheart.' Nel fixed her in his gaze, which was an unexpectedly soft and kind gaze, she thought. 'We're vehicles. Yeah, that's it. And yeah, I am one of them but I'm also not.' Another smile burst across his face. 'Throughout all of time, there have been us and there have been you. The bad ones...well, they went bad. One day, that heart stopped pumping red blood. It just turned black. That's an allegory, by the way. But it's also how it is. I can get into the black blood but I don't have to drink it.'

'So they just let you...observe?' Louise asked.

'Sure. We can't hurt each other. There's no point trying. That's why some of us just watch. Ob*serve*.' He over-phrased the second syllable.

'You can't hurt each other? What does that mean?'

'Exactly what I said. Take my word for it.'

'But Ged, he knocked me out. Twice.'

'Sure, he can do that. But you're not you, Joe. You're the echo. You're a used puppet, but I'm guessing they don't want you running around and they've got a pretty big reason to get you back to that farm.'

'So why don't they just activate me as a puppet again and make me walk straight back in there?'

'That, son, I don't know. That's the mystery. And that's why I'm here.'

'Great,' Frank said, he too now standing and reclaiming his place in the group. Nel stood too. 'That's just great. This is all just *great*. So what happens next?'

Frank seemed the most eager to know.

'Well now, I guess we go to that farm. I'll be honest with you. I'm just curious to see what all this is.' Nel winked at Louise, who didn't appreciate it one bit.

~~~

Alex didn't know how much time had passed. Maybe none. Could have been thirty seconds or a thousand years. His fingers, wrapped in the finest white satin, dancing over the exquisite ivory keys, playing music no one had ever heard before. It was beautiful. On either side of him stood a figure, dressed impeccably in dinner suits, tails still in the dead air. Each wore the mask of a pig.

Alex didn't look up at them but he could see their reflections – he was in rapture. His whole body surged with warmth, an almost aggressive happiness and contentment which seemed to be fuelled by the sound of the piano; the sounds he was producing from it.

A figure appeared behind the three at the piano. The two who flanked Alex turned and welcomed the new companion. Alex turned too. He saw a pair of eyes, bright lights in the darkness, staring back at him. He turned back to the piano. The three figures walked back past Alex and towards the single white door. One opened it and the three moved through. The door remained open and Alex's world went dark.

~~~

Paul Motta opened his eyes. He was sitting in a large red armchair – his legs folded at the shins, his arms at rest on the banks of the chair. His eyes adjusted to see a bright white room, with lights all around just below the ceiling, each about a metre apart. In the opposite corner – he noticed he was in a corner and could not see any exit in the room – was his reflection. In the other corners were two more armchairs, just the same. Each was pointed at the centre of the room. But it didn't look quite right. Something was off. It was *all* off.

Paul's body felt numb; he had gone through two odd transformations in a short time. His head had been full of warm satisfaction and now it felt cold, strangely empty. He didn't feel like he could move, but tried to lift his left arm. Nothing happened. He fixed his gaze on his reflection. It wasn't moving either. There was no expression on his face.

Paul tried to speak. His lips didn't open but he did manage a muffled croak. He realised that he couldn't move his tongue. There was no response anywhere in his body. But he could think – he was thinking right now.

'Hello.'

~~~

Frank hated the transition. It made his whole body *zing* like it was on fire. He imagined it was the same feeling as a cattle prod going up the backside; or more severely, being struck by lightning. In any case, he knew it wasn't over. He'd done it twice and now he would have to do it at least once more; possibly a hundred times.

'You don't have to come with me, Frank. I'm taking Louise somewhere safe.' Louise held Joe's left hand in both of hers. 'Nel. You and me. We're going to go and have a look, right? If they want me back there, I'll give them what they want, but on my terms.'

'Where's safe?' Frank asked, looking at Nel. 'These veins go everywhere, right? So how can we be safe?'

'Well, you'd be safe in the water, Frank. The veins don't work underwater. They don't even bother stretching out into it. The water kills it, see.'

'That doesn't make sense.' Louise frowned. 'How did Joe get to England? There's a lot of water between here and England.'

'Ah, now that's a good question. I'm glad you asked.' Nel paused and curled his top lip up a little, almost into a pout. 'Think of it as a blood clot. These veins, sometimes they hit dead ends, pools if you like. A pond, a lake; whatever. You can't see it – it's not water, but it's a little like a pool of water. So I can jump right from here to one of those pools, wherever. It's kinda hard to explain how I do that exactly. Not sure I really get it myself.' Nel chuckled again. Louise was really beginning to dislike Nel.

'But we're safe now, right?' Joe asked.

'You're with me. Each of us, we radiate a certain heat. Yeah, let's call it heat. Sorry, I'm not exactly used to explaining myself. This is kinda new to me.' Another broad smile, and in the moonlight Louise noticed Nel didn't have many teeth left. This made her dislike him even more. 'So this heat, I don't know exactly how wide it goes out, but that's how we find each other. Just no one ever tries to find me. I'm nothing.'

No, you're something, Louise thought.

'So what I'm saying is you're safe if you're with me. You're in my little bubble. My safety net. That is to say they can't find you, but if they came looking for me, here we all are!'

'Let's hope they don't then.' Joe poked his tongue out slightly, his teeth biting into it. 'So we're only safe if we go with you?'

'That's about the long and short of it.'

'Joe.' Louise stretched up to speak into his ear. 'I don't trust this guy. How do we know any of this is true?'

Joe looked thoughtfully out at the water. 'Lou, this is crazy. I know it is. But the whole day has been crazy. Trust me, yeah? If you trust me, you know I'm not making any of this up. I don't even believe it myself. But we... jumped. We did that, together. I found you and we're right here. Don't know how, but we are.'

'So we all go together,' Frank said. His expression was flat.

'No,' Joe said. The thought that had been trying to force itself to the front of his mind had finally made it. 'If you're safe with Nel, you stay with Nel. I'll go. This is all about me anyway, so it seems.'

'That's not the deal, sorry.' Nel smiled at Joe. 'I'm a watcher. I watch things. Damned if I'm going to stand here and watch these two while all the action's going on elsewhere.'

Louise squeezed Joe's hand. *We're in this together*, she thought. *Whether we like it or not.* Somewhere not quite at the back of her mind was a lingering doubt about her lover. Was he even a real man? An echo? What did any of this really mean? There was only one way to find out.

'Let's just do this, Joe. I'm ready.'

'Ready, Frank?' Joe asked. Nel closed his hand over Frank's shoulder. 'Okay. So how do we all end up at the same place? What's the navigation?'

'Close your eyes, Joe. Now visualise me; just me. Nothing else. It's real easy. This is how we do it.'

Joe closed his eyes. Louise closed hers too. Joe didn't see Nel's face; it was more like a glow – an orb of something that seemed to be Nel. The glow seemed to be moving further away in his mind's eye. As it grew smaller, Joe dived back into the vein, the skin splitting at the sides, a thick liquid parting but not splashing – and he and Louise were sucked in at once, folded into a whole; two entities bound together.

For a brief moment Joe lost sight of the image as bright white began to envelop them both. It disappeared immediately as he got the glow back and as it became larger, clearer, they stood facing him and Frank. The four of them stood at the entrance to the farm – a three-metre gap between two stone walls – and surveyed the area: a house over to the left; a barn to the right. It was dark but the moon was full enough to cast enough light on their immediate surroundings.

Frank turned to face Joe. 'Let's do this.'

~~~

'I said hello, Paul. Aren't you going to answer me?'

Paul's reflection grinned at him. A smug, satisfied grin.

Paul hesitated, his pulse beginning to race. His mouth didn't work. He tried again. This time something came out, the words bumpy and broken as his throat choked a little on the atmosphere. 'Am I dead?'

His opposite figure rose quickly from its red armchair and laughed with force. The sound died – there was no acoustic carry in this room. No door; no way out. His reflection moved closer.

'What's the matter, Paul? Can't get up? Cat got your tongue?' It laughed again.

'What...who are you? Where is this place?' The words came hard again; broken and throaty.

'That doesn't matter, Paul. Hey!' The reflection clicked its fingers – the lights went out and only a spotlight remained on its grinning face. 'You're in my house. Show some fucking manners.'

Paul was, in every way, helpless.

'You're me, Paul. I'm not you. You're me. See?'

It clicked its fingers again. Paul's own face, a twist of horrified bewilderment, appeared next to that of his reflection, given its own spotlight. The reflection face turned to that one and stopped, its left eye trained on Paul's seated embodiment. The figure turned slightly back, slowly, a smile widening across its face. Then it snapped back to the disembodied Paul, its jaws spreading open to reveal a giant mass of black – shiny; glossy even – a pulsating, giant globule of something. It rose out from the figure's mouth, like the crest of a wave and enveloped the head, snuffing out the spotlight.

Paul felt a searing pain in his brain – a sharp, stabby attack. He let

156

out an involuntary cough – sending a thick plume of smoke straight out. The smoke, looking a little like a black towel rolled up, hit an invisible wall and disappeared with a loud clap.

Reflection Paul clicked his fingers again and the lights came back on instantly. He walked nearer. This wasn't a reflection at all, Paul thought. *It's virtually on top of me.*

'Can I have me back now please? Go on. I'm asking politely. Actually, that's not fair. Why should I have to be polite?'

Standing, horrible Paul leaned in closer to sitting, immobile, scared Paul, their faces just two inches apart. Horrible Paul was still smiling but it flattened in a snatch. His eyes were a window to a pure rage; a dark fire; there was tangible power coming from the eyes. Sitting Paul could feel the force pushing against his mind, squashing it backwards into his skull.

Horrible Paul pulled away slowly and walked backwards, stopping just in front of his own armchair. Sitting Paul's mind released again as if it had been holding its breath.

'You know this isn't your fault. I don't hold it against you. You weren't to know.'

'Know what?' Paul's voice gained a little strength.

'Ah...some mistakes were made. I don't blame you. They weren't your mistakes exactly. England. What were we doing in England?'

'Not a lot. There was a murder. Some murders.' Paul struggled to find the words around the memory. The memory was a struggle too.

'That's right! That's right. And we were there. And what did we do there? What did we do?'

'We...I...I had a look around. I went up to the house. I chased a suspect.'

'A suspect!' Horrible Paul fell back into the armchair, laughing a cold, humourless laugh. 'Right. And this suspect – do we still suspect the suspect?' He laughed again, this time louder, *harder.*

'I'm still looking. For the suspect.' His voice was clear now. Clear but by no means confident.

Horrible Paul leaned forward, almost as if he was about to pounce. 'Right. We're still looking. Still...looking. And do we have any idea where to look?' His expression was flat again, cold; his brow crunched down.

'We lost...I mean I...lost him. We lost him.'

'Make your fucking mind up! Come on, was it you or us? Who lost the suspect?' He fell back again, head facing the ceiling and laughing in a nasty rasp.

'I don't know. I don't know who *you* are. I know who I am. Who the fuck are you?'

As the final phonetic tone died off from his last word, in a flash a hand closed around his neck. The force was unlike anything he had ever felt. Horrible Paul's nose squeezed into sitting Paul's, nudging further into his head. He backed up again but the grip remained.

'This is my house. You show some respect when you're in my house.'

Paul couldn't have said anything even if he wanted to.

'Who the fuck am I? I'm you in here and you're me out there. You're my corporeal representative! It's awfully jolly fucking-fuckety nice of you to walk back in here, all *I don't give a shit I'm just wandering about I can do whatever the fuck I like*. You didn't know what you were doing – it's almost hilarious!'

He loosened his grip and again sitting Paul let out a cough, this time wet. A thick plume shot forward and disappeared again as if it had hit a pane of glass.

'You see, ordinarily we don't have problems like this. We worked just fine, you and me. Us. We've been a good team. Making waves in Chicago. But then I lost you. Where did you go, Paul? What you been up to?'

'I...I don't understand.'

'Sure you don't. You're just a walking mound of fucking ignorance. I don't think you appreciate the seriousness of our little situation here.'

'What situation?'

'You found a back door. Some prick left the door open and you walked right into it. That's what we call a fucking cock-up! You're not allowed in the back door. It's a one-way street. Now I can't do anything to you. We're stuck like this.'

'I still don't understand.'

'You fucking twerp.' Horrible Paul adopted the voice of a whiny child: 'I don't *understand*. Please don't *hurt* me. It wasn't my *fault*.' He clicked his fingers and the room went black again.

~~~

'Let's stick together,' Joe said. He felt for his gun but it wasn't there.

'Hold on.'

'Where did he go?'

Only Nel didn't look worried.

Most of a minute passed. Joe appeared back next to Louise. 'We're not going back to our apartment any time soon. It's trashed.' He smiled at her.

Frank had now witnessed this odd phenomenon several times: a figure appearing; disappearing. There was no audio cue to signal it. No shower of sparks; no dust cloud. It was as simple as something just appearing or disappearing. He had never seen anything like it and imagined there really was nothing else like it anyway.

'I agree,' Frank said. 'Let's stick together.'

Joe handed him a pistol. He had another one in his hand. Frank almost smiled as he clasped it.

'I was about to say,' started Nel, 'that you won't need no guns in here. Guns kill humans. These guys...we ain't humans.'

'So *how* do we kill them?' asked Louise.

'Who says we're gonna kill anybody?' Nel retorted. 'You think this is about walking into hell with a gun in your hand, spraying lead into demons? No chance.' He chuckled. Louise really hated Nel now.

'I don't...'

'No, you don't. None of you do. Hell, I don't either.' Nel shrugged. 'This is the lions' den. I might be the only one who walks out of here.'

'No, we're all coming out,' Joe said. 'So what else can I do?'

'I guess Ged gave you – *re-awakened?* – the ability to get around. Maybe that's all you got.' He shrugged again. 'You know, the odds aren't amazing here. But the way I see it, you don't have a lot of choice. This is all kinda happening right now.'

'Let's just get on with it then,' Joe pointed at the house. 'There. We'll start in there. That okay with you, Nel?'

Nel shrugged a third time. 'You're the pilot, son. I'm just along for the ride. But one thing – don't get separated. You've all got to stay together once you cross over.'

Frank was out in front with Joe, then Louise close behind and Nel at the back. Reaching the house, Frank rapped on the door with the butt of his pistol. *Why am I knocking?* Three seconds later there were two bullet holes in the lock and the door swung open with a kick.

'Anybody home?'

'There's no one here,' Nel said. 'It's deserted. I'd know.'

'So why did we come here?' Joe asked.

'They're not here. They're over. We need to go over. I'll save you some trouble. It's in the barn.'

Louise was really losing patience with this odd, irritating man. 'Why didn't you say so before?'

'I'm just watching.' He winked at her for the second time.

Joe mediated. 'Leave it out, both of you. Let's just get in there.'

Again, Frank was first to the task. He pushed up the latch, swung the door open and waved the others inside. The barn was dark. Frank switched his pistol's torch on. Joe did the same.

'Trapdoor in the corner,' Nel said.

'And you know this *how*, exactly?' Frank asked. He was becoming a little suspicious too.

'Because I've been here, stupid. The only way in is through that trapdoor.'

Louise found the light switch and bathed the barn in a soft, orange glow. Joe and Frank turned their torches off. It was cold in the barn. Really cold, Louise thought.

'And where does it lead?' Frank asked. Joe stood with him, a foot from the trapdoor, looking down at it. 'Are you telling me this trapdoor, in this barn, leads down into some hellish place where guys like you, but evil guys like you, roam around plotting giant fires? This is bullshit.'

'Sure sounds like bullshit, friend, but it ain't. I can assure you that down there, that's where the action is. Joe should go first.'

'Right,' Joe said. He squatted down, found the half rusted handle and yanked the door upwards. It came up heavily but easily enough and he set it down gently on the barn floor. He peered in and edged over backwards and dropped into the hole. There was a small opening that appeared to lead into a tunnel. He brushed aside some earth and what looked like roots and squeezed through.

Frank was next down. Louise shifted a glance at Nel – she wasn't comfortable being left alone with him. He didn't notice.

'Come on down, Lou,' Frank called.

She did as she was told. Nel watched her move into the tunnel. He knelt down slowly and closed the trapdoor. He heard some muffled shouting. *Humans complaining*. He had done his part. He shifted over so that he was kneeling on the trapdoor. Eyes closed, he placed his hands on the wood and started rubbing them backwards and forwards. The first splinter went into the skin easily. He pressed down harder as the first few trickles of blood spread underneath; his gruesome finger-painting had covered most of the surface after a minute. He stopped and looked at his palms. Most of the skin was loose; a bloody mess. The shouting stopped.

Seventeen – The House of Pigs

'We're fucked,' Frank said. 'Up, down and all around. Left, right and centre. F. U. C. K. D.'

'What about the E?'

'Joe, we are so fucked that there isn't an E. The E is fucked too. The E has gone and it's not coming back.'

'We need to keep moving,' Joe said.

'I knew he was trouble.' Louise glanced back. The opening they had come through was gone. There was just a wall of earth all around them, apart from a narrowing tunnel that had no light at the end. The three of them were huddled up, a triangle of despair. Frank and Joe's torches were their only lifeline.

'Everyone is trouble,' Frank said. 'Everyone.'

'This is all my fault,' Joe said.

'Yes, it is.' Frank shrugged. 'No two ways about that.'

'It's not your fault, honey. You're just who you are.'

'Or maybe not,' he said, quietly. 'Well, we're in here now. Whatever will be will be. Come on – single file.'

Joe edged past Frank and pushed forwards, Frank and Louise following closely. 'Shit,' he said. 'A dead end.'

Frank shone his torch up. 'No, there's another door there. Look.'

'Give me a boost, Frank.'

Frank cupped his hands. Joe stepped up and pushed the door open. It swung easily and thudded on the ground the other side. Frank pushed and Joe climbed out.

'You go up next, Lou.'

She did. Joe helped her up. Her knees scraped against the edge of the hole as she tried to look around. It was too dark to see anything. Joe's torch shone back into the hole.

'Joe,' called Frank. 'I don't know that I can get up there. It's too wide down here to get a foothold. How far can you reach down?'

Joe leaned in, setting his gun down at his side. Louise bent to pick it up. He stretched his arm down a little too far than he should and felt a burn in his shoulder. His fingertips were still over a foot from Frank's.

'I can't, man. Try a running jump, flick off the wall.'

Frank backed up a little. He didn't feel confident at all about it.

Louise was searching the immediate area. 'Lou,' Joe said, 'can you see if there's anything – a rope maybe?'

She shone the torch straight ahead, her finger wrapped tightly enough around the gun to let off a shot if she needed to. Even as a glorified receptionist she had gone through weapons training. She had never had cause to shoot anyone though.

'Joe?'

'Yes Lou?'

'I think we're back in the barn. This looks like the same place. There's a light switch somewhere.' She set off towards the barn doors.

'Huh?' Joe looked up to see the torch light flickering off behind him. 'Come on Frank. Hurry up.'

He looked back into the hole. Frank's light was off.

'Frank?'

No answer.

'Frank, quit messing around. Get up here.'

No answer.

Joe shuffled back a little. 'Lou? Can you bring the light back here?'

He rolled over onto his left side and looked towards her. But her light was off too. 'Lou – this isn't funny. Put the light back on.'

No answer. Joe's eyes widened. He couldn't see anything at all. He reached his left hand back to the hole and put his hand in. His fingers touched something wet. He snapped his hand back and rolled up to sit and then stood – almost stumbling backwards.

'Hello again, Joe!'

The barn – he could now confirm Louise's suspicion – was immediately light. A handsome man, dressed in a dinner suit, complete with red bow tie, stood eleven feet from him. Behind the man was a ladder leading up to a small balcony level.

'I suppose you don't remember me, friend. Oh boy, we had some good times.' He smiled broadly.

Joe felt for his gun. *Damn it.*

'Don't you worry about that now.' The suited man turned around and mounted the ladder. 'No time for shooting practice. We've much to do!' He climbed two rungs. 'Oh, how rude of me. Sorry. I'm Edward.' He began to climb further.

Joe turned to see the trapdoor gone. There was a red mess in its place; straw and something congealed.

'Helluva time getting you back here, Joey!' Edward was at the top now. 'Come on up, anyway. Something to show ya.'

Joe stayed in his spot. He had nothing.

'Don't be shy, feller! Come on up. I won't bite. Promise!'

Joe stepped forward, glanced behind him and carried on. His hands were clenched into tight fists. He reached the ladder and started up it.

'That's my boy, come on up.' Edward was kneeling; doing something. 'We've all missed you. Really, really.' He let out a childlike giggle.

Joe reached the top. Edward had his back to him.

'Et voila!' Edward leapt off to the side and Joe fell back, putting both hands out to stop himself. His left missed the floor and caught the ladder, gouging a small cut in his palm. 'What do you think of my *art*?'

Joe turned his face away and looked at Edward.

'You don't like it? Aw, that's sad. I did this just for you, Joey. Look at it. *Look…at…it.*'

Protruding from the corner of the barn was a large body, hanging off four long, sharp hooks – two on each side, through its chest. There was a bloody gouge from the neck down to between the legs – and down there, just entrails.

'He messed up, see. It was his fault. All his fault.'

Joe felt a surge of something in his throat. He stayed crouched back, his hand clutching the top of the ladder. He now noticed the smell – like a bullet of rotting flesh aimed straight at his face. It washed over his head as his body lurched forward, spewing a mess of vomit onto the dusty floor.

A tiny spray came off the floor and attached to the toes of the body's right foot. Joe looked straight back at Edward with a helpless expression.

'Oh, you don't even know who this is, do you? So sorry. Well, this is Hat. He messed up last time. This is his punishment.'

'I…punishment for what? I thought you couldn't hurt each other.'

Edward laughed. 'Very good. Well, who told you that porkie pie? If we couldn't hurt each other, how else would Hat here have has dick ripped off and shoved up his arse?'

Joe felt another surge of something hot and silvery at the top of his throat. Edward stopped smiling and aimed a deadly serious glare at Joe. His face cracked suddenly and he began to laugh again.

'You crack me up, Joe. Every time!' Edward stood up, brushing the dust off his trousers. 'Ah. Now we're on speaking terms, my good man, shall we get out of here?'

Before Joe could answer, Edward shot an excited grin at him and clicked his fingers.

~~~

The lights came on. Paul felt lighter. He tried to move and found that now he could. His evil reflection had gone; as too had the red armchair. Paul's own seat was the only one left in the room. He stood up uneasily. To the left was now the thin outline of a door with a small round, red handle. He walked to the door and grabbed the handle. It felt warm, soft even. He turned it.

The door was heavy, like pulling against the wind. A sharp sound of rushing air came as he felt himself thrown forward, the door shutting fast behind him. This was the room he had entered earlier. The piano was just to his right; the double doors maybe forty or fifty feet straight ahead. In front of the doors stood a figure in a dinner suit, the mask of a pig, shaking its head slowly. It raised an arm and pointed at Paul.

The piano played but there was no one sat at it. Paul stepped forwards and the figure did too, head still shaking. It had the momentum of a pendulum, as if attached to the ceiling by some unseen string. Paul took another step. The pig took two steps forward. It seemed to gesture now for Paul to turn around.

Paul turned and saw the door was open again. Another pigman stood the other side, beckoning him inward. He turned back and saw the pointing, head-shaking pigman was back at the double doors. He turned back and took a step through the door he had just come through. The pigman faded from view, as if he was on wheels and a rope and someone had tugged him backwards. There was a spotlight across an otherwise black room; the spotlight was small, but focused on something shiny.

Paul walked over to it, noting that his footsteps made no sound, and bent down. He put his hand into the light and picked up his old Chicago police badge. A scene burst into life all around him.

'Motta – Motta! Get moving. Code 56 down town. You're with Stacey.'

Paul was disoriented. This was – what, five years ago? Last year?

When had he left Chicago? He couldn't place the time. In his hand was a pistol; his holster and badge on the table in front of him.

'Motta! Come on!'

He ran out of the office, down a short flight of stairs and out of the back door. A car was waiting. Other cars were filling up and driving away through a large metal gateway.

'Paul. Get in. Come on. What's with you today?'

He climbed into the car, belted himself in and asked where the code 56 was. Rod Stacey told him: the perp was holding his wife and son hostage. Apartment block, fifth floor. Perp was threatening to shoot them both unless he got what he wanted. But he hadn't said what he wanted.

They arrived to find an awkward crescent of police cruisers, a line of handlers holding the public back and redirecting them around to the other side of the road. Paul looked up to see the seven-floor block.

'Motta, Stacey. Over here.' Paul turned to see Sergeant Gullidge waving at them to join him. He was stood just outside the apartment lobby. A group of armed officers were behind him and over beyond them he saw a news reporter talking to camera. He and Stacey walked over to the entrance.

'What the fuck are they doing here?' Stacey asked. Paul was staring at Sergeant Gullidge. 'Paul? Hey Paul.' Gully snapped his fingers in front of Paul's face. 'Anyone home?'

'Oh...I'm...oh, sorry Joe. Sorry.'

'Whatever's up with you, snap out of it. We're going in. Twenty seconds.'

Paul nodded. He looked at Stacey, back at Gully and did a twirl to take the scene in. When was this? Was this real? He didn't remember it at all.

'We're go. Team one, on me. Team two, elevator. Go.' Joe pointed at a man holding a large shield. The man set off into the building. The others followed. Paul followed Joe.

They briskly climbed the stairs – eight flights – before stopping. The man with the shield turned but held the shield behind him, facing the door onto the fourth floor. Paul saw his badge said 'Hanratty'.

'Okay guys, we're at one-zero. We go left, cover three doors down and I want two at the far window. No escape, okay?'

There was no verbal affirmation; everyone nodded. Paul looked back

down the stairwell. There were at least twenty officers. He turned back to see Joe smiling at him.

'This is it, Paul. Ready?'

Paul nodded.

Joe pressed a small button on his collar. 'Okay. We are go.'

Hanratty advanced up the final two flights and drew the door open with one hand while keeping the shield up with the other. Gully, Stacey and Paul huddled in behind him, almost scurrying down the corridor. Paul counted the two doors as if making sure and they reached the third. Hanratty set the shield down between them and the door. Six officers ran past them, three going another twenty feet down to the far window; the others stopping just past the huddle.

'Paul, you're with me. Come on.' Joe led and Paul followed. A group of officers took their place behind Hanratty and his shield. Joe and Paul rounded a corner half way up the corridor, going left and around. Joe smiled and nodded at Paul, who looked back in bewilderment.

'What the fuck is up with you today man? Here, get the window.'

Joe opened the window and Paul put his hand in to hold it up. Joe slid out onto the fire escape and replaced Paul's hand with his. They advanced as far as the next window. Joe reached into his belt and pulled out a digi-mirror. He carefully angled it to see inside the apartment.

'It's clear,' he whispered, depressing the button on his collar again. 'Gully with Motta on fire escape. Kitchen clear. Entering.'

The window was locked.

'Paul – open it.'

It felt like a punch in the gut. Paul looked at the window blankly.

'Open the fucking window, Paul. Come on. *Tick-tock.*'

He moved past Gully to the window and stared through it. He shook his head as if clearing a fog, and looked down at his belt. His eyes bounced over various items and settled on a digi-pick. He took it out, flicked the casing open and thrust it into the frame, finding the lock. The pick whirred for two seconds and the lock came free. He risked a look back at Joe's belt. Joe was facing the other way, doing something on the wall.

'Bout time. Let's get in.' Joe pushed over to the window. Paul carefully drew the window up and Joe hoisted one leg over, then the other.

167

'What...what's that on the wall, Joe?'

'Shut up man, you know what it is.' He took the window as Paul climbed over. 'You can do the next one.' He pointed to the far wall where a door was slightly ajar. Paul could see it led into a bathroom. 'Here.'

Joe put a small black device in Paul's hand. He looked down at it and realised it was a package of C4 explosive. 'Over there, Paul. Come on. The door's opening in T45.'

Joe moved over to the other door. It was closed and coming from the other side were muffled voices. Paul attached the device to the wall and joined Joe.

Joe slipped a tiny bendable cord attached to a small screen unit under the door and flicked up the screen. Half a second later a tiny red light flashed and the image came up. Paul looked down at it and saw a woman lying on the floor in a pool of blood. It seemed to be coming from her stomach.

Over to the left was a boy – maybe pre-teen – also lying down, straddled by a heavy-set man holding a paperweight in one hand while his other gripped the boy's neck. He looked ready to strike the weight down.

Joe quickly withdrew the camera cord and threw it behind him. He nodded to Paul, grabbed the door handle and the two men stood up. He mouthed *one...two...three...*and swung the door open, putting two shots in the man's head just before the paperweight would have smashed the boy's skull open. Over the other side of the room, the front door crashed open, with Hanratty, his shield and a swarm of police following behind.

'Perp down,' Joe said into his collar button. Paul looked at the boy. He was smiling. *Punch.* He felt it in his gut again. Why was the boy smiling? *Punch.*

Paul couldn't breathe. His heart was doing its best to emerge through his jacket. His bowels felt weak. There was a wet sensation in his pants. He looked up at Joe, who winked back then down at the boy again. The boy winked at him.

'Eddie, stop!' Joe put his hand up towards Hanratty, who did as he was told. 'We've found a device. You need to get out now.'

'Sir!' Hanratty turned and ushered his troops back out the door. He took a second to look back. 'Joe – the kid?'

'We need him. He might know.'

Hanratty nodded and took position outside. Joe got Paul's attention away from staring at the boy and threw him another pack of C4. 'Over there – quick.'

Paul followed the instruction and placed the C4 on the wall that led to the bedrooms. He turned back to Joe and nodded. He felt like smiling. Then he did smile. The boy caught his eye and they winked at each other.

'That's it – we're out.' Joe led with the kid and Paul followed behind. They left the apartment, went back down the stairs and made it outside. Two women were screaming. The news report was still broadcasting. Joe looked at Paul and nodded. They led the kid out, pushed through a sea of civilians and entered Joe's cruiser.

The kid got in the back with Paul. He started to laugh. Just as some faces appeared at the cruiser windows, Joe pulled away. Paul started laughing too.

As they drove away, the fifth floor of the apartment block blew out, up and down. The explosive sound made Paul's ears ring, but he carried on laughing. He turned to look back and see the carnage. It was very dusty. He couldn't see it very well. It didn't matter.

~~~

'Now, Joe. Wake up. Wake up, Joey boy.'

Edward stood over Joe, who was in the foetal position on top of a large metal grate. Opening his eyes, his sight adjusted. He was peering down, beyond the grate into a long, dark hole. Chains hung from the grate. They looked wet. There was a horrible low hum; a sensation of vibration.

'Just get it over with. Just kill me.'

Edward laughed heartily. 'Kill you? Oh no. That wouldn't be fair at all. I have no desire to kill you, Joey.'

'What do you want then?'

'There you go, being all uptight again. Sheesh, calm down mister! We just want our Joey back, that's all. The clock's ticking, you know.'

'I don't know anything,' Joe retorted. 'Where are we?'

'Why, we're on our way to the party, of course. Up you get.'

'I didn't put my glad rags on.'

'Don't worry about that. We'll make sure you look the part.' Edward winked at Joe. 'Come on then.'

He rounded behind Joe and gave him a light nudge forward into a corridor. The walls were black stone. Like the chains, the walls looked wet.

'Where's Louise and Frank?' he asked, stopping in his tracks.

'Oh, they're waiting for us. You'll see. Hurry along.'

Joe reluctantly carried on. They came to a thin curtain. 'Go on,' Edward said. Joe stepped through the curtain and into a red and white room. Edward joined him. The room was busy – a party indeed. Ladies dressed in beautiful gowns and men in dinner jackets. A jazz band played. Over to the left was a bar with glasses of red and white liquid. A man stood behind it, smiling.

'Welcome home, Joe.' Edward clicked his fingers. The music stopped dead. Everyone stopped dancing. They looked over at Joe and began to applaud. Frank and Louise were there too, smiling and clapping. They looked at each other and giggled like children. Ged was there with a woman. She looked like his dog, Joe thought.

'See? This is your home; this is where you belong,' Edward said. 'Why don't you get yourself a drink and mingle a little?'

Joe looked over at the bar. Edward snapped his fingers again and the music began instantly. The dancing resumed. There was something *horrible* about the rhythm of the music. He looked back at Frank and Louise, who appeared to be tangoing. They seemed rapt in each other.

He walked over to the bar.

'Hey, Joe. How you doing?'

'Just… uh, I'm good, thanks. You?'

'Sure thing, just same as always!' The barman was cheerful. It made Joe feel a little cheerful too. 'Everyone's happy to see you, Joe!'

A tap on his right shoulder – a beautiful woman, smiling serenely at him. 'Hey Joey, we've all missed you.' Her voice was like velvet. She leaned closer and kissed him on the lips. A surge of comfort washed over him. She reached down and put her hand on his crotch and kissed him again, rubbing her hand around. He responded and opened his mouth.

He felt another hand on his head, stroking his hair back. A body pressed up behind him, gyrating slowly. It appeared to be a male body. He thought he didn't care. A voice in his head. *No, Joe. No. Don't let this*

170

happen. Joe. Fight it. Fight it.

He let his mouth close and edged back from the woman. She looked hurt; pained. 'Hey Joey, what's the matter?' She leaned in again. He put his hands up against her shoulders. 'Come on, Joey.' Her voice was beautiful; exquisite. She reached down to his crotch again.

'Get off. Just get off.' He pushed her hard and fell back a little. The body behind him fell onto the floor. A few of the dancers saw the commotion and stopped.

'What are you doing, Joe? Don't turn away from me.' The woman opened her mouth wide – a wet, pulpy mass of black *something* congealed began spilling out. He backed up further and glanced at the barman, who looked confused. His eyes were clouds of red and black, like oil in water.

'No, Joe. That's not right man.' The barman's mouth was spilling black ooze. 'Come on, Joe. Have a drink, yeah?'

Joe backed up as far as he could go. The man he had knocked backwards was still on the floor, wearing an injured expression. Joe glanced over at the dancers. Most had stopped although the music kept going. It sounded more urgent than before, as if heading for a crescendo. Edward was at the far set of double doors talking to a man in a white suit. The man pointed and Edward turned around. The beautiful and handsome faces had become a sea of sickly, twisted expressions.

Joe lurched forward, pushing the velvety-voiced woman out of the way. He came to a door, opened it quickly and disappeared into the next room, shutting the door behind him. The new room was dark but for a spotlight a few feet away. He went over to it and knelt down to see what was on the floor. It was a small cap gun; black metallic. He recognised it. *This is mine.* He reached down and picked it up.

'Joey? Joey! It's lunchtime.'

It was his mother's voice. Joe stood up and surveyed his battleground. His knees were red and marked from kneeling on the deck. The goodie troops had advanced far enough and all but wiped out the baddies, but for one small group hiding out in a bunker. Action figures of varying size and repair were strewn over the battlefield, their plastic limbs contorted awkwardly to reflect the chaos of their demise. The goodies had lost a few good men and some more were recovering from injuries in the first aid tent. Joe's force always had a medic as back-up. It was one of the reasons he never lost.

'Joey? Did you hear?' His mother called again.

'Yeah – coming!'

He reached into his trouser pocket and found his trusty cap gun. Taking aim at the bunker – the last outpost of resistance – he was about to squeeze the trigger but then decided to leave them be for now. They would keep. Just two or three of them were no match for his forces, who would keep the situation under control while he retired for lunch. He lowered his gun and turned towards the cabins.

Joe loved being on the boat, moored more than moving. It was more like a house when it was safely tied to land; the land being its huge, never-ending garden. Being on the boat was being free. No school, no confrontations. It wasn't that he was scared of being on the boat out on the water, but it felt like anything could come at any time. He always wondered what was underneath – some unseen force circling, following, waiting and then one day jumping up and devouring the vessel and everyone on it. It was an unsettling feeling. His bladder would weaken every time the boat left land. The water was bottomless. There could be anything down there.

He skipped over the deck, rounding the helm and hopped down onto the lower deck, another hop down to the seating area where his father was sat in front of a table full of food and drink, consumed by his newspaper.

'You winning, Joey?' He looked up briefly, smiled at his son and went back to the paper.

'Always, dad. But I didn't finish it. There's one last...'

His mother interrupted. 'Put that thing away, Joey. Not at the table, dear.' He did as he was told and put the cap gun back in his pocket.

'Thank you.' She smiled down at him, setting a jug of orange squash in front of him. 'Now dig in, boys. And Joey, you have to eat some vegetables.'

'Yeah, yeah.' He smiled up at his mother, who sat down opposite him. She said: 'Carl, please put the paper down. Just for a minute – while we eat.'

Carl looked up slowly from the paper and directed a stern glare at his wife. 'Charlie – how about you worry about what you're doing and I'll worry about what I'm doing.' His hands scrunched the paper in at the sides. Charlie broke the stare and got back to selecting some ham, a couple of cheese slices, some tomato quarters and a thick lump of bread to sandwich them all into. Joe looked quickly at his mother, then father, then back at his empty plate.

Carl brought his hands together aggressively, the paper crumpling in his grasp. He fashioned it into something ball-like and tossed it behind him, over the side of the boat and into the water.

'Honey, I...'

Carl interrupted: 'Honey I...I'm so sorry. I'm so sorry honey.' It was a whiny tone – deliberately antagonistic. He looked at Joe. 'Son, let me tell you something about women. Women are...' He paused and looked up at the sky, then down at his tumbler of whiskey on the table. He picked it up, swigged back a large measure and gently placed the glass back on the table. 'Son, women are dangerous creatures. They pour you a drink then tell you not to drink it. They buy you a goddamned newspaper and tell you not to read it.' He fixed his wife in a steely glare.

Joe put his hands on his lap and began picking at a loose piece of skin on his thumb. He kept his gaze on his empty plate.

'Son, I'm talking to you. *Look* at me when I'm talking to you. You're as bad as your mother.'

Joe kept picking at the skin. He looked to the right, meeting his father's mean eyes. 'Sorry, dad. Sorry.'

'That's okay son. That's okay. Now eat your fucking lunch.'

'Carl!'

He shot his wife a *don't you dare*. 'You eat your fucking lunch too.' He stood up, his knee knocking the table up. His whiskey tumbler upended, spilling a tiny drop – sending a rivulet heading in no particular direction across the surface. He picked the glass up and walked over to the cabin, opened the door and went inside.

'Mum,' Joe whispered. 'I'm sorry.'

She reached her hand over to him. He stopped picking and put his hand in hers. 'It's okay, Joey. It's just when he has a drink. You know he loves both of us so much.'

'I know, mum. I don't like it though. He scares me.'

'Don't be scared, Joey. He'll never hurt you.' She turned to look at the cabin, absently placing a slice of cheese on top of another.

A punch in the gut. Joe's head snapped backwards and he felt like he'd been awoken from a dream. He looked at his mother...*when is this?*

Where am I?…and then behind him, catching sight of a sailing boat far out on the lake. It was all peaceful. Barely a sound to be heard. Then the cabin door swung open, his father emerging from it with a half-full tumbler in one hand and the whiskey bottle in the other. *Punch.*

Joe's hands returned to his lap and he resumed picking at the skin. A piece felt loose enough to pull, so he pulled it. It went down from the tip of the thumbnail and cleared the nail all together, stopping just before the joint as he ripped it upwards and off. *Ah.*

His mother turned back towards him. 'Joey?'

He didn't answer. He watched his other thumb and forefinger rolling the skin into a ball and then let it drop to the floor. It bounced off his foot. He looked at the wound on his other thumb. There was a sliver of blood next to the nail, slightly bleeding onto it. He put the thumb in his mouth and began soothing it with his tongue. He felt the sting all the way down in his stomach. The metallic taste was familiar and comforting.

Carl swaggered back to the table and uneasily put the bottle and tumbler down. He sat and reached into his pocket. 'There!' He slammed an old revolver on the table, making Joe and his mother jump.

'Carl! What are you...'

'Where's your little one, son? Go on, get it out. Let's see who's got the biggest, huh?' Again he silenced the woman with a *look.*

Joe reached into his pocket and took the cap gun out. He placed it on the table next to his father's gun. It was tiny in comparison, barely matching the size of the butt. He looked up at his father with wide eyes. His legs were trembling.

'See, son? You'll have one of these someday. A real man's weapon. Stop anyone doing anything with this baby.' He put his hand down on it and swivelled it. The gun spun on the table, stopping to point back at the cabin.

Charlie eyed the direction of the barrel suspiciously. A few degrees further and it would have been pointing straight at her.

'Lucked out there, honey!' Carl boomed. He let out a throaty laugh and put his hand back on the tumbler. 'You want to hold it, son?'

Joe shook his head. 'Nu-uh.'

'Ooh, scaredy cat. Come on, son. It ain't gonna kill you. Might kill somebody else if you're not careful but it ain't got teeth and it ain't got a brain so just pick it up and see how it feels.'

Joe tentatively reached for the gun, his fingers reluctant to touch it.

'You be careful with that, son. Couple of bullets in there.' His father took another swig of whiskey.

Joe picked the gun up and squeezed his hand tight around the butt. It was just too big to fit snugly but it felt good; heavy. He looked at the cap gun lying on the table and all of a sudden felt repulsed by it. *That's for babies. This is for men.* He smiled at his father. Carl didn't notice. He finished the whiskey in his tumbler and leant back, his arms following his shoulders. His left arm landed on Joe's neck, wrapping around. It was close to affection. He closed his elbow around Joe's throat and gave it a squeeze.

'There, Joey. How'd you like the feel of that beauty?'

Joe nodded enthusiastically while trying not to acknowledge his mother's worried stare.

'See?' His father snatched the gun from Joe's hand, picked up the cap gun in his other and said: 'That's for babies. This is for men.'

Punch. Joe was brought back out of himself again, like a coat snatched from a hook. He took in his surroundings again. Why were his mother's eyes filling with water? He looked back at his father, who was pointing the gun at his own head. 'Hey honey, wanna play? Remember what happened last time?' He winked at her and laughed. *What happened last time? What's happening now?* 'Carl, please don't. Please don't.' His mother held her hands up, gesturing for him to stop, to put the gun down. Joe's head began to fill with warmth. He could feel a smile breaking out. *Punch.*

'What do you say, honey? Us three, one bullet?'

'Carl! Stop it.' Charlie screamed. 'Put it down, now!' She looked at Joey, stood up and reached for him. Carl swatted her hand out of the way and fell awkwardly into Joe's lap. Joe sat straight up, missing his mother's grasp, and threw his arms up. Carl pushed against Joe's legs and returned to his seat.

Charlie turned on the spot and ran for the cabin door, just making it through and to the other side by the time Carl was up. He had the gun pointed to the sky. 'You're gonna regret this, Charleen. Come back out!'

Punch. Joe watched his father grab the cabin door handle. He stood up and walked calmly over to the door, catching his reflection in the bridge window. He was smiling but there were tears running down his cheeks, one making it as far as his chin and ready to succumb to gravity. His father went into the cabin, pushing the door wide open as if to beckon his son in. Joe reached the doorway and saw his mother backed up against the corridor wall. His father turned back to him. 'This is fun, ain't it kid?' The words came muffled, somehow slower than normal. His father's eyes were smoky – black and red wisps floating out and upwards, dissipating into the atmosphere.

'Give me the gun, Carl. Please! Give it to me.' She was sobbing and screaming – a cacophony of despair. The scene slowed down further. Carl strode aggressively and put the gun barrel in her neck, his other hand grabbing her hair behind and yanking it down. 'Carl! Please!' She screamed again.

Eyeliner and tears created a black river down her face, the river flowing awkwardly over her cheeks, pooling by the nostrils and sending a dark waterfall down onto Joe's father's arm. He stepped back, releasing her hair and wiping his hand on his shirt. Slowly withdrawing the gun from her neck, he traced it down between her breasts and leaned in, kissing her.

'Sorry, honey. I'm sorry.' The vowels rang out like a record slowed down to a quarter of its original speed. His father was crying too. 'Just kiddin' around. Just a bit of fun.' He traced the gun into her hand, let go and stepped back. Joe's smile broadened. His father turned around to face him.

'Just a bit of fun, kid. Just a bit o...'

His head moved over just enough to see his mother's face. She had her fist up in front of her mouth, her elbow stretched out towards him. *Warmth spread down to Joe's chest.* Her lips moved and he thought he heard her say *I'm sorry*, but it was stifled. Her thumb flicked backwards and he recognised the click from a thousand Westerns.

The bullet took less than half a second to reach the wall, on the way penetrating her gum and jawbone and taking a path through the bottom of her brain, slicing a couple of millimetres away as it then smashed through the skull and into the wooden and fibreglass wall.

The gun fell to the floor and thumped like a bass drum in a cave. Father and son stood motionless, staring into each other's eyes. Joe's gaze drifted beyond and down to see his mother's body slumped on the floor, a messy red line on the wall plotting her course.

He fell forwards, knocking against his father's leg and stumbling down to where she lay.

His father was right behind him. He leant down and picked the gun up, throwing it back out of the cabin onto the deck. It landed and spun three and a half times. His father wrenched him upwards and screamed something. It was all too slowed down for Joe to understand. He was thrown back up the corridor and stumbled on the first of the three stairs leading back to the deck, and fell forwards onto it.

More shouting – Joe tried to clamber up towards the gun but was pushed past and over it, performing an involuntary somersault and coming to rest awkwardly against the safety railing. His father picked the gun up, strode over to Joe and yanked him up, manipulated him around and shoved his head and chest over the railing.

Joe's view blurred. The water seemed to be trying to get him. He felt a heavy object dig into his head. His hands were wrenched back and forcefully clasped together as his father put all his body weight on Joe's back.

The click. Another passage of words, even slower now. It sounded to Joe like a helicopter's rotor. The weight came off Joe's back and he felt something heavy hit the back of his leg. He looked up to see his father splash into the water, his head going in first. A hand closed around his, pulling him up and around.

'It's okay. It's okay.'

The sound returned to normal speed. The man put his arms around Joe and pulled him inwards. *It's okay. It's okay.* Joe looked up and saw a kindly face smiling sympathetically back at him. He smiled back. The sympathy drained quickly from the man's face. Joe's smile broadened.

'I'm Edward. Pleased to finally meet you, Joe.' He backed away and Joe did the same. They smiled at each other. Joe turned to look over the railing into the water. 'He's dead. They're both dead.' A dark patch covered his father's head. The rest of the body floated like a sack. 'I took his throat,' Edward said. *Punch.*

The spotlight faded and the room was all black. The cap gun was not in his hand any more. For the first time in his very short lifetime, Joe – *echo number X X of Joe* – understood. He closed his eyes and visualised Louise. There was nothing. No feeling of reaching out. He tried Frank, then Tom. Still nothing. He visualised himself – a stare into some interior mirror – and caught a waft of colour. He tried to focus on it and the waft became a mist, then an outline. His shoulders edged backwards and he thrust his head forward.

As light came back into the world, Joe stumbled forwards, knocking his left shoulder against something hard and bumpy. His feet and ankles felt wet. It was a dim light, but better than total darkness. Joe had experienced more than enough darkness recently.

He stood back up straight and saw he was in a corridor, much like the one Edward had led him down from the metal-grate-pit a few minutes earlier. He walked into a circular area and looked up to see a dim, murky cloud of something, with the image of the grate just poking through in the distance, fifty or so feet up. Back at eye level were four passages, one with some light in it, but not immediate – possibly around a corner. He stepped into the passage and followed it as it narrowed, leading around a slight curve to the right. He came to a door – roughly shaped to fill an odd hole. He reached for the handle and pushed it gently open.

Joe fell to his knees, wetness enveloping them and lapping up at his thighs. Ahead of him, hanging from the black stone wall, was what he knew – he felt – was his own body. The head was rounded, hollowed out, as if someone had just lifted his face off and cut everything behind it out of the shell.

When the lights go out and you can't see, just close your eyes and wait for them to come back on.

His mother's voice sounded clear, soft. Joe let his body slump down, his head stopping with a bounce just above his knees. *Okay*, he thought. *Okay.*

He walked back towards the pit, crossed it into the corridor and made his way to the end. As he drew nearer, the wall became a mesh; the curtain effect he had seen before. He pushed through it, although it took no effort.

Back in the red and white room, he saw the same scene as before: dancing, beautifully dressed men and women; a jazz band; a bar. He went over to the bar and picked up a glass. Warmth rushed over his face, almost burning back into his skull and then down into his chest, thighs and beyond. He raised the glass and emptied it into his mouth, swallowing yet more warmth. The liquid felt thick like a placenta – a mess of birth – creeping down his throat in the most exquisite way.

A tap on his shoulder – Tom's kind face, eyes red and black and smoky, lips wet and black. Tom's hand reached down to Joe's, clasping it. Joe looked down to register this and then back at Tom. Joe smiled. Tom shook his head.

Joe took another drink and walked to the back wall, sitting down on the velvet bench. Tom stayed at the bar but kept his gaze on Joe. A few seconds later Tom walked over and sat next to him. A figure appeared, hazy against a backdrop of dancing black and white, who sat down on his other side. Joe looked at both of them, long enough and with care to study their appearance, and was satisfied they looked good. They looked just right for the party. He smiled at Tom, who chuckled and patted Joe's leg. He looked over at Frank, smiling and nodding at each other.

Joe leaned over and spoke into Frank's ear. Frank nodded and grinned. They both looked over at Tom, who nodded and smiled.

'I'm not Tom,' he said.

After a while the band stopped.

Epilogue

A single blemish appears. Black, solid, as far as every horizon. Everywhere. The infinite abyss. This is not space. No light exists. No stars shine through the darkness. The blemish turns into a ripple. There is no ear to detect its herald. No throat to gag at its scent. The ripple spreads, a tiny bump growing, heading slowly towards boundaries that do not exist. From the ripple comes a protrusion. It grows longer, like a worm searching above ground. Another protrusion appears nearby. This one looking for the other. They slide across a surface – two loose ends tying, weaving together. More protrusions, more worms. Each moving towards another and into the growing mass. The mass begins to pulsate, still growing.

Somewhere nearby a rush of wind carries voices. Swirling and directionless, silvery and slippery.

It is almost there. I can feel it.

I can feel it too.

Is the room full now?

Yes. We should tell the others.

The circle will be complete…

www.ingramcontent.com/pod-product-compliance
Lightning Source LLC
Chambersburg PA
CBHW030336180626
46810CB00003B/1381